NOW YOU OWE ME

NOW YOU OWE ME

a novel

❧

Aliah Wright

🐔 Red Hen Press | *Pasadena, CA*

This is a work of fiction. Names, characters, places, and incidents are either the product of the author's imagination or are used fictitiously. Any resemblance to actual persons, living or dead, events, or locales, is entirely coincidental.

Book design by Mark E. Cull

Library of Congress Cataloging-in-Publication Data

Names: Wright, Aliah D., author.
Title: Now you owe me: a novel / Aliah Wright.
Description: First edition. | Pasadena, CA: Red Hen Press, 2024.
Identifiers: LCCN 2023057025 (print) | LCCN 2023057026 (ebook) | ISBN
  9781636281568 (paperback) | ISBN 9781636281575 (e-book) | ISBN 9781636282688
  (library binding)
Subjects: LCSH: Serial murderers—Fiction. | Kidnapping victims—Fiction. |
  LCGFT: Thrillers (Fiction) | Novels.
Classification: LCC PS3623.R48 N69 2024 (print) | LCC PS3623.R48 (ebook)
  | DDC 813/.6—dc23/eng/20231222
LC record available at https://lccn.loc.gov/2023057025
LC ebook record available at https://lccn.loc.gov/2023057026

The National Endowment for the Arts, the Los Angeles County Arts Commission, the Ahmanson Foundation, the Dwight Stuart Youth Fund, the Max Factor Family Foundation, the Pasadena Tournament of Roses Foundation, the Pasadena Arts & Culture Commission and the City of Pasadena Cultural Affairs Division, the City of Los Angeles Department of Cultural Affairs, the Audrey & Sydney Irmas Charitable Foundation, the Meta & George Rosenberg Foundation, the Albert and Elaine Borchard Foundation, the Adams Family Foundation, Amazon Literary Partnership, the Sam Francis Foundation, and the Mara W. Breech Foundation partially support Red Hen Press.

First Edition
Published by Red Hen Press
www.redhen.org

Printed in Canada

For women who die at the hands of men.

NOW YOU OWE ME

What is the way to the abode of light? And where does darkness reside?

—Job 38:19

PART ONE

PART ONE

CHAPTER ONE

1998

Flying down a potholed highway, Corinthia and Benjamin Zanetti jostled against each other beneath a filthy tarp in the bed of an old, black Ford F-150. For now, their father Jason, driving the truck and still wearing the checkered shirt and blue jeans he had on when he was released from prison earlier in the day, was unaware his seven-year-old twins had stowed away in the back. But when fumes from the exhaust washed over them, Ben coughed.

"Shhh!" Corinthia said, pressing a small finger to her pursed lips.

"It's hard to breathe under here!" Ben grumbled. A slivered moon cast just enough light through jagged tears in the canvas for them to see each other in the darkness.

With their pale blue eyes, fair skin, and plump lips, Corinthia and Benjamin were mirror images of each other—save for the texture of their sun-kissed blond hair. Hers fell in ringlets across her shoulders. His was cropped shorter and framed loose waves around his cherub face.

Both were far from angels.

"I know that!" Corinthia snapped. "But if Daddy catches us . . ."

Ben cut her off and finished her sentence. "He'll kill us." He paused. "I don't know why I let you talk me into . . ."

Corinthia, older than Ben by a minute, pinched him.

Ben's hands flew to his mouth, and he suppressed a youch.

She sucked her teeth and exhaled. "I didn't talk you into coming," Corinthia spat. "You're always following me and every time you follow me something always goes wrong and I have to fix it. I hate it when you do that. You make me sick!"

Ben fumed. "Call a doctor then!"

"Shut up!" both twins said simultaneously.

"No! You shut up!" Their whispered argument grew more heated—until the old pickup screeched to a stop.

Ben clutched at his chest. His eyes grew wide, and he blanched.

"What's wrong with you?" Corinthia mouthed. Her voice went up a slight octave and her face reflected her concern. It softened when she raised her eyebrows.

"I'm scared!" he whispered back. "I'm just gonna tell Daddy I'm sorry we followed him."

When he tried to move, Corinthia dug her fingernails into his forearm and scolded him. "Are you crazy? If you do that, we'll just get into more trouble."

"You're hurting me, 'Rinthia," he said.

"Oh, I'm sorry, Benji," she whispered, releasing his arm. "But you know I'm right."

She watched him nod in agreement. A single tear rolled down his cheek. He trembled so hard the tarp began to shake. Instinct took over. Corinthia reached over and wiped the tear away.

"He's coming," Ben told her, his voice filled with his fear.

Corinthia's voice was comforting when she said, "Calm down, little brother. Just be still. OK?"

Ben nodded and took a deep breath. His sigh was soft, resigned.

When their father opened his door and marched to the back of the truck, the twins went rigid. Corinthia shifted her shoulder and torso out of her father's way just as he reached beneath the tarp.

Ben held his breath when he saw Jason's fingers grasp a large and heavy pipe.

"Lenny!" Jason shouted. "You out here?"

The twins heard a voice.

"Yeah, over this way." Suddenly the night grew brighter—their father must have clicked on the truck's headlights. Emboldened by the presence of another adult, Corinthia and Ben rolled over onto their knees, lifted the tarp, and peered through the cab's back window. Through the windshield, they watched Jason step into twin pools of light.

"Where's my money?" Jason asked. He ran a hand over the stubble on his cheek and tucked a lock of his blond hair behind his ear. At six foot four, olive-skinned and muscular, Jason towered over the slight, rail-thin man who moved out from the shadows just beyond the headlights.

The man was scratching his arms so fast, it was like ants were biting him. "Well, I ain't got it right now, but I'm a . . ."

Jason raised the pipe high above his head like a baseball bat and smashed it across Lenny's mouth. Corinthia and Ben both gasped. Lenny staggered in front of the truck, screamed once, spit out teeth, and raised his hands in defense. But he never said a word while Jason struck his head with the pipe, over and over again.

Blood sprayed until Lenny stopped moving.

Ben flinched and winced beside his sister. He raised a small fist to his mouth and moaned. But Corinthia's blue eyes were wide open in wonder. Transfixed, she removed the tarp and jumped down onto the deserted gravel lot. She watched a livid Jason huff and puff.

His face was beet red. His hands were slick with gore.

"Corinthia?" he asked, a hint of incredulousness in his voice.

Without a word, his baby girl approached Lenny's body, face down on the ground in his own blood. A tentative Corinthia nudged Lenny with her white-sneakered foot, staining it red.

When she looked up at her father, his face freckled with blood, she recoiled. Her features scrunched into a mask of heartbreak.

"Is he dead, Daddy?" she sniveled.

Bits of Lenny covered Jason's button-down, green-and-gray-checkered shirt. The ruined pipe still in one hand, Jason peered at his daughter. Her bottom lip was trembling and she looked on the brink of tears. He scooped her up with his free arm and shushed her when she twisted and whimpered. "Don't look," he told her.

Then, "Where's your brother? I know he's out here somewhere, too. Ben!"

When Jason bent down, Corinthia slipped from his grasp, backed away from the man's body, turned, and threw up on the ground. Ben climbed out from underneath the tarp. His blond hair was streaked with grime. A dark smudge stained his soft chin.

"Sir?" His voice quivered. Jason, who was prone to violent outbursts, could be as cruel as he could be loving. The twins never knew which Jason would show up—especially after he'd gotten out of jail, which he had been in and out of their entire lives.

Jason shook his head from side to side and sighed. When his daughter wiped her mouth on the back of her left hand, he took a deep breath and exhaled before giving both children a look of frustration. "Both of you get in the front and be quiet."

The twins did as they were told.

Jason turned his back. When the pipe made a clattering sound against the pebbles after it fell to the ground, Corinthia jumped in her seat next to Ben, spooked. Without thinking, Ben put an arm around his sister. She flinched before burying her face in his shoulder; her silent tears soaked his T-shirt.

Jason dug through the dead man's pockets. He pulled out a wad of money and counted it. "It's all here?" he marveled, kicking the dead Lenny in the ribs. "Meth head, lying piece of . . ."

Jason walked back toward his children and barked at them, "Get out. Ben, grab that tarp out the back. Help me." Ben pressed his fingertips above his eyebrows and wiped them down his temples and across his cheeks before rubbing his wet hands on his thighs. He climbed out of the truck.

At their father's instruction, the twins spread the tarp out evenly on the dark ground. It was a warm summer night and, deep in the Pennsylvania mountains, far from their home, there wasn't a soul in sight. With their meager help, Jason rolled the body and the pipe inside the canvas sheeting. Sweaty and smeared with even more blood, he towered over his quaking children and waggled a finger at them.

"Don't say anything to anyone about this—especially your mother, you hear me?"

"Yes sir." They nodded in concert.

An hour later, Jason stopped the vehicle in a secluded spot beneath a bridge on the edge of the Schuylkill River, in North Philadelphia. He heaved the body and the pipe into the water.

The three of them watched Lenny sink.

"Now," he said to his twins, "take off those dirty clothes."

They looked at each other. "Huh, Daddy?" Ben asked.

"Take 'em off. Leave on your underwear. Corinthia, give me both of your shoes. You can keep your socks on." The twins stripped out of their tiny tops and shorts, and Jason removed his blood-splattered shirt, too. He drove a few more miles downstream and threw everything into the water.

When they returned home, well after 2:00 a.m., the house was quiet and dark. Jason roused both sleepy twins from the cab of his truck and helped them down. Their mother, Jenna, and their four-year-old brother, Luke, were upstairs sleeping.

"Don't turn on any lights," he told the pair. "Just wash up and go to bed."

Corinthia ascended the stairs, taking them two at a time, but Ben lingered in the shadows nearby. Curious, he watched his father tap white powder from a small vial onto the back of his fist and sniff it before opening a mini bottle of Jameson Irish Whiskey that had been under the kitchen sink. Jason tipped the bottle to his lips and drained it. He cleared his throat and snatched the handset of the phone from the wall, punched some numbers into it, and spoke to someone on the other end for a good twenty minutes.

Whoever it was did most of the talking.

"No. He didn't have the money," Jason purred into the receiver after a few moments. Then a long pause.

"What do you think happened? Yeah. Yes! I know that," he growled.

Ben sat on the bottom of the stairs. His leg bounced up and down.

"I took care of it. What? Tomorrow? OK, fine."

Jason hung up, rounded the corner, and caught Ben inching back up the stairs.

"Didn't I tell you to go to bed?"

Ben turned to dash up the stairs, but Jason was faster. With both hands, he grabbed his oldest son by the neck and lifted him up against a wall, almost to the ceiling. When Jason exhaled, the smell of alcohol wafted over Ben, assailing his nostrils. Suspended in midair, moonlight pouring in through the windows, the boy's feet kicked as he clawed at his father's hands. Ben didn't know which was worse: staring into Jason's reddening eyes while his fingernails dug into his flesh, or the fact that his father's hands were squeezing so hard he could scarcely breathe.

In measured tones, Jason whispered: "Never defy me, follow me, or speak about tonight to anyone. If you do, I will kill you. Just like I killed Lenny. You hear me, boy?"

Ben nodded, and Jason dropped him. He fell to the floor with a loud thump. Ben clutched at his throat, coughed, and crawled up the stairs toward the room he shared with his sister.

A showered Corinthia was lying on her bed in her favorite pajamas playing with a cigarette lighter when a blubbering and gasping Ben entered the room. She threw it under the bed, but he saw it anyway.

"You know if you set the bed on fire again, we're really gonna get it!" he croaked before bursting into tears.

Corinthia crinkled her eyebrows. She sat up and flicked wet hair behind her ear.

"What happened?" Her voice was heavy with worry.

Ben's shoulders heaved up and down. He took short, quick breaths when he told her what their father said.

"Oh honey, don't cry," Corinthia said, imitating their mother. She got up, grabbed his hand, and led him to his bed. When Corinthia climbed in next to him, Ben blew air from his quivering, pink lips. She pulled him into her arms, shushing him, and waited for his shuddering to stop. They lay there in silence for a moment, holding hands.

"You're always so warm," he told her. He inhaled. "You washed your hair with Mommy's strawberry shampoo, didn't you?"

"Mmhm," she answered. Ben rested his head on her shoulder and twirled his fingers in her damp, golden hair. He liked that she never complained when he played in her hair, something he always did when he was upset. She kissed the top of his head and ran her fingers through his hair too for a few moments, before placing a hand on his back. She rubbed it in small circles. His heart was rattling so hard he felt like it was ready to burst through his shirt. He knew she could feel it.

"Are you OK?" she asked, concerned.

"Daddy killed that man," Ben said, his voice barely above a whisper.

"No, he didn't," she said, matter of fact. "I can prove it."

"What? How?"

"Later, Benji," she said, yawning. "I'm tired. Go take a shower. You stink."

The day after they'd helped their father dispose of Lenny, a tiny baby skunk they often played with wriggled and squeezed its way through the wooden fence to their backyard. They lived on the outskirts of Philadelphia in a mostly integrated suburb filled with sprawling homes and lots of woodland creatures—deer, foxes, possums, squirrels, and skunks. Corinthia had discovered that if they fed some of the animals, they could pet them too. But the first time they'd seen the skunk a few weeks earlier, Corinthia had said, "Yuck! I'm not touching that thing!"

"Don't be a stupid head, Corinthia. Remember last year when the people at the petting zoo told us baby skunks don't spray until they're much older?"

"Oh yeah, I forgot."

"Just don't tell Mommy," Ben continued. "She'll get mad. You know we're not supposed to have any pets."

"Yeah, I know," she laughed. "Mommy said we got each other. We don't need any pets."

"I think a pet would be nice, though," he said under his breath.

"I'll be your pet!" his sister said before she leaned toward him and kissed his cheek. When he hugged her back, the squished skunk mewled and they both laughed.

Today, Ben picked the skunk up and it snuggled against his chest. The twins debated a long time in their secret shared twin-language what should become of it.

Corinthia popped a Raisinet in her mouth. "Let's kill it."

"What?" Ben clutched the animal closer to his chest and turned away from her in a half-hearted attempt to shield it from his sister. Corinthia meant well, but sometimes she could be, well, cruel.

She smacked her lips and swallowed. "I'm going to prove to you that it will come back to life. Just like Lenny came back to life. Uriah Washington on Eyewitness News said Lenny was just missing."

Ben exhaled and frowned, stroking the skunk's black-and-white fur. "But we know he's dead. And anyway, a dead skunk won't come back to life," Ben said with confidence.

"Oh, yes it will!"

"I dare you to see if it's true!" Ben said.

"No, I double-dog dare you!" they said in unison. Corinthia jumped up and down.

"Jinx!" she shouted first. "You owe me a soda!"

Ben pouted and waited for his twin to say his name to break the curse.

"Fine!" Corinthia said a moment later. She wiped chocolate on her jeans. "Go get the bucket."

"No."

"Benji, just get the bucket!" she said, laughing. "It's not going to die. Not really, you'll see. Give it to me." Ben stared at her a moment, unconvinced. Against his better judgment, he handed her the wriggling animal. He watched her play with it for a few minutes before he ran into the kitchen to retrieve their mother's mop bucket. It was big, yellow, stained, and heavy.

Two thin metal spokes on either side of the plastic white handle held it in place. From outside he heard her yell, "Bring me some more Raisinets!"

Ben turned the bucket upside down, climbed on top of it, and snuck into the stash of chocolate his father kept hidden in a cabinet above the sink. He sank two yellow and orange boxes of the chocolate-covered raisins into his back pocket and hopped down. The bucket banged against the back of Ben's legs when he lugged it across the kitchen's checkered linoleum floor and outside into the yard through the grass.

"Get the hose," Corinthia commanded, motioning toward the long green garden hose attached to the side of the house. Once the bucket was full, Corinthia dared Ben to submerge the skunk, which she rocked like a baby while it lounged in her lap, nibbling bits of grass from her hand. It squealed in delight like it always did when she hummed to it and scratched its belly.

"No," Ben told her. His hands were shaking. "I dared you, remember? You do it."

She stopped swaying for a moment. "I think you should do it."

"I think you shouldn't take a dare if you're scared."

"I am not scared!"

"Yes, you are."

"Am not!"

"Are, too!"

"Fine! Fraidy-cat!" Corinthia said.

She stood and seized the skunk by its tail.

"No!" Ben had changed his mind. He lunged for the animal, but Corinthia twisted away from him. "It's not going to die, Benji! You'll see!"

Then a bold Corinthia submerged the surprised, mewling animal into the cold water. It thrashed and clawed at her, tearing long, deep, bloody scratches up and down her arms.

Ben stood spellbound.

She gasped at the pain and shrieked, "Help me!"

Air bubbles appeared in the water. A foul stench wafted up from beneath the surface.

"Oh! Pee yew!" Corinthia said, unbowed by the baby skunk's faint musk. "Hurry up!"

"I thought you said it wouldn't spray!"

"I didn't think it would!"

Ignoring her, Ben plunged his hand into the bucket and tried to retrieve the animal. He cursed and jerked his hand out after the baby skunk bit down hard and tore a tiny chunk out of his flesh. It clawed at him, too, its talons ripping Ben's skin from wrist to elbow.

"Ow! That hurts!" He cried. He snatched his left hand back and wrapped it in the bottom of his T-shirt.

"Dammit," Corinthia said, parroting their father. "I have to do everything!" Before the weakened skunk could crawl out of the deep bucket, she slammed it beneath the water with one hand and hit it in the head with the other. Her clothes were drenched. Undaunted, she punched the skunk once more until the wet, matted animal was still.

The twins peered into the bucket.

The water was pink.

Corinthia backed away from the mess. Her chest rose and fell from exertion. She frowned and whispered, "Is it dead yet, Benji? Did we kill it?"

Ben pinched his nose between his thumb and forefinger. "I think so." With the other hand, he pulled the motionless skunk from the water by its tail.

"Ugh, it stinks."

When he handed the drenched, limp animal to Corinthia, she placed it on the ground, careful, in an attempt not to disturb it further.

"It'll come back to life, Benji. Just watch!" They poked it with sticks.

"It's dead." Ben said after a few seconds. "It's finished."

"No. It's not!" Corinthia screeched, upset. She prodded it with her sandal. "Look it! It moved!"

Ben scoffed. "That's 'cause you kicked it."

She burst into tears and got on her knees, pressing down hard on its cold, wet fur.

"Please God," she whispered. "Don't let it be dead." Blood ran down her arm. The skunk didn't move. But the back gate did, and in strolled their neighbor, old Mrs. Miller. She spotted the twins in the corner of the yard. Her hand flew to her nose.

"What is that awful smell? Corinthia? Honey, are you bleeding?"

Just as she peered over the twins' shoulders, the tiny skunk leapt up and jumped on Mrs. Miller's chest before scrambling down her arm and into the hedges. The old woman screeched so loud Corinthia pushed both of her hands against her ears. A startled Ben took two steps back.

Jason rushed outside from the house. "What the hell did you two do now!"

Even after they apologized to Mrs. Miller for "giving her the fright of her life," and after their mother Jenna begged him not to, later that night Jason spanked them. While they lay in her bed, Corinthia held Ben's head close to her chest. As always, he responded by twirling his fingers in her long, yellow locks. They hummed their favorite hymn, "Jesus is Tenderly Calling."

When she began weeping, Ben looked up and into her eyes.

"It's OK," he whispered to her. He held her hand and kissed her cheek. "It'll stop hurtin' after a while."

"I'm not sad 'cause we got spanked." She sniffed, rubbing snot and tears across the back of her hand before wiping it on the pillowcase.

"I'm mad because we got caught. You know how I hate getting caught."

During those hot days of 1998, the twins were always in trouble—mostly because of their growing obsession with death.

Quite a few animals died that summer. And Corinthia shed tears over every last one—even when Ben, who often joined in, begged her to stop. But she was determined to prove they'd come back to life, like the skunk.

Like Lenny.

One of the twins threw rocks at a car window the next block over, breaking it so they could drag out a small Chihuahua in the back seat. It bit Corinthia without breaking her skin before running away, though. While on a playdate with a classmate, one of them took a heavy book to a friend's hamster when the little girl's back was turned, smashing the animal's hind legs.

"It was an accident!" Corinthia told the crying girl. Ben rolled his eyes when both girls wept in each other's arms. When their parents were at the market with their little brother, the twins tried without success to drown and suffocate a kitten, putting its shivering, wet body in the garbage cans outside. After a few minutes, Corinthia opened the can, pulled it out and set it free.

"We can't kill it, dummy!" Corinthia scolded him. "You want Mrs. Miller to find out?"

"Don't call me a dummy!" Ben yelled. "This was all your idea in the first place!"

"You don't have to yell at me, Benji!" she sobbed, before running back into the house.

They did other things, too. When Corinthia wasn't around, Ben got caught peeping at their cute, brunette babysitter through the bathroom keyhole while the door was closed.

"It wasn't me!" he screamed in protest when his father tore into him with a belt. Later that day, Corinthia climbed on the roof and got Ben to help her launch water balloons at the neighbors. When they were found out, she convinced her brother to take the blame. Ben alone was punished for that.

While he lay across his own bed hours later, still smarting, Jenna, his ivory-complexioned mother, sat down. At five foot seven and lithe, Jenna was raven-haired and was as dark as her husband was blond. Her eyes were a washed-out kind of green. She smiled down at Ben and smoothed his blond hair.

"Benjamin," she said, "you have to take better care of Corinthia. She's your sister."

"Mommy," he told her, "I'm trying to be good. I am. But sometimes Corinthia . . . she just . . . she always winds up getting me in to more trouble. She keeps saying she's not, but I can't make her be good. I can't! Sometimes she's mean and she doesn't care about things or animals or people like I do."

"She says the same things about you, Benji. People tell us all the time both of you are really bad kids." She sighed. "It was never my goal in life to raise little monsters."

"I'm not a monster," Ben retorted. "She is."

"Neither of you are. You just need to make better choices. You and she are the same, Ben."

"But we're not."

She shook her head from side to side, and Ben inhaled the perfume from her flowing hair.

"You're just alike. You know each other better than anyone else in the whole wide world. You even share the same spirit."

He didn't say anything after that.

"Ben," his mother continued, "you and Corinthia are very blessed. I didn't have a sister or a brother or a mother when I was your age."

His eyes grew large and he sat up. "How come?"

"Because my parents died when I was two years old. I grew up in foster homes, which is where they send kids without moms and dads. I wish I had what you have. You should be grateful."

"But what about Grandma?"

"She's your father's mother."

"How come she never visits?" he asked.

Jenna took a deep breath before exhaling. It was a few moments before she spoke again. "Your grandmother and I don't get along," she said, seeming to choose her words with care. "She . . . well, she thinks I should raise you differently—take you to church more often. But I like our church lessons at home, don't you?"

Ben nodded. He thought about the one time they went to visit his grandmother a couple of years after Luke was born. She was a pretty, fair-haired older lady who lived alone in a great big house. She even had a second, smaller house behind that one, too.

His mother continued. "She thinks that just because she's living in a mansion with plenty of money, she can tell us how to live our lives, how to raise you." Jenna sighed. "Anyway, you still get to talk to her on the phone on your birthdays, and she sends all of you nice Christmas presents every year. You don't need to see her too much."

"But she's always asking us to go to church with her."

Jenna bristled. "Jesus is always with us. 'For where two or three are gathered together in my name, there am I in the midst of them,'" she quoted Scripture. "You need to pray more, Benji."

"I know, Mom."

"You pray for your daddy, especially. He's got some . . . evil in his blood, something he inherited from his father. Pray, too, it never touches you."

It was dusk when Ben stood next to his sister on the porch later. Corinthia looked at him and muttered something.

"What did you say?" he asked.

"I'm sorry," she repeated. "For getting you in trouble."

"No, you're not."

She blinked and sniffled and wiped at her eyes. "Am too."

He shrugged. They were watching their neighbors play. When one of them shouted, "Who's up for hide-and-go-seek?" Ben shot past Corinthia. "I am!"

The other kids turned to face him, surprised.

Ben didn't know why, but none of the neighborhood kids liked playing with them. Probably because Corinthia, who started out as everyone's friend, would almost always wind up pulling the girls' hair or picking fights with the boys. Because he was her brother, he guessed he was guilty by association.

He skipped toward the kids while his twin sister watched. When the ringleader, a brown-haired eight-year-old girl, asked him to be seeker, Ben nodded. He put his hands over his eyes and counted.

Corinthia stood next to him. "Ooh, maybe the first one found loses!" she shouted. Ben smiled at her and repeated her taunt. They ran off together in search of their playmates and found Owen Pizicopski first. When the game was over, an angry Owen jumped in Ben's bewildered face.

"Why is your sister the boss of you?" he asked, pointing to Corinthia. "She's not even 'it'! You don't have to do whatever she says. Maybe you should wear the dresses!" The other kids snickered.

Ben's eyes swam with tears.

But before he could say anything, Corinthia slapped Owen across his face. "You can't make fun of my brother! Take that back!" she roared.

Owen's hand flew to his stinging cheek. He turned and ran away, crying. "That's right! Go home to your mommy, you little cry baby!"

Ben rounded on his sister. "You didn't have to do that! I don't need you to fight for me!"

One hand flew to her chest and her mouth fell open. She put both hands on her hips when Ben stalked off. She pouted. "Well, I was only trying to help!"

When Owen's mother told Jenna that Corinthia had slapped her son, she marched the pair to his house to apologize.

"I'm sorry I slapped you," Corinthia said, her face flushed, while shifting from one foot to another. She stared at the ground while Owen stood in his doorway, smirking at them.

Owen's mom poked him. "I'm sorry I made fun of you," he told Ben.

"It's OK," Ben said.

"There now," Jenna said. "Mrs. Pizicopski, I want you to know these two will be grounded for what they've done. But I wanted to make sure they apologized to Owen."

Owen's mother nodded.

"But I didn't even do anything," Ben whined. His mother slapped the back of his head.

The twins were grounded. And for the rest of the summer, their mother confined their playing to their large backyard.

∽

"Jason!" Jenna cried out the window at their father one August day, as summer came to a close and all of fall yawned before them. From high in the tree house, Ben and Corinthia could see and hear their parents. Jason lay under the Ford truck, changing the oil. He sat up abruptly and banged his head. He rose from the ground with a curse. Corinthia frowned. Ben said nothing when his sister climbed closer to the ground but stayed among the branches.

Jason wiped his hands on a dingy rag. "What now, Jen?"

"Those kids are going to be the death of me! Luke fell out of that tree—again!"

The pair could hear Jason stomping through the living room, the dining room, and the kitchen before he emerged from behind the screen door and appeared in the backyard.

"Corinthia! Benjamin! Both of you come down right now!"

Ben slid down the huge oak tree so fast that he skinned both knees and his right leg. Jason scowled at Ben's grimace. Corinthia, unfazed, hung upside down by her knees, her favorite pink-and-white dress with big yellow flowers billowing lazily in the breeze. Her hands were linked behind her head. Her pink-and-white panties were showing.

"Girl, what are you doing?" her father yelled up at her. "Bring your ass down here, too!"

She took a deep breath, hoisted herself up, gripped the tree branch tightly with both hands and let her legs and her dress fall. She hung from the lowest branch, a good four feet off the ground, dangling by her arms.

She let go, landing like an Olympian in an artful crouch.

"Sir," she said, a questioning expression on her face.

"What happened to Luke?"

"He fell," Ben said, a little too quickly.

"That true, girl?" her father asked.

She gave her father a long even gaze.

"No, sir. I pushed him."

"Why'd you go and do a thing like that?"

"'Cause."

"'Cause what?"

"He squished Henry," she lied.

"Who the hell is Henry?"

"My pet caterpillar. I was waitin' on him to turn into a butterfly."

Jason turned his head slightly, stifled a laugh, and went back inside.

Ten minutes later, Corinthia was hanging by her hands from the tree again. This time she was higher up, deep within the branches, but just outside their tree house. "I bet we could kill Luke and he would come back to life just like that skunk did. Like Lenny did," she said.

Ben was standing inside the tree house, looking out through the open window at his twin sister. "That again? You almost killed him a few minutes ago! Besides, that's stupid."

"Why is it stupid?"

"Because it won't work, dummy. It's a miracle we didn't kill that skunk!"

"We did kill it."

"We didn't!" he corrected her. "And it was bad enough we had to get all those rabies shots at the hospital, bathe in tomato juice and everything! Plus, we still stank! Besides, we killed a whole bunch of animals and not one of them came back to life. We cannot kill Luke."

"Why are you such a fraidy-cat!" She laughed. "He won't really die, dumb dumb."

"I said no," he responded.

Corinthia ignored him. "Luke!" she called to their baby brother on the ground. "Come up here."

Ben went to the door of the tree house and stood on the large branch that held his sister. "No!" Ben yelled at Luke. "You stay right where you are!"

Luke craned his four-year-old neck, looking up at his big brother and sister. He shrugged and continued making mud pies in the dirt.

"Honey, it would be easy," Corinthia said, trying to convince Ben in the same tone their mother used when she wanted them to eat spinach, which they both hated. "He's little. I can push him out of the tree house. It's higher up than he was before."

"No!" Ben demanded. "And if you try, I'm going to tell Mommy!"

"I hate you!" Corinthia screamed.

"I don't care. I'm going to tell on you."

"I'm going to tell on you," she mocked him in a voice identical to his. "You won't tell anyway," she continued in a childish, singsong lilt.

"I can! And I will!" he screamed.

"You can't! Daddy said you can't tell anyone about what happened to Lenny! And if you tell Mommy, I'm going to tell her that you told me Daddy killed Lenny and then Daddy will beat you till you die!"

"Just shut up! You're such a bitch!"

That's when Ben jumped up and down on the branch holding his twin sister some fifteen feet in the air.

Corinthia shrieked before she fell, her small body hitting two thin tree limbs before she sailed through the last branch. She landed face up in the mud at her baby brother's feet.

"'Rinthia?" Luke asked. He looked down at his big sister and screamed. Jenna and Jason rushed outside. Corinthia didn't move. Her father knelt down next to her.

"She's still breathing."

"Jason," Jenna said. "We need to take her inside!"

Jason scooped up his unconscious daughter and ran upstairs to the twins' bedroom. Both boys followed. Inside their room, their mother knelt beside her bed.

"Shouldn't we call 911?" Ben asked, breathless. "That's what they taught us in school."

"No," his father said, his voice loud, firm.

His mother nodded. "She's just had the wind knocked out of her. Come here, let's pray."

When the boys knelt, they bowed their heads and began praying "Our Father which art in heaven . . ."

Thirty minutes passed. Ben's parents were now whispering behind closed doors in the twins' room after sending the boys downstairs. When his parents appeared and went outside, Ben ran back up the stairs and looked down at them from a window in the hallway. He could hear snatches of their conversation.

"But we should . . ." his mother was saying.

"I said no!" his father thundered.

Scared, Ben went into the room he and Corinthia shared. She was still, so he climbed into bed next to her. "You gonna be OK?"

He saw her eyes flutter open. "You thought you were going to get rid of me. Didn't you, little brother?"

"No," he said, ashamed and looking away.

"Good. 'Cause you are never getting rid of me—not after today. Know why?"

He shook his head.

"Because now you owe me."

CHAPTER TWO

O ne month later, Jenna and Corinthia sat on a bed in the twins' room preparing for church.

"See? If you do it just like this, your hair will gleam in the sunlight," Jenna said, brushing her daughter's hair. Corinthia shrugged and tugged at her scratchy and uncomfortable dress.

"I bought that for today's service, young lady, so please don't wrinkle it."

"Yes, ma'am," Corinthia said, her eyes on the floor, her legs dangling over the edge of the bed. When Jenna stopped to rummage through a dresser drawer in search of her daughter's stockings, Corinthia began twirling her fingers in her hair.

Summer was gone. The drama of the tree house fall was a distant memory. Ben was contrite—his mother's way of saying he was still being punished for causing Corinthia's accident—so he wasn't allowed out.

"Why are we going to church all of a sudden?" Corinthia asked her mother.

Jenna sighed. "I've explained this. Mrs. Miller saw you fall from that tree and I'm sick and tired of her and everyone else asking about you. Better if they see that you're just fine."

Corinthia was silent for a moment. "I think Benji should go. I don't want to go."

Her mother slapped her. "Don't you dare say that! Little girls go to church with their mothers!"

Corinthia gasped. She held her hand to her tingling cheek. While her mother often struck Ben, she had never hit her before—and certainly not in the face. In shock, she whimpered, "Yes, ma'am."

"Besides, we need our girl time," Jenna continued, as if nothing happened. She tossed the stockings at Corinthia. "Put these on, please. We're leaving shortly."

Jason, who had taken Luke fishing, never prayed or went to church with them. Corinthia couldn't understand why.

"I hate spending time with her," Corinthia said aloud, moments after Jenna had left their room.

"She keeps saying it's a miracle that fall didn't kill you," Ben said.

"I almost wish it did," she muttered. "She never lets me out of her sight. Can't even play outside in the yard anymore. She makes me sick."

"Have fun at church," Ben told her before leaving her alone. She pulled a face and turned back toward the mirror.

Two hours later, Corinthia discovered church didn't make her feel any better either. Her mind wandered, as it often did, to Ben. How could her mother be so . . . cruel toward him? She sat on the hard pew next to Jenna, her hair tucked beneath a stupid bonnet. When Jenna handed her the hymnal, Corinthia sighed and tugged on the bottom of her dress.

"Stop pulling on it," her mother said through clenched teeth.

The pianist began to play, and their voices rang out when they sang the hymn "Take My Hand, Precious Lord."

After service, the pastor smiled down at Sister Zanetti's child and pointed toward the large tan bandage visible beneath her white stockings.

"Scraped your knee there, huh?"

"Yes, sir," Corinthia whispered, staring at the floor.

Her mother laughed. "My little girl is as tough as nails."

The pastor smiled, nodded, and moved to speak to another congregant.

Later, Jenna took Corinthia to the mall for more clothes.

"Why'd you get rid of all my pants?" Corinthia asked her. "I don't want to wear dresses all the time."

"You don't need slacks. Your tomboy days are over."

"But you're not buying anything for Ben, Mommy. He needs . . ."

Jenna cut her off. "What did I tell you about him? You worry about you. I'll worry about Ben."

Later that night, Ben awoke with a fright after Jenna slipped into their room, shears in one hand, his privates in the other.

"You're a bad boy, Benjamin Zanetti," she whispered in the darkness. "You corrupted your sister. I wish you had never been born." She squeezed his penis. "I should cut it off."

Ben screamed until his mother dropped the scissors and ran sobbing from the room.

"Are you OK?" Corinthia asked quietly. He nodded. "I hate how she treats you now, Ben," she whispered. "I feel like . . . it's all my fault." Ben was silent.

Corinthia made him lock the door after that. But it didn't really matter. Jenna's insane rage was boundless after the accident.

One day, she asked him to retrieve something from the basement. When he was halfway down the stairs, she kicked him square in his back. Down he went, toppling limb over limb until he was at the bottom, looking up at her when she slammed the door in his face. He lay there for a few moments, numb. When he got to the top of the stairs and twisted the doorknob, he found it locked.

"Mommy?" he whimpered. "Mommy!" He banged. He yelled until he was hoarse. Several hours later, his father let him out.

She locked him down there for days afterward. And he would wait for Luke or Jason, who were rarely home, to return and release him.

"Come on, Luke," Jason would tell his baby boy. "Let's go fishing. Want to go camping? Hunting?" Luke would nod and away they'd go, away from Jenna, who behaved more irrationally each day.

Seasons flew by and the children grew—all behind closed doors.

"I wish we could go back to school," Corinthia whispered under her breath one day. Jenna heard her.

"I can teach you just as well here," she said. "Besides, there's no religious instruction down at that school. Keep being smart, and I'll smash all these TVs. It rots your brain, and your daddy keeps watching garbage on it anyway."

That garbage was pornography. The summer after Lenny's death, the kids didn't see much of their father. When they did, he was high and passed out on the couch—garbage blasting from cable television—much to their mother's ire.

Once, Ben heard their parents argue after one of Jason's friends was killed at an Italian eatery on South Street.

"You don't know a damn thing, Jenna!" Jason had said, snorting and rubbing his hand across his nose. "Don't ask me about my business."

"I don't want my kids around it. You have no idea how being around that crap affects them!"

Jason scoffed. "I'm not the one driving them crazy, Jenna! You're doing that all by your damn self. Locking that boy up in the basement."

"I'll stop, then. You need to leave the drugs alone! But just tell me, where do you take Luke?" she demanded. "Why just him?"

"You know why."

Jenna was quiet. From the open doorway of his bedroom upstairs, Ben could hear their every word. He hated it when they argued.

Then Jason said, "Jenna, you're sick, baby. Let me get you some help. You can't keep taking what happened out on Ben. He's my son, Jenna. My boy. Benji is . . ."

Jenna shrieked. "Jason, I don't want to hear it again!"

A short while later, Ben heard Jason stomp out of the house. He went back into his room, stood at the window, and watched his father leave.

It was the last time Ben ever saw his father.

A few years later, Jason came and got Luke. After that, both had disappeared for good, leaving behind a mother who was losing her mind.

"It's like she doesn't care about me anymore," Ben whispered to Corinthia one day. Jenna went back to work, but when she wasn't working, she spent most of her time with Corinthia. She doted on her, buying her fancy dresses and shoes and, as she grew older, padded bras and expensive accessories. She ignored Ben—who was relegated to his father's hand-me-downs and the barest of essentials.

"I will never forgive him for hurting you," she had told Corinthia. "He was supposed to protect you. You are more important to me than anyone else on this planet."

"But it doesn't matter, Mommy," Corinthia pleaded. "Everything's OK now." Jenna just gave her a blank stare before leaving the room. Ben emerged from the shadows a few minutes later.

"I can't take much more of this," he said.

"Me, either," Corinthia agreed. "Promise me one day we'll run away."

Ben nodded. "I will always take care of you, sis."

She smiled. "I'll always take care of you, too, little brother."

The incessant knocking on the front door one afternoon while Jenna was working took the Zanetti household by surprise. No one knocked. Not even the deliverymen from Amazon. When Corinthia opened the heavy wooden door, a petite white girl with ashen blond hair stepped into the foyer.

"Hi! I'm Jane." She thrust her hand out to Corinthia, who stared at it like it wasn't real.

Jane laughed. "This is the part where you shake it."

Corinthia smiled, shook Jane's hand, and introduced herself.

"Corinthia," Jane repeated it. "I like it—kinda old-fashioned. It's pretty, like you." Corinthia's blush deepened. Pretty? she thought. She didn't know what to say. No one had ever paid her a compliment.

"You don't look like a Jane. Not a plain Jane," Corinthia stammered, trying to flatter her back. "That's for sure."

Jane grinned, and Corinthia did too.

"Wanna come hang out at my house?" Jane asked, tossing her hair over her shoulder. It floated in the air for a moment.

Corinthia's heart continued to tango against her chest. "Sure! Wait right here! Let me put on some shoes." She ran up the stairs, taking them two at a time until she reached her bedroom.

"Where do you think you're going?" Ben asked her. Corinthia fell to her knees, looking under the bed for her sneakers.

"Out."

"Don't let Mommy catch you," he cautioned.

"Don't tell Mommy, Benji, and I won't get caught."

"Don't be fresh," he said, mimicking their mother's voice. Laughter followed. Then Corinthia pleaded, "You know, you could cover for me if she comes back and I'm not here."

She dug through her dresser drawer and pulled out a bra. She turned her back, pulled the straps of her dress down to her shoulders and struggled into it. Then she pulled the straps up.

Corinthia glanced in the mirror, pleased at her reflection. At thirteen, her blond hair was straighter now and hung all the way down her back. She brushed her hair on the left side first, then the right, alternating until it gleamed. Satisfied, she opened her dresser drawer and pulled out a tiny tube of pink lipstick. She applied it with care, pursing her lips to even out the color. She took a small tube of mascara and brushed it on her eyelashes. Her blue eyes sparkled when she smiled. She gripped the sides of the dresser and closed her eyes.

"Cover for you? How?" Corinthia heard Ben say. She opened her eyes.

"Just tell her I'm in the basement folding clothes or something. She never goes down there anyway."

He laughed. "You know I can't do that. Besides, she never comes home from work in the middle of the day anyway."

Moments later, side by side in the sunshine, Corinthia and Jane skipped down the street. It was a mild spring afternoon, and Jane's purple-and-gray bag was slung over her left shoulder.

"Nice book bag," Corinthia said.

"How come I've never seen you at school?" Jane asked, looking into Corinthia's face.

"My mom homeschools us."

"Us?"

"Yeah, me and my brother, Benjamin."

"That's weird."

"Yeah."

"Was that your brother I heard you talking to upstairs?"

Corinthia nodded.

"How old is he?"

"Almost fourteen. We're twins."

"Wow," Jane said. "Guess you don't look alike since you're fraternal, huh?"

Corinthia shrugged. "People say we do. He hates it though, looking like a girl. How old are you?" Corinthia asked her.

"I'm fifteen, but I'll be sixteen in a few months," Jane said. "Don't you guys ever get to hang out?"

"Not really. We're not allowed to. You got any brothers or sisters?" Corinthia asked.

Jane shook her head no.

They continued their walk in silence before Jane turned to Corinthia again. "I'm not supposed to have anyone over at my house unless my parents are home. Only, they're hardly ever at home. My dad travels a lot and sometimes my mom goes with him."

"OK," Corinthia said. "I'll get in big trouble too if my mom finds out I'm gone."

"Guess we won't let her find out." Jane winked. Corinthia laughed.

For three months, mostly in the middle of the night, long after her mother was sleeping, Corinthia would sneak over to Jane's house. The pair would giggle over magazines, talk about TV and YouTube (which the twins rarely watched), boys, and makeup.

"What's high school like?" Corinthia asked her one day while Jane showed her the proper way to apply lipstick. Jane burst into laughter.

"It's a nightmare!" she said. Corinthia's mouth fell open. From Jane, Corinthia learned about the minutiae of day-to-day schooling and re- lationships, the tediousness of study, and the rigors of testing. Through Jane's complaints she learned, too, about the angst that forever seemed to plague teenagers.

Jane's bedroom was on the first floor in the back of her house, abutting some woods. Some nights, she'd crawl in through Jane's open window.

"Look at Rapunzel! Come to let down her hair!" Jane would say each time Corinthia climbed through. They'd sit on her bed talking for hours. Jane did most of the talking, while Corinthia sat in awe, wishing she could switch places with her.

"You have to help me!" Jane said late one night. She grabbed Corinthia by the hand and yanked her so hard through the window Corinthia fell on the floor.

"Ouch," she said, rising before she sat opposite Jane on her bed, tugging on her shorts. "Help you with what?"

"Sienna Black says CJ Ramirez likes me and might ask me to junior prom!" Jane was breathless. Her blue eyes pierced Corinthia's. She plead- ed, "Will you help me?"

Corinthia had no idea who or what she was talking about. But Jane had been so kind to her that she simply smiled and nodded and asked, "What's a prom?"

Without taking a breath, Jane explained in rapid detail what prom was and how much it meant.

"How am I supposed to help?" Corinthia asked.

"Well," Jane said, pausing for dramatic effect, "I've never kissed a boy."

Corinthia clutched a small yellow throw pillow in her lap. "And?"

"I need to practice."

"OK," Corinthia said.

"On you, silly!" Jane said, punching her arm.

Corinthia's eyes widened. "You want to practice kissing? On me?"

Jane nodded.

"But I'm not gay."

Jane laughed. "It's not about that!" she said, waving her hand, dismissing Corinthia's complaint. "Girls kiss other girls all the time! It doesn't mean anything."

Corinthia stared at her for a moment. "I don't know." Then she raised an eyebrow and shook her head no. "I don't think my first kiss should be with a girl. I mean . . . no offense," she stammered.

"None taken! But you did promise to help me. Besides," Jane said, pausing, "you might like kissing me."

"I told you, I'm not . . . I wouldn't even know how." Corinthia's blush was deep, staining her cheeks bright pink.

Jane moved closer to Corinthia. "How do you know?"

"I . . . just know."

"Can I tell you something, Corinthia?" Jane asked. She took a wad of strawberry-flavored bubble gum out of her mouth and stuck it to the back of her hand.

"Sure."

"I want to be the first person you've ever kissed."

Corinthia frowned. "Why?"

"Because I like you. I have ever since the first day I saw you sitting at your window. I would walk by and wonder who the very pretty girl with the long hair was. I wondered if she would let me kiss her."

Corinthia licked her lips, and her blushed deepened. Her entire face was red. "You really think I'm pretty?"

Jane edged closer to her. "I think you're beautiful."

And before Corinthia could protest, Jane leaned in and kissed her. Corinthia closed her eyes. Jane's lips were soft and moist when she brushed her mouth across Corinthia's.

"See? Not bad," Jane said in a small, soft voice. Her breath was bubble-gum sweet. Corinthia's eyelids fluttered when she looked into Jane's eyes. The older girl pressed forward and whispered, "Now let's do it like they do on TV."

Their blond heads together, Jane kissed Corinthia with an ardent zeal that made the younger girl's heart fly around in her chest like restless butterflies. Jane puckered her lips, murmuring her pleasure in tiny, breathy sighs. The room came to life with slight smacking sounds. Jane gave Corinthia very wet, passionate kisses, and much to her surprise, Corinthia began to moan. Jane bit Corinthia's bottom lip gently and seconds later she sucked on her tongue. Corinthia abandoned her doubts and surrendered.

Jane tasted of strawberries and smelled like gardenias.

Corinthia was bewitched—until she felt something that startled her. Desire.

Sensing Corinthia's alarm, Jane grabbed the back of her head and kissed her with a level of intensity that left the younger girl breathless.

Then, in a rush, Jane whispered against her wet mouth, "I don't really like boys, to be honest, Corinthia. Our bodies can be so much more exciting. Let me show you."

When she brushed her hand across Corinthia's bra, the girl pushed Jane so hard she fell back into the pillows. Corinthia stood and whirled away from Jane, letting the pillow in her lap fall to the floor. Without a word, Corinthia turned her back on Jane, crouched low, and climbed out of her window.

"Hey, Corinthia! What's wrong?" Jane hung in the window and shouted, "Don't go like that! Come back. I'm sorry!"

Corinthia stalked back down the street toward her house. She'd never felt anything like that and didn't know what to make of it. Halfway down the street she could hear Jane's voice following her along the breezy route home. She could still feel Jane's soft lips pursed against hers, still feel Jane's tongue.

Corinthia's mouth now tasted like strawberries.

She never spoke of what happened, and she didn't go back. Not even after Jane rang the doorbell two days later and spoke to Benji through the closed door.

"I don't know what else to say," he told Jane. "She said to tell you not to come back."

CHAPTER THREE

One cool, quiet night a few months later, well after her fourteenth birthday, Corinthia pushed the living room window open and climbed outside on the porch. Dressed in a dark blue hoodie, a pair of her father's old rolled-up jeans, and her new pink sneakers, she was off to explore and pleased to have the time to herself. Walking without a destination, she let the moon light her way. She crept between the houses and peered into open windows. Without thinking, she found herself behind Jane's house.

The driveway was empty, which meant Jane's parents weren't home. However, the windows were open and the lights were on. Dressed only in her bra and panties, Jane was on her phone. Corinthia marveled at her skin, the shape of her breasts, how her little derriere dimpled her panties. How she wished she could be her! Just for ten minutes—to attend school, to have places to go and friends to talk to. She winced at the memory of their kiss.

Jane threw her head back and laughed at the caller; then she put the phone down and unhooked her bra. Her full, perky breasts bounced out, and Corinthia, hidden in the trees, gasped. With her eyes she drank the older girl in. She felt a strange revulsion and then, out of nowhere, Corinthia heard a familiar voice.

"What do you think you're doing?"

Corinthia's heart sprang to her throat. She jumped.

Ben.

"You scared me! Why are you even here?"

He shrugged. "I always come here. Every night, just like you, for months."

Corinthia shook with rage; her voice rang with more than a hint of disbelief.

"You're watching her? You've been following me?"

"Of course. As much as Mom still blames me for nearly killing you, you think I'd ever let you out of my sight? I follow you. And I watch you watch her," he said, jutting his chin, nodding toward a topless Jane.

Corinthia couldn't look at him. "Girls aren't supposed to like girls, Corinthia," he teased. "What would our mother say?"

Her cheeks reddened as if exposed to a bright hot lamp. Scriptures flooded her brain in her mother's voice. "'Even their women exchanged natural relations for unnatural ones.'" She stared at the grass then looked up just in time to see Jane hang up the phone and turn out the lights.

"I don't like her," Corinthia snapped. "Not like that."

"Oh, yes you do," Ben said. Beneath the stars his countenance darkened and a mischievous shadow fell over his eyes. He poked his chin toward the window. "I saw you kissing her. I know you liked it."

Corinthia's eyes were like slits. "You don't know anything, Benjamin."

"I know," he said. "I can smell the need wafting from you now, sister dear."

Corinthia wanted to strangle him, but that would have been impossible. "I don't know what you're talking about."

He laughed. "I understand you better than anyone else in the whole world. You loved kissing her. You just didn't like the way it made you feel, did you?"

Blood drained from her face. "Leave me alone, Benji," she said, walking away.

He ignored her. "I know what you want now."

She whirled around and took a confrontational stance. "What?"

"You want to make her pay for making you feel . . . like a sinner. You won't, for some reason. But I will."

Ben began to climb the steps that led to a porch beneath Jane's open window.

"Stop it, Benji!" Corinthia whispered. "You can't go in there!"

"You are not my mother, and you cannot tell me what to do!" he taunted her. "Her parents aren't even here. Their car isn't in the driveway."

"What are you doing?" she said.

"What do you think? It's not a sin for me to kiss her!"

Before she could protest, Ben disappeared through the window. Corinthia slipped into the room with him. In silence, Ben approached Jane's bed. In the shadows, the room didn't appear to be that dark. In fact, Jane's bedroom was always cast in a dim yellow glow. It came from a small night light on the floor in the outlet next to her bed.

"I've had it since I was three," she had told Corinthia once. "It's always on when I sleep. I don't think I could sleep without it."

Ben's voice was quiet when he spoke to his sister.

"Look at how pretty she is when she's sleeping, Corinthia. Just like you when you were little." He leaned in and found her scent enchanting. "Mmmm. She smells like . . ."

Corinthia cut him off and finished his sentence. ". . . Strawberry shampoo. The same kind Mommy buys me."

In the semidarkness, Jane's eyes flew open in surprise, and she flinched. Before she could cry out, Ben jumped on top of her and clamped his hand over her mouth.

"If you scream," he whispered, "I will kill you. Do you understand?" Eyes wide, Jane nodded. Ben pressed his hand down harder over her mouth and grinned. Jane squirmed.

"Don't scream," he warned. He loosened his hand, hovering it over her mouth. He smacked her hard.

She blinked rapidly. "Please," she gasped. "What the . . . ? What are you doing?"

Ben leaned closer to Jane and whispered, "I want the kiss you gave my sister."

"What?" Jane cried, confused.

Ben pressed his hands into her small Adam's apple and squeezed hard. Jane coughed and thrashed. Eyes bulging, she kicked and wailed. He jerked her up to a sitting position before slamming her back against the wooden headboard. Tears filled her eyes.

"What's wrong with you? Why are you doing this? I was only ever nice to . . . argh!" When his hands tightened around her throat, she recoiled and wrenched without success. She clawed at him in a futile attempt to stop him. But Ben was stronger. He could feel her heartbeat quicken between her breasts.

"Did you know I've been watching your little peep show for months, Jane? I bet you did! I mean, who takes off their bra in front of an open window with the lights on?"

Jane balled her fists and began beating at Ben's arms and his chest. She scratched his face, scraping his skin beneath her fingernails.

"Dammit!" Ben yelped. "I wasn't going to hurt you! But now you leave me no option!" He punched her hard on one side of her head and she wailed in agony.

"I'll stop if you give me that kiss," he said. She swallowed hard and nodded. He forced her against the sheets. With one hand he held both of her wrists above her head and leaned in close. His blue eyes never left hers. Jane wept when she kissed him.

"Mmmm," he whispered. "I want that tongue, too."

Their kiss was hesitant, slow, almost . . . tender. He was so gentle that for a few minutes, his hands relaxed. Still, Jane stiffened beneath his touch. He noted that her mouth, dry as cotton, was salty with her fear. It made him euphoric, lightheaded. He stood and backed away.

"I think she's had enough," Ben said to his sister with a touch of remorse.

That's when Corinthia straddled Jane.

"What are you doing?" Ben said, alarmed. "I got my kiss. Let's leave!"

"No," Corinthia told him. "It's my turn!"

She put her hands around the beaten teenager's throat and choked her until she passed out. She snatched one of Jane's scarves from the floor and tied her hands to the headboard.

"Don't tell me you're jealous?" Ben said, his voice taking a tone of disbelief.

"What? I'm not jealous!" she scoffed.

"Corinthia, you need to stop!" Ben told her.

But she ignored him. Over and over, Corinthia played with Jane, choking her to the brink of unconsciousness before slapping her awake. Ben grew tired of begging Corinthia to quit. Each time Corinthia throttled her, Jane thrashed on the bed, coughing, sputtering. Jane's pretty complexion turned flushed and blotchy.

Her hair was tousled. Through anguished sobs, she begged Corinthia to stop until her voice was strained and harsh. In silence and wonder, Corinthia shuddered with pleasure; to Ben, it seemed like she was . . . savoring Jane's pain.

"Why are you doing this?" Ben asked.

"I'm just playing the same game you did, little brother. Why should you have all the fun?" Corinthia asked him, her voice brimmed with excitement. "You know what Mom says, 'Share and share alike.'"

"Please," Jane cried, wrestling against Corinthia in vain, trying to escape.

"Please, you're hurting me! I won't ever come to your house again! I promise. I won't tell anyone!"

"Kiss me now," Corinthia demanded. She stared into Jane's eyes, gaping at the sudden and steely determination that bloomed across the girl's face—despite her obvious fear.

"No," Jane said, her voice weak, her eyes weary. "No more kisses."

Corinthia punched her in the throat. She mimicked Ben's cadence. "You must want me to kill you." Gasping and dazed from the blow, Jane shook her head no. Her voice was bitter.

"What do you want?"

"I want you to beg me, Jane," Corinthia said. "Plead for your life."

Jane begged. "I don't want to die! Please don't kill me!"

Corinthia stared into Jane's eyes. "Ben," she said. "Should I let Jane live?"

"You're crazy!" Jane sobbed.

But Ben was paralyzed from within. He wanted to be appalled, horrified, but he wasn't—and that scared him even more.

"I always knew you would do this again," Ben told his sister. "Stop it, Corinthia. You're going too far! She said she wouldn't tell."

Corinthia turned her head slightly to the left, but her gaze remained on Jane.

"Don't you see, Ben? We can't take that chance. I have to fix this. I know her way better than you. She'll tell. I know she will."

Suddenly, Ben was seven, standing on a thick tree limb, watching Corinthia plot Luke's demise. Today, however, more than anything, he wanted to be upset. But deep down he found Jane's fear enticing. It shrouded him in a weird, contemptuous bliss. Every scream, every sob, every plea, every painful moan was rapturous. And he knew his sister. He knew she felt it too.

When Ben swooned from the sight of Jane's torture, Corinthia swooned with him. Ben was sure he had never known pleasure like this—and it sickened him. Corinthia would later tell him that it sickened her too. But he didn't believe it.

"Corinthia," he said, his voice hesitant. "Let's just leave, please."

Then Corinthia banged the final nail into the coffin of Ben's guilt.

Her eyes never left Jane's face. "Remember, you still owe me, little brother."

Ben exhaled. He hung his head in defeat. "Just finish it."

Jane's eyes widened once more and she gave a last, panicked cry. "You're insane! Please! Don't!"

And then, before Ben could change his mind, Corinthia Zanetti began strangling Jane Winters.

Corinthia looked down and marveled when Jane's stunning features morphed into a detailed mask of horror. A small voice whispered one word in her ear: stop. She ignored it. Just a few minutes more, she thought to herself. In utter wonder, Corinthia noted the surprise and terror in the teenage girl's eyes. Struggling for breath, Jane broke her restraints, gasped, and feebly clawed at the hands choking off her air supply. For a fleeting moment, fear about the consequences of her actions crawled across Corinthia's skin. But so, too, did a sense of euphoria when the lack of oxygen made the blood vessels near Jane's corneas pop, streaking the whites of her eyes with fine red lines.

"OK," she told Ben, her voice resigned. "I'll stop in a minute."

But she didn't.

"Promise me you won't tell!" she said. "Promise!" But Corinthia's hands were fixed to Jane's throat like cement—all while the blond kicked and struggled without success. Corinthia squeezed harder, leaned in, and buried her nose in Jane's hair, unaware the girl's lips were turning blue. She took a deep breath, and the scent of strawberries and a sense of peace washed over her. Beneath Corinthia's tightening grip, the light behind Jane's eyes began to fade. The petite teen went limp. When Corinthia released Jane and looked down at her, she gasped. Jane didn't look right. She looked . . . odd. Corinthia slapped her and called her name. "Jane!" She sniffed. "Jane? Come on! We were only playing!" But Jane was still.

Corinthia frowned at first. And then the realization of the magnitude of her actions dawned on her with a rapidity that left her breathless. Frantic, Corinthia shook Jane over and over again.

But the girl didn't move.

Corinthia gulped, "Jane! Oh no! Jane? Jane?" Then, "I . . . I didn't mean to!"

Corinthia stared at Jane for a moment before she placed one final kiss on Jane's forehead and staggered when she rose from the bed in the girl's empty house.

In her shock, Corinthia's mind darted back to the moment her father killed Lenny. "I think I'm going to be sick."

Ben blinked. With one hand, he reached out and grabbed Jane by the jaw and moved her head from left to right. Jane's sightless eyes were open; drool ran down her chin. He lowered his ear to her lips.

"She's not breathing," Ben marveled. "You should be ashamed of yourself, Corinthia," he whispered.

Corinthia's heart whipped fast and quick against her heaving chest. Blood drained from her face and fresh tears spilled from her eyes; her cheeks were hot and flushed. She felt a sour, sinking feeling in the pit of her belly.

She realized then that she had heard those words before.

From whom? Her father.

When they were five years old, they had watched a moth inside a jar battling in vain to escape, to feel a single breath of air kiss its powdery white wings. Jason had left the decision to open the jar up to her. But she had not. In silence, they waited while the moth pulverized its tiny body to pieces against the glass prison, trying to get out.

You should be ashamed of yourself, daughter dear. Little girls are supposed to be more loving.

That's what Jason told her before he snatched the jar away and his little girl burst into tears.

Corinthia sniffed. "At least now we won't get into any trouble," she whispered back to Ben. With the back of her hand, she wiped the tears from her cheeks.

Ben's silence was deafening.

"I didn't mean to!" she told him, her voice hollow. Without warning, her face contorted and she fell to her knees and howled like a wounded animal. "Jane!" she cried.

"Oh, Ben," she whispered. "Why did I do that to Jane?" She buried her hands in her face, retched, and trembled so hard her entire body shook.

Ben turned on his heel, and before he retreated out of the window, he muttered over his shoulder to his weeping sister, "Now she's just like Lenny, Corinthia. She's not coming back."

Much later, Ben alone crept back in through his living room window, one of Jane's scarves tucked in his back pocket. He had one foot on the floor when the lights came on.

He froze.

Jenna was sitting in a wing-backed chair. "Where have you been?"

Startled, Ben turned white. "I . . . went for a walk."

Jenna rose from the chair, crossed the room, and slapped him so hard that part of his upper lip started to swell. Ben coughed and stared at the floor.

He shook his head from side to side. Defiant, he looked down and gazed into his mother's eyes. At fourteen, he was a foot taller than her now. When he wiped his hand on the back of his mouth, he tasted blood.

"You know you're not to leave this house without my permission. You are not supposed to go out, looking . . ."

Ben cut his mother off and spat, "Did you think I would live here trapped in this prison for the rest of my life? Did you think I wouldn't, what? Grow up? One day I'm going to leave and never come back!"

Jenna recoiled like she had been bitten by a snake. "Don't say that! You know, there are days when I think I should leave you here where you stand."

"Not if I leave first!" he shot back.

"Oh? And where are you gonna go?"

"I can go live with Grandma!"

Jenna erupted into peals of laughter. "Your grandmother—if she's even still alive—is crazy! That demented old woman can barely take care of herself—last I heard she had Alzheimer's."

"What's old timers?"

"Alzheimer's. It means she's deranged, Benjamin."

"Well, then I'll go live with Daddy!"

She laughed again. "Your father? As if he wants you? Nobody knows where he is. He went to your grandmother's, stole all her money, and ran off with Luke. If the cops couldn't find him, what makes you think you can?"

"You can't keep me here forever!"

Jenna raised her hand to strike him again, but Ben caught it in mid-air. He pushed her so hard she fell to the floor, stunned. Without another word, Ben stepped over Jenna, kicked off his shoes and climbed the stairs until he reached his room. When he opened the door, the bedroom was empty. He slammed the door shut and lay across the bed and finally nodded off. Hours later, a light breeze awoke him, and his ears began to ring.

With his eyes closed, he said to his sister, "How'd you get past Cruella?"

When Corinthia didn't respond, Ben tried a different question.

"Why did you kill her?" he whispered.

"I didn't mean to, Benji. But . . . you know she would have told. You would have gotten in trouble. We both would have."

"You don't know that," he whispered.

"Why did you have to crawl through her window!" Her voice was bewildered, angry.

He pushed his head into his hands. "I just . . . can't believe you killed her," he whispered. A hush descended over the room. Ben broke the silence. "We have to leave."

"I know," she replied, her voice filled with concern. "Are you afraid we'll get caught?"

Ben laughed. "No. That's not why. I can't stand our mother anymore. She hates me. Sometimes I can't . . ."

"Breathe," Corinthia said, finishing for him.

"That's why Daddy left. He couldn't take it anymore, either," Ben said.

"Do you think . . . Daddy and Luke are still alive?"

Ben sighed. "I don't know. I don't care."

"Where will we go? When should we leave?"

"I'll go first," Ben said. "Find a place, then you can follow me, just like always."

Corinthia sank her head in her hands and murmured, "OK."

In a quiet voice he leaned forward and said, "We have to love each other, Corinthia. Mom and Dad don't. Don't you trust me?"

"Do I have a choice?"

"No, you don't. And I can fix stuff, too, you know."

"Yeah, OK," she said. "We'll see."

CHAPTER FOUR

Ben glanced at the address on the faded Christmas card envelope in his hand and leaned again on the doorbell to the large, stately home.

"Please God," he whispered. "Let her still be alive."

His breath caught in his throat when the door swung open. A familiar, wizened woman with papery pale skin and long blondish-gray hair squinted at him and gasped.

"Ma'am, are you Mrs. Alma Zanetti?" he asked.

"Ben?" She peered at him from behind a pair of thick glasses. They made her eyes appear twice as large. With tiny amethyst earrings on her lobes, she was dressed in a purple-and-blue dress with white piping. It matched the sensible purple velvet ballerina flats on her feet. Her gnarled fingers were covered in rings, including one made of three tiny emeralds and a diamond solitaire.

"Hi, Grandma."

"Praise Jesus!" she shouted, snatching him against her. Her suddenly familiar scent of Chanel No. 5 was as warm and inviting as her embrace. She peered around him.

"Come on in!" She dragged him inside, closing the door behind her.

"Where's your mother? Where's your sister?"

Fourteen-year-old Ben cleared his throat. "About that . . ."

When he finished telling her about his mother's repeated abuse and her threats to abandon him, his grandmother began trembling in anger.

"Let me get the phone!"

Ben took her hands in his. "Please, don't call anyone. Mom ran off, and Corinthia and I are both scared." Tears pooled in his eyes. "We're not supposed to leave the house—especially Corinthia. It's why I came alone—in case Mom comes back. We weren't even sure you were still alive. We didn't know if you would take us in—it's just . . . well, when we ran out of food last week . . ."

"Nonsense! Of course I'll take you both in! Come on in the kitchen. I'll make you something to eat." For twenty minutes, while his grandmother moved between the cupboards and the refrigerator, Ben listened to her rail against Jenna.

"I told your father many times not to marry that woman. I knew she wasn't wrapped too tight! You must live with me from now on."

Ben frowned. "But what about our house? What if she comes back and finds it empty?"

"Don't you worry about the house." She patted his arm. "I bought your parents that house when they got married, and it's still in my name—even though she hasn't allowed me to set foot in it since you were little. I'll send caretakers to look after it. Even if she comes back, they'll let her know where you are. From now on, this is your home." His grandmother hugged him again. "It's so good to see you, Benjamin! I can't wait to see your sister."

Ben collapsed against her. "Thank you, Grandma. I can't tell you how grateful I am." The pair sat side by side on a large forest-green sofa.

"Grandma," he asked between bites of the sandwich she made him, "have you seen my Dad and Luke?"

She nodded. "Your thieving father did bring Luke here," she sighed. "But that was years ago. He emptied out one of my accounts and took off with your brother. I called your mother and the police. I haven't seen him since and don't care to."

When Ben slanted his eyes and creased his forehead, she leaned in and kissed him.

"Don't get upset." She rubbed his back. "I'm sure wherever they are, Luke is fine—the way your father doted on that boy." She sniffed. "Your mother's leaving is a blessing. I got my grandbabies back."

He nodded and hugged her. "And I get to know my grandmother better."

Soon after, Ben discovered his mother had been right: his grandmother's dementia became more apparent. She was forgetful, repeated questions over and over and misplaced things. She also often mistook Ben for Corinthia.

One day, on a stroll, Ben said to Corinthia, "It's really nice out today, isn't it?"

"Yeah, it's really beautiful," his sister answered.

The sprawling, luxurious five-acre estate in Glenside, a tiny hamlet on the outskirts of Laurel County in Central Pennsylvania, was situated on rolling hills and dotted with dozens of trees and shrubs. It was a huge resplendent single-family home with a soaring, steeply gabled roof with chimneys at either end.

The property also included a neighboring guesthouse.

"You can't see it from here. It's several hundred yards away at the end of the driveway behind the house and down a narrow path," Ben's grandmother had said, handing him keys. "Take a look inside. Keep the key. I have extras. We entertained here so much when your grandfather was still alive, but he hated an overcrowded house so he had it built to accommodate guests."

Isolated in an open field at the end of a winding road, several large, majestic oak trees shrouded the view of the guesthouse from the path that approached it. Constructed completely of cobblestones, the front door opened onto a fully furnished living room, complete with a fireplace and large bay windows. Opposite the living room and across a narrow hall was a sunny eat-in kitchen, fully stocked with appliances and pots and pans. Further along the hall, on either side, were two bedrooms. A master bedroom was at the back of the house, and across from that was a full bath.

"Remind me again. What did you think of the guesthouse, Ben?" Grandma asked. She was getting a glass of water in the kitchen.

"I'm not Ben, Grandma. I'm Corinthia!"

"What?" she said, staring at her granddaughter through her thick glasses. "You two look so much alike; it's like seeing double," she chuckled.

Corinthia beamed. "The guesthouse is nice, just like the rest of the house. Here, let me get that glass for you." She took the drinking glass from Alma, filled it with cold tap water and handed it to her. Now, take a seat," she said, leading the old woman to the kitchen table. "I really hope we get to stay here—even if Mom comes back."

Her grandmother patted Corinthia's hand after she sat down. "Well, we'll just have to wait and see, won't we?"

As the years passed, however, they never heard from Jenna again.

❧

Ben and Corinthia loved living with their eighty-two-year-old grandmother. For the twins, it was like moving from hell to heaven. She re-furnished her guest rooms for them in shades of pink and blue, let them order new clothes and shoes from Amazon, and indulged their whims like a wealthy Santa Claus. She taught Corinthia how to bake bread and make pasta from scratch. She also encouraged them to learn how to drive. They, in turn, did the yard work and chores and made sure she kept her many doctors' appointments and took her medicine on time. And she would regale both with fascinating stories about their grandfather and her child-hood. And they, well, they adored her.

"This was a good decision—coming here," Corinthia told Ben after they'd been there a few months. He smiled and nodded. "Can you imagine how much different our lives would've been if we had grown up here?" she asked him.

He nodded.

"Corinthia!" her grandmother called out to her one day from outside. "Come help me in the garden."

"Sure, Grandma!" Corinthia said, opening the front door.

Wearing jeans, the sun beating down on them, Corinthia and her grand-mother planted wisteria along the back of both houses. They then planted vinca as ground cover and tiny budding pink damask rose bushes along the path to the main house and in the backyard.

"They were your great-grandmother's favorite," her grandmother said of the roses. "She had at least a half dozen of these bushes in her garden in Augusta, Georgia. In fact, these came from her gardens."

Corinthia looked up at her from the ground where she knelt in the dirt. "Do you think I could grow roses like this someday for my kids, Grandma?"

"Of course, honey," she said, patting her granddaughter's shoulder with her gloved hand. "All of this," she said, waving her hand over the estate, "will be yours someday—you and your brothers. Would you like that?"

"Yes, ma'am." She grinned. "I'd like that very much."

Her grandmother's eyes sparkled when she winked at her granddaugh-ter. She sniffed and cleared her throat. "I'm so glad you're here, dear. I have always wanted help planting these. Pay attention to how the wisteria grows. See here," she said, pointing to the brick wall. The teenager squint-ed into the sun, gazing at her grandmother's pointed finger.

"Vines with the most beautiful lavender and purple flowers will snake up along the back of this entire wall," Grandma said. "I can't wait for you to watch it grow. Every year it will grow more and more. It's beautiful, and it smells divine."

Two hours later, Corinthia wiped the sweat from her brow with the back of her left hand and rubbed both earth-covered hands across the front of her jeans.

"Are we almost finished, Grandma?"

"Yes. Help me up," she said, grunting when Corinthia helped her to stand. "Let's go inside and have some of that lemonade."

Once inside, though, she neglected to get a drink and instead reached for a bottle filled with pills.

"Grandma, stop! You took that already!" Ben placed his hand on his grandmother's arm. She had nearly made the lethal mistake of taking a double dose of medication. She paused and burst into tears.

"I don't know what I'd do without you."

Ben put his arms around her. "Don't worry, Grandma. I'll take care of you."

"You know, I believe the Lord doesn't make mistakes," she told him, her voice a bit sad. "I think He sent you back to me for a reason. I never even realized how much help I needed until you showed up."

She reached into her apron, pulled out a handkerchief, and dabbed at her right eye.

"We needed you too, Grandma. It's . . . nice to be wanted." And Ben meant it. When he first arrived, he had been relieved she'd taken him in. To him, she was almost a stranger. But to her, he and Corinthia were family—the family she felt had been denied to her for far too long. She had even said he reminded her of Jason so much it was scary. That had surprised him. Ben hadn't seen his father in so long, when he recalled him it was like the man that fathered him was little more than a dream. A bad dream who had drifted in and out of his life. Jason was, after all, the man who abandoned him to the cruelties of his mother. The man that had taken his beloved little brother away and left his eldest son to fend off a disturbed mother often alone. And for that he would never forgive him. But in his grandmother, he had found—for the first time in his life—a real home. It was filled with an unconditional love that surprised him every single day. And their grandmother had mellowed Corinthia, too. They treasured her, this woman who never raised her voice or hand to them and who saw only the good in them—and cherished it.

She peered at him through her owlish glasses and brightened.

"You know after your father stole from me all those years ago, I changed my will so only my grandchildren can inherit my estate. Did I tell you that?"

"Yes, Grandma, you've told me that quite a few times."

"Oh," she said, deflated. "I hate being so forgetful." She sighed. "Well, don't forget. Neither your mother nor your father is entitled to a penny. Just promise me you'll give Luke his share?"

"I promise," Ben told her. "But Grandma, you're not going anywhere for a long time," he said, kissing her cheek. "We don't need your money."

As the roses grew and the wisteria climbed the walls of the houses, Ben got taller, but his frame remained slight. Corinthia began experimenting with all kinds of expensive foundation, blush, and eye shadows. She also developed an obsession with dark red lipstick.

Each summer, Corinthia would go outside and cut dozens of fragrant roses from the bushes, filling the house with their scent, delighting their grandmother. Some days, she'd walk behind their house and along the narrow path that led to the back of the guesthouse. Sure enough, clumps of stunning purple wisteria hung like large teardrops along almost the entire back wall of both houses. Bunches of fist-sized blossoms curled within the thin green leaves.

"Grandma was right," she said to Ben. "They're breathtaking. It reminds me of something out of a fairy tale."

Four years after their arrival, their grandmother died in her bed while an inconsolable Corinthia held her hand. True to her word, Alma Zanetti appointed Ben her executor and bequeathed all five acres of her property and her entire estate to her grandchildren. So sizable was the inheritance, which went uncontested, that neither had to work.

That was when Corinthia suggested they move into the guesthouse.

"Granny's house is too big for the two of us, Ben, and it's too much to clean."

He sighed his agreement. "Should we rent the other house? Some of the property?" Ben asked his sister.

"Nah. Let's just leave it and decide what to do with it later. I'm thinking of buying something in New York, anyway." She winked.

The neighborhood had changed. A Produce Den Farmer's Market sprung up not far from them, and what was once an empty field on the edge of town now included a movie theater, restaurants, shops, and gour-met grocery stores.

Corinthia swiped through her phone. "Says here they're trying to build it up for the students at Glastonbury U." Ben nodded, craning his neck to see the new developments while driving.

The local university was a few miles away.

By 2013, when the twins were almost twenty-two, Ben had long been settled into the guesthouse.

Isolated and far from the road, he found it was the perfect place to take his girls.

Ben froze. The TV blared an old cold-case show.

"Even though fingerprints were found all over the dead girl's bedroom and the apparent killer's DNA was beneath her fingernails, the person re-sponsible for Jane Winters' death continues to elude authorities."

Ben's ears rang, and he held his breath when the camera panned to the front of what used to be Jane's house.

"Detectives tell us, however, that because neither any prints nor any of the recovered DNA is in any criminal database, they may never know the culprit's identity," the show's host continued.

"Neighbors who remember the girl called her friendly and outgoing. Her parents found her strangled to death in her bed in 2004. And although it's been nearly ten years, the death of Jane Winters may never be solved—un-less her killer strikes again, leaving DNA and fingerprints behind."

Ben stood up and switched off the television.

By now, four other women had gone missing in Laurel County and the news was paying a lot of attention to their disappearances—much to Ben's growing consternation.

Still, after all, as even the program had to admit, they had never found Jane's killers.

"I'm calling it a night," he yawned.

Corinthia was already sound asleep.

The next day Ben rose and went for a three-mile run. He entered the house and peeled his sweaty shirt off and mopped his forehead with it. He sensed his twin was near.

"Happy birthday, little brother!" Corinthia blurted in a singsong voice. "Did you enjoy your birthday present last night?"

He smiled weakly and pressed a finger up to his right ear and rubbed it with vigor.

"Happy birthday, sister dear!" He knew the reference to his "present" and the enjoyment thereof would lead to a fight. He bristled and strode down the hallway toward the bathroom.

"I need a shower," he mumbled.

Delicious, hot water rained over his head, down his neck, and across his back.

He had held his "present" in his arms for most of the night, playing in her hair, trailing his fingers up and down her warm skin. He had promised Corinthia that this would be the last girl.

Air whooshed out from his mouth, and he felt his tension dissipate. The heat from the shower relaxed him. His eyes were closed, and he inhaled deeply. Tendrils of steam rose around him and curled in the air. He didn't hear the door open, but a slight breeze caressed the nape of his neck.

The shower curtain billowed a bit and the air shifted.

"We can't keep this one," Corinthia said, her voice soft. Ben's body grew rigid. He shuddered ever so slightly. Here it was again. The same argument. Her justification for murder.

"I know," he said. Ben took a step back and his head emerged from the water, which was still beating against his chest. He did not open his eyes. "But we'll keep her just a little while longer."

"You always say that," she snapped.

He put a wet fist to his mouth and sighed. "We have time."

"I don't think so. They're looking hard for this one."

"I said I know that!" He flung himself forward, pressing his entire body beneath the water again, relishing in its sudden, stinging warmth.

Moments later, he shut off the shower and reached for a towel and rubbed it across his face. When he opened his eyes, he was alone in the bathroom. Ben dried off and got dressed. He went to the room in the guesthouse, where their latest catch remained tied to the mattress on the floor, asleep in a chloroform haze.

He stared at her from the doorway.

This girl had been hitchhiking—a habit she had after drinking all night. Corinthia had done her homework, so Ben knew all of her habits. When he first brought her home, he had climbed into the back seat of their car with her, covered her eyes with a black silk fabric, and played in her golden tresses. Pressing damp lips to her cheek, he sat there a long time and watched in near fascination while her soft blond tendrils fell through his fingers. Edging closer, he caressed her and pressed his nose into her hair and gasped. Strawberries. She, too, used strawberry shampoo?

"What a pleasant surprise," he had murmured. He inhaled, wishing he could drown in her scent.

Much later, back in the room, Ben climbed on the bed next to the young woman and played idly with a tactical pen between his fingers. Corinthia had said this one's name was Tallulah Montgomery. Her snoring was soft. He set the pen on the floor near a desk he kept in the room and closed his eyes. It was night now and nearly quiet—save for the frogs that still croaked outside beneath the strains of what sounded like thousands of crickets. They hummed to each other, creating a symphony beneath the moonlight. It was a sound he adored, that and the occasional roar of airplanes soaring overhead as they made their way toward the Harrisburg International Airport.

Ben snuggled closer to Tallulah and stroked her arm. He closed his eyes. He could feel Corinthia hovering nearby, but she didn't say anything. Ben sat up and removed Tallulah's blouse and miniskirt. Her skin was warm and pale in the room's ambient light. He ran his hands up and down her young, firm body.

He whispered to his sister, "This one I'm going to cherish."

Over the years, his twin had helped feed his insatiable need to kidnap women, and Ben tolerated her desire to "fix" his mistakes by permanently disposing of them. But as the years passed, Ben wanted to keep them indefinitely and Corinthia did not. She grew jealous of his attentions toward them—that he knew. And their disposal was the source of many arguments. He knew that despite her help kidnapping this one—his last one for his birthday—he would have a devil of a time convincing her not to dispatch Tallulah.

"Ah, what a musical name you have," he whispered.

Ben yanked Tallulah's T-shirt up. She wasn't wearing a bra. He removed the rest of her clothes and shoved her panties into his back pocket. He grabbed a large bottle of strawberry-scented lotion and dumped some of it into his hand. Ben massaged the lotion into her skin, her breasts, her arms, her legs, and her feet, gently, as if she were virginal, innocent.

He stood and went outside to his car.

When he returned, Ben dressed her in a new frilly summer sundress, just like the ones Corinthia wore as a little girl. He pulled the panties out of his pocket, shoved them between the girl's lips, and secured a brand-new handkerchief over her mouth, careful not to cover her nose so she could breathe. He propped Tallulah between his legs and slowly began braiding her hair into one of Corinthia's favorite hairstyles—a French braid. Satisfied, he began the elaborate process of restraining Tallulah to the mattress in the center of the room. Both her arms and legs were tied with rope that had been inserted into four sturdy rings of metal nailed to the floor—one at each corner of the bed. When she was properly restrained, he lay next to her and smiled. She was soft now—just the way Corinthia had been when she was little. He snuggled up to Tallulah, caressing her cheek and twirling the braid with his fingers. Through it all, a drugged Tallulah did not stir and Ben fell asleep, his nose buried in her berry-scented hair.

Hours later, on the other side of the door and down the hall in the house's small kitchen, Ben wondered if Tallulah could hear them screaming at each other. It was morning now—the day after their birthday—and he and his sister were having a recurring argument.

"Ben, what the hell are you doing?" The voice was shrill and very upset.

"Calm down, Corinthia. Please," Ben whispered. "She'll hear you."

"Don't tell me to calm down!" Corinthia shouted. "You've finished with her already." She pointed her finger at him. "You promised me this was the last one . . ."

"It could be. If you stop killing them."

"You think I like doing this, Ben?"

"Yes," he said. "I do."

"Oh, Ben." Her voice dripped with disdain. "Listen to yourself. Are you upset because I have the guts to do the things you won't do? If you stop bringing them, I'll stop getting rid of them."

"You make them sound like trash. You make them . . ." Just then, Ben could hear the sounds of thumping coming from the room down the hall.

"See! You woke her up, 'Rinthia!"

Corinthia snorted, picked up her grandmother's old teakettle, and walked toward the stove.

"She was going to wake up anyway, stupid. What were you thinking?"

Ben winced. Corinthia filled the kettle with water. "I wish you wouldn't talk to me like that."

"How else am I s'posed to talk to you? You keep doing this dumb crap. Why can't you be like me? You don't see me always dragging skinny dumb blonds around."

"She's not dumb! She goes to college!"

"She goes to college!" Corinthia mocked him. She filled the teakettle, but when she picked it up, it clattered to the floor, hurting her hand. "Dammit!" Corinthia winced as she waved her injured palm back and forth.

"Now see what you've made me do!" she said. "Get a mop and clean up this mess!"

Ben grabbed the mop from the pantry.

"The entire house always smells like frickin' strawberries! And you KEEP giving them my Raisinets! What the hell, Ben?"

"What?" he asked, alarmed. "You love Raisinets. And did you see?" He implored. "I did her hair like yours. I dressed her up just like you used to dress."

"Those girls are not me!" In a rush, Corinthia begged, "Let me just get rid of this one. Tonight. Please?"

"No," he bristled. "I'm sorry. I can't just yet. She's so pretty."

"Aren't I pretty enough for you, Ben? Why can't I be enough?"

Ben stared at the wet floor, unable to look at his sister.

"Yes," he said. "You are enough! But I . . . you . . . I can't touch you like that," he whispered. "It's not the same."

Corinthia inhaled and exhaled sharply. "But you promised."

Ben began mopping up the mess. "We've been down this road before."

"Let me kill this one tonight, Benji. Besides, she doesn't even look like me!"

"We don't have to hurt her. She doesn't even know what we look like! She's blindfolded."

"She knows our names, dummy! And it's all over the news. The FBI is looking for her!" Corinthia screamed at him. "Kidnapping is a federal crime!"

"You can't keep doing this, Corinthia!" he yelled back. "We can let them go. We don't have to kill them."

She ran her fingers through her hair. "Ben, all the problems I've had my whole life have been because of you! Did it ever occur to you that maybe I might want to go to college? Have a career? Start a family? I've had no life because of you!" She continued like she was talking to a small child, "Don't you see? Even if we start letting them go, they will bring the police right to our door and they'll find out about the rest. It's too late now. We have no choice."

"We do have a choice."

"We don't. We can't reverse the irreversible, Ben!" She rolled her eyes. "Tsk! I can't believe you! This was all your idea in the first place. Remember Jane?"

"That was a mistake."

"That's a lie and you know it," she seethed. "You climbed through Jane's window! You choked her first! You almost killed her yourself! I have told you over and over for years now that if we let them go—we will both get in trouble. I couldn't bear it if you went to prison," she said, her eyes pleading.

"Ha! Why would I go to prison? I'm not the one killing them, Corinthia!"

"Little brother, you are just as complicit as I am and you know it," she said, before imploring him once more. "You are all I have! I'm getting rid of them for you. For both of us!"

He pursed his lips and shook his head from side to side. "You're not though, Corinthia," he said in a quiet voice. "Not really."

She was silent. "Ben," she said, her voice slow and deliberate. "When you stop bringing them home, I will stop getting rid of them. Nothing's changed."

He shrugged. "Maybe I have." And it was true. After all, they were just kids when they killed Jane and there had been more girls since. But before they begged Corinthia not to kill them, they would plead with Ben not to rape them.

Of course, he never quite did, even though they had no way of knowing they weren't there for sex.

They were there to comfort him in ways Corinthia wouldn't anymore.

"You can change, Ben," he heard her say after a long pause. "People change."

He stared at the floor. "If I could change, I would leave you here alone, but I can't change, and that scares me."

While she jabbered on, Ben's thoughts turned to Cassidy Fisher—something they always did when they argued about a victim. Cassidy was the seventeen-year-old they'd kidnapped four years earlier. She told Ben she had an eight-month-old baby at home. She had shown him photos of the little boy and begged for her life—for her child's sake. Despite gnawing misgivings, Ben was silent when a blubbering Corinthia choked her to death with a belt. She had kissed the girl's forehead and whispered over and over, "I'm sorry. I'm so sorry."

When he closed his eyes, Ben could still see the tears on his sister's cheeks, hear the anguish in her voice when she complained that the girl's death was all his fault. He remembered how Cassidy's eyes bulged just before her face turned purple.

When it was over, Corinthia vomited all over the floor.

"It's too late now," Corinthia was saying, pulling Ben from his memories. "It's all about you and satisfying your need to . . . to feel them up! Fine! Can I help it I have this . . . compulsion to kill them for our own protection?"

"I knew it!" he said, slapping his hand on the table. "You have been telling me you're doing this just to keep us from getting caught, Corinthia. But that is a lie and you know it! You like killing them because you're jealous of them."

She scoffed. "I am not."

He decided to try a familiar path. "We need help," Ben whispered. "Why won't you let us get help?"

"Help from who?" she thundered. "The police? We keep going in circles, Benji." She jabbed her finger in the air, her voice breaking. "I love you. But I am not going to jail for you."

For years, she had tolerated her twin brother's baser instincts, watching with a sense of dread when he bathed the girls, shampooed their hair, and rubbed their entire bodies with scented lotion before snuggling with them. Their captives' fear of not knowing what her brother would do to them next knotted her stomach. And that was because she knew the only solution to his needs was their deaths. Ben wanted to keep them. But that was far too risky. What if one escaped? Those girls would bring the law and it would be the end of them both.

Besides, didn't they have each other? Like always. Why couldn't that be enough?

But if Corinthia were completely honest, she had no qualms about doing what had to be done—doing what she knew Ben could not do. And deep down, even though it sickened her, it thrilled her, too—something she would never admit to Ben. Hell, she could hardly admit it to herself. And she hated it—this conflicting feeling that burned like acid in her stomach. Hearing their last, dying gasps when their lives faded away moved her both to tears and ecstasy. It was for the greater good—their greater good. But during the actual act? Well, nothing else mattered.

Not sex, not food, not the probability that they would one day be caught—something that worried her every single day.

If she had to be honest, Corinthia cared, and she didn't care. It was . . . an abhorrent circle she embraced long ago; their victims' deaths brought her both a feeling of revulsion and wonder.

Nothing scared her now, except the growing apprehension of one variant singularity—which was that Ben wasn't in this with her anymore.

Ben closed his eyes. "You don't have to kill this one, Corinthia," he muttered.

"I don't want to, Benji."

He sighed. "We could easily get caught getting rid of her body."

He heard her voice, soft and breathy.

"OK. I won't hurt this one. Promise."

Corinthia was silent a moment and finally crossed her arms. "Are you sure she won't tell?"

Ben put his head in his hands and ran his fingers through his blond hair. "Yes. I'm positive."

"Swear on our love for each other that she won't tell."

"You know I can't do that."

"Swear it!" she demanded.

"OK. I promise she won't tell."

"How can you promise that?"

"Why is it impossible for you to just trust me?"

"Because that's not good enough, Ben."

Ben glared at the ceiling. "I'm not talking to you anymore! Just keep your promise."

"OK, Ben!" he heard her say. "I'll spare this one. But I'm begging you, please don't bring anymore home!"

In an instant, he was a petulant child again, putting his hands over his ears, trying to shut out his sister's voice to no avail.

"Don't kill her and I won't!"

62

Ben stomped down the hall toward the bedroom. He opened the door and walked over to the makeshift bed staked to the floor.

Ben lay beside Tallulah and caressed her body. The prone figure on the mattress whimpered as if in agony and recoiled from Ben's touch. It didn't bother him one bit. He removed her blindfold and stared into her lovely blue eyes.

"I'm so sorry you had to hear that, love," he whispered. "So sorry."

When Tallulah began to weep, Ben removed her gag. "Don't scream," he warned. "She hates screaming." The girl swallowed.

"Why," she whispered, "are you doing this to me?"

Ben sighed. "I don't have a choice, honey. I can do the things to you that I can't do with Corinthia. She's my soulmate. Do you know what that means?"

Tallulah shook her head no.

"Do you know who Plato is?"

She grimaced. "Greek philosopher, right?" Her voice was hoarse.

"You sound thirsty. Are you thirsty?"

She nodded yes.

"I'll be right back."

He left. Ben returned moments later with a glass of ice water. The cubes clinked against each other in the glass when he held her head up off the bed and pressed the drink to her lips.

"Plato wrote that there were three genders on Earth—men, women, and the Androgynous, who were once more powerful than gods," he said while she drank. "They were like humans, except they had two of everything: arms; legs; heads; and genitals, both male and female. But just one soul."

Ben wiped a tear away from his captive's cheek. He kissed her where the salty trail had been and pulled her into his arms.

"Afraid that they would kill them like the Titans tried and failed to do, the gods split the Androgynous in two, weakening them and separating their souls—each half forever yearning for the other. Soulmates are real. I was so blessed I was born with the mate to my soul. Most people never meet their soulmates. Did you know that, Tallulah?"

He was hypnotized, watching the hairs on her arm stand at attention.

"How do you know my name?" she whispered.

Ben's tone was nonchalant. "Because I've been following you for almost a year," he said against her hair.

Tallulah's shuddering caused the entire mattress to vibrate.

Ben inhaled the enchanting fragrance coming from her hair. He smiled. "I saw what you did," he told her.

Tallulah gulped. "What?"

"The hit-and-run," Ben said, without a whit of artifice. "Back in February? You hit that little girl on her bike and took off."

Tallulah became so still it was like she had stopped breathing.

"Is . . . is this about that?"

Ben shook his head. "No, of course not. That little girl died, by the way. It was all over the news. Never did find the driver."

Tallulah swallowed. "I know," she said, her voice very quiet.

"Well," Ben said to her, "I didn't take you because of that."

"I'm so sorry," she wailed.

"Oh, honey," he said, holding her close. "I know you are! You didn't do it on purpose. But you got away with it." Ben cocked his head to the side. "I wonder, though, is that why you hitchhike everywhere now? Can't stand to drive?"

Tallulah nodded.

"Well, your secret is safe with me," Ben whispered, his chin resting atop her head. "I guess you could consider 'this' payback?"

He was silent when she trembled in his arms.

"Anyways," he continued, "my soulmate and I shared a womb, and even after we were born, we slept together throughout our childhood. We have shared so many intimacies. But, of course, we could never have sex with each other. Incest, after all, is a sin, and our love is unlike any other. It's pure. I would never defile my sister. And so I won't defile you either."

He kissed her forehead and squeezed Tallulah tighter against him.

"You look so much like her," he sighed. "I will treat you like a sister. She was so soft, long ago. So sweet." He exhaled, his voice childlike. "Now, I can't touch her or play in her hair. But I can do that with you. You're my Corinthia all over again, strong, beautiful. And your skin is so warm. It's like you're her. Only better." He sniffed. "Less mean."

He was ecstatic. "You can make me happy, Tallulah. I'll keep you a little while and then you can go, my perfect little birthday present! And I know you won't tell anyone because, well, then I'd have to tell on you, wouldn't I? But we have to be careful not to make Corinthia angry."

Tallulah sobbed.

"Please don't cry!" Ben said. "Look, I'm going to gag you again and put on your blindfold. Corinthia doesn't like for you girls to look at her." He sighed. "I have to go. But you are safe here with me—with us. I mean it. Corinthia won't hurt you. She promised. I'll bring you back something to eat and we can cuddle some more. OK?"

She was silent.

"OK?" he repeated, this time with menace in his voice.

Tallulah nodded.

"Good," Ben said, standing. He blew her a kiss. "Don't go anywhere."

CHAPTER FIVE

From the time they were tots, the twins had knock-down, drag-out fights—but never as bad as the one they'd had over Tallulah.

Corinthia knew Ben was right. He was always right. So this one would live; she pressed both fists to her forehead in irritation. And he wasn't wrong, after all. Trying to dispose of her body after there was so much attention on her disappearance could be to their detriment, especially since she'd been all over the news. Despite Ben's argument, she knew his real reason for not killing her. He loved extending his pleasure—this weird affection for human touch. And that was repulsive. Why wasn't she enough? Why did they have to look like her? It was just so . . . creepy. After Ben's departure, she turned toward the captive who was blindfolded and staked to the mattress on the floor. Corinthia had a bad feeling about this girl.

She paced the room a few moments more before she threw the window open. She smiled when Tallulah began shivering in the cold on the bed. She had promised Ben she wouldn't kill her. She didn't promise to make her comfortable.

Sure, Corinthia was conflicted about killing them. She was human after all, and women are natural nurturers, aren't they? But deep down? She had to admit, she liked to tango with death. Scratch that. She loved it. But could she really stop if Ben stopped bringing them? Would she be able to?

Maybe. "Yes, I can stop," she said aloud.

I guess I owe it to him to try, she thought to herself.

She hadn't really contemplated it because deep down she knew his compulsion to kidnap was just as great as hers to kill. Of that she was certain—and even though she felt a muted sense of shame once the deed had been done, she 100 percent enjoyed watching the light of life diminish behind their dying eyes.

Ben, ever the romantic, liked to douse them in berry scents and play Beethoven's Moonlight Sonata. Corinthia rolled her eyes when he did that melodramatic crap. After all, she was the one performing the true master-piece. And her rituals were way better.

Grabbing a handful of hair, she would rip the bandana from their eyes so she could better absorb their horror and surprise. Oh! How she delight-ed in their shock. They never expected their killer to be a woman!

How she loved throttling them to the point of semiconsciousness, yank-ing a beautiful, lolling head to one side, and drinking in the girl's visage. Just the thought of it made her quiver with delight. The best part was when Corinthia's prey looked up at her, eyes dark with fear, pleading for her life, never knowing that was the last time she'd ever ask for anything. Corin-thia was their punisher, their slayer. They had to die, she often reasoned, so she and Ben could be safe. Safe from scandal. Safe from recriminations. Safe from repercussions.

Corinthia shook her head and thought about the best part—the nearly orgasmic pleasure that swept through her during the act itself. She fash-ioned herself a merciful angel of death. Didn't she kill them as fast as pos-sible so they wouldn't suffer? And her justification for killing them was resolute. It was her divine right not only to end Ben's weird little trysts with these mini-Corinthia replacements, but to make certain there was no evidence of his crimes—their crimes. There were many reasons why she and Ben couldn't be closer. And so, if they were truly standing in for her, well, that was plain wrong! Ben didn't deserve that—not after all the crap he had put her through.

No brother should want to touch his sister the way he wanted to touch them. Or put her in a situation to have to clean up his messes to protect him. If only she could just leave! But that was impossible. And besides, she loved her little brother. Ben needed her. He wouldn't survive in a world without her.

Still. Brothers don't massage their sisters when they're stark naked! Corinthia had told him this, over and over again. It was sick. It was twist-ed, whether he was a virgin or not. And if he kept kidnapping these girls, toying with them in the home they shared, among their things, where their victims could easily lead the police and destroy their lives, well, their deaths were very necessary. How could he not see that?

Never mind that she also enjoyed it. Sometimes. Well, most of the time. But she was really conflicted about it.

Sometimes Corinthia stabbed them.

Ben hated that.

"Too messy," he'd complain, and she agreed. But often it was essential. Those girls weren't always weakened by lack of real food and immobility. On more than one occasion she'd been nearly overpowered. Somehow, a few of those girls had managed to survive off just Raisinets and Pepsi—Corinthia's favorite snack—some for weeks!

Strangling them was better. She had Googled it.

While the veins in a girl's neck were compressed, her blood pressure would rise before causing her heart to stop beating. She memorized every detail of their flabbergasted faces while the mask of death descended over their once-beautiful mugs. By the time Corinthia was finished, each of Ben's playthings would be a nasty sack of meat—face puffy from tears; the whites of their open, dead eyes splotched from protruding blood vessels. She would never tell her brother this, but Corinthia enjoyed reducing them to ghastly beasts that no one would want to touch—including Ben.

Nothing disgusted him more than a corpse.

Oddly enough, it sickened her, too.

Corinthia took a deep breath. Her exhale was very loud and pronounced.

She was resigned. "I'm not going to kill you," she told Tallulah, her voice filled with sadness and a touch of regret. "But only because Ben asked me not to."

Then, on the other side of the house, a gunshot rang out. Corinthia froze.

Dammit, she thought. Hunters are on the edge of our property again. She tilted her head to the left and pressed a finger behind her ear, straining in vain to hear. Another shot rang out. It sounded like they were right outside.

And the window was open.

That's when Tallulah, fighting against her restraints, freed one hand and ripped off her gag.

"Help me! Please, they've kidnapped me!" Tallulah's cries grew louder.

"Shhh!" Corinthia panicked. She straddled Tallulah and placed her right hand over the girl's mouth. When Corinthia leaned over the captive and whispered, "Be quiet," Tallulah reached up and grabbed a handful of Corinthia's yellow locks and gave a mighty yank. Corinthia wailed when she felt strands of her hair being ripped from her scalp. In a bastardized attempt to conceal both their cries, Corinthia reached in her pocket and whipped out her iPhone.

"Hey Siri!" she commanded. "Play Michael Jackson!"

"Sure thing. Here's some music from Michael Jackson," Siri responded.

Without warning, Tallulah used the heel of her hand to punch upward. While Michael wailed the lyrics to "Bad," Corinthia heard a crunch and saw stars. The blow caught her directly on the nose—her phone skidded across the hardwood floor.

"Damn you!" In pain and surprise, Corinthia reared back and scrambled to her feet. One hand flew to her face, which was now smeared with blood. Incensed, Corinthia stumbled to the window and slammed it shut. When she turned around, she was surprised to see Tallulah sitting up, snatching the fabric from her eyes and mouth.

The girl's eyes widened in shock. "I'm going straight to the police! You will not get away with this!"

"Like you got away with killing that little girl?" Corinthia taunted her.

"That was an accident!" Tallulah hissed while she bent over to undo the ropes at her feet. "This is way, way worse! We'll just see what the cops have to say when I tell them how your crazy ass killed all those women!"

Corinthia's jaw dropped. "Crazy?" she spat. Without thinking, Corinthia lunged toward the desk and grabbed one of Ben's tactical pens.

While the girl's head was bent over the ropes, Corinthia reared back and stabbed Tallulah in the side of the neck.

Tallulah flew backward on the mattress. Fear and panic lit her pretty blue eyes.

"No, no, no, no, no!" Corinthia stumbled backward and, in startled surprise, raised a fist to her mouth. "I . . . I didn't mean to! Ben is going to kill me!"

Tallulah struggled for breath and clawed at her neck, trying to rip the pen out. Blood oozed around the makeshift weapon, etching a jagged red line across her collarbone toward her breasts.

Corinthia jumped back on top of Tallulah, pinned her shoulders to the floor with her knees, and yanked the tiny spike from her throat.

Tallulah slapped both hands over the wound in an attempt to stem the blood flowing down her chest. In one final act of defiance, she kneed Corinthia between the legs and her captor howled in agony.

An angry Corinthia raised the implement high in the air.

"You ungrateful little . . ." she said in a low voice, her eyes darting toward the window. In a swift motion and before she knew it, Corinthia brought the pen down and, one by one, she gouged out Tallulah's eyes.

The thrashing girl's mouth formed an "O" from which no sound emerged save for the gurgling of blood from the puncture in her neck. Tallulah's now crimson-stained lips turned gray while Corinthia stabbed her over and over.

"You bitch!" Corinthia cried out. "Look what you made me do!" She didn't stop stabbing Tallulah until both of the girl's eye sockets were a grisly mess.

Corinthia panted and tried to catch her breath.

"You made me break my promise! Damn you! We were gonna keep you! Let you live!" she roared before flinging the pen across the room. "Why did you have to ruin it?" Hands coated with the young woman's gore, Corinthia pressed her knees into Tallulah's chest and squeezed hard against the tiny hole leaching blood from her throat. Corinthia closed her eyes and shuddered when she began crushing the girl's windpipe. Tears rolled down Corinthia's cheeks.

She leaned over the girl and whispered against her hair.

"I'm so sorry," she wheezed, kissing her cheek. A weakened Tallulah flailed on the bed, gasping for air while she tried without success to remove Corinthia's hands from her neck—hands that were now warm and sticky. "It wasn't supposed to be like this!" Tallulah's blood oozed between Corinthia's knuckles, staining the bed, the floor, and both of their clothes.

Blood dripped, too, from Corinthia's smashed nose.

There was so much, Corinthia's mouth tasted like copper.

Face contorted, she pressed her puckered lips harder against Tallulah's blood-smeared cheek. She whimpered empty regrets in the dying girl's ear. From the corner of the room, where her phone had slid, Michael Jackson began singing "Can't Let Her Get Away."

Bawling and shuddering, Corinthia choked Tallulah so hard she began lifting the girl's body off the bed. When Tallulah went limp, Corinthia gulped and enveloped the dead young woman in her arms. "Ben loves me, not you. Me! Not you." She repeated it again and again while rocking Tallulah back and forth like a babe.

Several hours later, in the middle of the night, Ben turned on the lights and entered the room. He was shocked.

The neat room was now a disaster. The ropes were unraveled; a pair of black panties was the only thing left on the blood-splattered mattress.

Were those footsteps behind him? He turned and caught a reflection in the mirror. Streaked in blood, his twin peered back at him. She looked like the very definition of homicide.

He whirled around. Tallulah was gone. His stomach roiled. He hadn't seen this much blood since, well, since his father made quick work of Lenny when they were children.

Ben saw red—and not just blood, either.

"What have you done?" Ben said, his voice calm. "You promised me you wouldn't kill her. I wasn't done with her yet."

"I . . . didn't mean to," Corinthia said, trembling.

"You promised me, Corinthia, you wouldn't do this anymore."

"I know," he heard her say, her voice soft. Her face twisted in anguish. "This will be the absolute last time. I swear it."

Ben narrowed his eyes and huffed. "Where have I heard that before? Look at the mess you made! You know I hate when you do this—look at all this damn blood! Why?"

Corinthia spoke so fast, her words seemed to trip all over each other when they fell from her lips. "I didn't want to kill her. It just happened! She tried to escape! There were hunters outside, Benji," Corinthia pleaded. "They were closer this time, too. And the window was open. What was I supposed to do?"

"You could have knocked her out! You didn't have to kill her."

"Did you hear me?" Her tone grew indignant, argumentative. "The window was open. She was yelling for help! I did not have a choice."

"You could have just closed the window, Corinthia! What's wrong with you?"

"The same damn thing that's wrong with you."

"I can't help it," they said simultaneously. Silence swept between them for a moment.

"I'm sorry," she whispered. "I know you wanted us to stop—that this should have been the last one."

Ben's voice was thick with fury. "You will help me get another one, Corinthia."

She blinked. "I should be enough, Benji."

"You will never be enough!" he bellowed.

A furious Corinthia mumbled, "She had it coming anyway."

"What did you say?"

"She killed somebody's child, Benji."

"And you killed somebody's mother."

"Who? Cassidy? You said you wouldn't bring that girl up again!" she whined. "And her death was all your fault! You knew she had a kid when you brought her here."

Ben pursed his lips, threw his hands in the air, turned, and stormed from the room.

PART TWO

Behold, I will do a new thing; now it shall spring forth; shall ye not know it? I will even make a way in the wilderness, and rivers in the desert. —Isaiah 43:19

CHAPTER SIX
Halloween, 2015

S tanding on a dusty mat in the basement of a dilapidated gym in the mountains of Laurel Valley, Pennsylvania, twenty-year-old Amanda Ebony Taylor was paying rapt attention: "If someone's trying to choke you," the self-defense instructor told a group of female students, "the first thing you'll feel is fear."

Like her, he was African American. A middle-aged former cop, he was bald and stocky. He often gave his lessons in an unrestrained fashion. "First instinct: your hands go up toward your throat to stop him." He crossed his hands atop one another when he moved them up to his own neck. "But don't do that! Instead of grabbing his hands, if he's facing you, reach between his legs, grab his privates, and twist hard."

He stretched a hand out in front of him, pantomiming the gesture. "Punch him down there or, better yet, take your knee and smash it into his groin," he said, raising his knee fast and high. "He'll double over. Once he lets go, clasp both hands, raise them above your head and bring them down hard against the back of his neck. That should disable him."

"And if he's behind you?" Amanda asked.

"Same thing," the instructor answered. "Reach behind you, pull or punch. Like this," he said, demonstrating. And then, as if they were in middle school, a loud bell rang, signaling the end of the lesson.

Amanda gathered her things. She was an enchanting woman with shapely hips and luminous brown skin. All of five foot three, Amanda had thick and curly shoulder-length hair. Each of her earlobes held four tiny silver studs. She smiled when she glanced in her compact, astonished by how much she had changed in two years. The high schooler who didn't care about makeup was no more. Now, whether it was for self-defense classes or sitting in class, Amanda rarely went out without "beating" her face. When she didn't get a makeup hookup from one of her friends who worked at the MAC Cosmetics store in the mall, she swiped through Instagram and bought beauty palettes from @thecrayoncase and lipstick from @thelipbar. As a result, along with her signature black combat boots, she was never without dramatic eye makeup, highlighted cheekbones, bright red nail polish, and chunky silver rings on either thumb.

She licked her lips—her lipstick still looked good.

Amanda closed the compact, reached inside her faded Black is Beautiful T-shirt, and pulled out the jewel-encrusted cross her dad had given her. It dangled between her breasts from a long silver chain. Equal parts sweet and short-tempered, Amanda was a walking paradox who always smiled before narrowing her dark brown eyes when she was angry.

When her parents came to collect her from college for the holidays during the winter of freshman year, they were startled by her transformation.

Gone was the plain, dark-haired bookworm with waist-length hair extensions that they had dropped off three months earlier. In her place stood a rebel.

A studious rebel—one who now embraced her ethnicity. She ditched the weaves for her own natural hair, sometimes styling it with braids, finger coils, or wash-and-go twist outs she learned to do herself courtesy of the many beauty influencers she followed on Instagram like @thechicnatural, @lyssamariexo. And now, thanks to @aieshatae, she was debating getting Sisterlocks, too.

Sweat slipped down her back as she headed toward her car. The sun was setting beneath the drab clouds, and it smelled like it might rain. Amanda grinned when she flipped the sun visor down and looked in the mirror to dab her forehead with NYX blotting paper. Satisfied, she turned on the radio and began singing along to Beyoncé's "Grown Woman."

Bobbing her head to the music, she drove east for ten miles through the basin of Laurel Valley, across winding mountain roads toward home—Glastonbury University.

In the distance, soaring above the clouds, were the castle turrets of the school. They came sharply into focus, dominating the landscape. The closer she drove, the more mind-boggling the view became.

Glastonbury was a private, rural university about a hundred and five miles from Philadelphia with few minorities—but that wasn't something

Amanda paid particular attention to. Amanda had grown up in a not-too-dissimilar area on the outskirts of Englewood, New Jersey—not far from its former resident, comedian Eddie Murphy.

GU's castle was constructed in the late 1900s by the heir of a wealthy industrialist. People had flocked to the school during the height of the Harry Potter films because some jokers online had said Hogwarts was its exact twin. But that wasn't why Amanda was there. Her first choice, after years of growing up in suburbia, had been Howard University in the heart of Washington, DC; her second was NYU. But her parents—both doctors—were adamant she attend GU—their alma mater. It was where they had met twenty-two years earlier. "It's also safer," her mother had said.

Amanda threw her books on the bed in her apartment-like dorm and called out her best friend's name.

"Fiona!"

No one responded.

The dorm they lived in was a lackluster 1940s-era apartment building that housed twelve girls in six small bedrooms, a living room, an eat-in kitchen, and a sitting room. There were four bathrooms—each with three shower stalls that always seemed to be occupied.

But not today. Amanda smiled when she realized the apartment was empty. No girls meant no fighting for the shower—or hot water. In a flash, she was naked. She grabbed a towel and headed for a stall. Twenty minutes later, she stepped out of the shower to hear someone calling her name.

"Amanda? You in here?"

Amanda emerged from the hallway to find it was Fiona.

When they had met after freshman orientation in their shared dorm bedroom, Amanda couldn't believe how fashion-model beautiful her new roommate was—inside and out. It was like the girl had climbed out of a Clairol hair color ad. Her waist-length, honey-blond hair swept suggestively above her curvaceous derriere whenever she walked. Her arresting sapphire eyes were streaked with flecks of gold.

Fiona faced her roommate, her hair floating around her. She shot Amanda a questioning look. Amanda's shrunken tresses were wet, dripping from the shower. She was clad in a towel.

"Why do you always do that?" Fiona demanded. "Why can't you put a towel on your head like normal people? You're getting the floor all wet."

Amanda shrugged and slipped, half-naked, past her friend and into their bedroom. "Couldn't find one."

"Again?" Fiona cracked a smile. "Come with me tonight to Dukes. I want to get lit."

"Nope. Gotta study, and then I gotta work." Amanda whipped the towel away from her body, bent over slightly and dashed it over her thick wet hair. She rubbed it until it was damp, relishing her nakedness—a trait she picked up from Fiona, who flounced around their bedroom in various stages of undress all the time.

"You could call out—just this one time."

Amanda grinned at Fiona and then shook her head no. Clad again in the towel, she sat on her bed, slicked some Carol's Daughter Hair Milk through her natural hair and began parting it in sections with a thick black comb so she could plait it for a braid-out later.

The pair had been friends for almost two years. Both were raised by well-heeled religious parents. Both grew up sheltered in the suburbs—Amanda in Jersey, Fiona in Maryland. While Fiona was boisterous and outgoing before college, Amanda spent the last two years of high school hidden in her room, studying and envying people online—until her dad put a camera in her hands on a trip to Alaska. During her last winter break before senior year, Amanda took hundreds of photos—one of which got 200,000 likes on Instagram. When she hung some of the poster-sized photos on her dorm room wall, Fiona was the first person off the Internet who recognized her.

"Oh my gosh, you're the EbonySnowKween?" Fiona had shrieked with pleasure, referring to Amanda's Instagram account. "I just started following you!"

They'd been fast friends ever since and so alike they fit like gloves. Amanda hadn't had a best friend before—not someone who knew her inside and out and liked her anyway. If anything, in Amanda's mind, they were more like sisters. Theirs would be a lifelong friendship, of that Amanda was certain. They borrowed each other's clothes, jewelry, and perfume. Fiona had even come close to convincing Amanda to get the same kind of tattoo Fiona had on her ankle—three interconnected hearts. Amanda had laughed before refusing.

They walked to breakfast each morning before separating for class and dined together at night. They shared their desires for the future. In Fiona,

Amanda had found a confidante who had helped her overcome her fading shyness—and who could identify with her about the continued overprotectiveness of their parents.

When they met, Amanda had been the quiet, studious type who did whatever her strict mother demanded. Fiona, an aspiring therapist, was the complete opposite. Boisterous, bubbly, empathetic, and argumentative, Fiona spouted profanities at her parents over the phone almost every time they spoke.

"I could never speak to my mom like that!" Amanda had said once after Fiona told her mother to mind her own damn business and then promptly hung up on her.

"Yeah, you can!" Fiona had laughed.

"Uh, no I can't. My momma ain't like your momma."

Fiona waved her hand. "Look, we're grown and in college! Study. Get good grades. But you're not living at home anymore, and you are officially NOT under your mother's thumb."

That was one thing Fiona told Amanda over and over: "We're allowed to have some fun."

It was Fiona who had encouraged Amanda to party more and to ditch her thick glasses for Lasik surgery—much to everyone's surprise. As a result of their friendship and Fiona's influence, Amanda spoke her mind more, and her attitude had started to become a lot more cavalier, except where her studies were concerned.

"Awww, come on, Mandy!" Fiona whimpered like a little kid. "It's Saturday night, and it's Halloween! We'll have a blast! You can't stay cooped up in here. At least come before you have to go work."

"Oh, yes I can," Amanda said, her mellifluous voice stern. "Seriously, I've got a test on this crap on Monday," she said, jutting her chin toward an anatomy book on her bed. "I'll see you guys at the diner once the bar closes anyway."

Amanda worked part-time as a cashier at Joyce's, a twenty-four-hour diner on the opposite end of campus. Her shift began at 11:00 p.m. and she wouldn't get home until way after four in the morning. Some of the other students working at the diner found those hours brutal, but Amanda liked it because at that time of morning it was easier to get tips. The after-party crowd was loud, but they tipped way better than the funky gym rats and assortment of other weirdos, like the one she called Quiet Girl, who came in to sip coffee and stare at their phones at 7:00 a.m.

While Amanda finished her plaits, Fiona was in the closet. "My red leather jacket? Where is it?"

"Right where you left it, hanging on the back of the door."

Fiona smiled and peeked behind the door. "Snake it wudda bit me."

"You say the weirdest things."

"And you don't?" Fiona scoffed.

"Not out loud."

Amanda grinned, stood, and put on a long black T-shirt emblazoned with the words "Need More Sleep" in red-and-black glitter. "Dammit," she said, rummaging through her dresser drawer. "I thought I had some clean panties in here."

"Just go commando," Fiona said.

"Everybody can't be like you."

Fiona laughed. "Say, what happened on your date last night?"

Amanda groaned. Both girls were using dating apps to date—without success.

"That guy?" Amanda asked. "Really cute redhead, but a complete nerd."

"And you're not?"

Amanda paused mid underwear hunt. "Fair point, but this guy has spent the past seven years in college, studying medicine. And now works as a pharmacist."

Fiona began changing her clothes. "So? There's nothing wrong with that. They make good money. At least he wasn't weird."

Amanda snorted. "Well, I'm not finished. One of his hobbies is playing that game Universe of Wardom, where he's some grand pooh-bah or something. He even said that's why he didn't finish his residency, because he takes his commitments to 'online warmongering' seriously," she said, making air quotes.

"Oh, ewwww! People still play that?"

"Apparently," Amanda said, pulling some jeans over a pair of black panties.

"Can I borrow your Run-DMC T-shirt?" Fiona asked.

"I don't know if it's clean."

Amanda watched as Fiona found the white shirt with red letters, sniffed it, shrugged, and slipped it on. She tugged the bottom of the T-shirt down so it rested low across her dark blue jeans. Half a dozen silver bangles clanged together on her wrists when she reached under the bed and pulled out a pair of red-and-white high-top Converse sneakers, which she laced up before snatching her red leather jacket off a hook. The buckles and zippers jangled when Fiona moved to snatch her purse from the knob of their bedroom door.

"That doesn't look very Halloweeny to me," Amanda said, frowning.

Fiona chuckled and whirled around in a circle. "What? Are you saying you don't think I can double for Iggy Azalea in this outfit?"

"Oh, please! You look more like Michael Jackson."

The pair laughed again and continued chatting while Fiona touched up her makeup. Amanda sat cross-legged on her own small bed, highlighting sections of her textbook, *Gray's Anatomy*.

"I don't know how you read that thing."

Amanda grinned. "I like the pictures. Besides, it beats reruns of the TV show."

They were laughing again when one of their roommates popped her head in to ask a question, bringing in the hallway sounds of girls rushing in and out of dorm rooms on a Saturday night. A slight breeze from the open window at the end of the hall lifted Fiona's hair from her shoulders, seductive, alluring.

"Sure you won't come to Dukes with me, Amanda? I'll wait for you to change."

Amanda shook her head no. "You go ahead. Wash that liquor down with some candy for me. I'm in for the night. Besides, maybe you'll get lucky with Mark."

"Yeah, maybe," Fiona said, rolling her eyes and then winking. "Maybe. I am feeling lucky tonight."

Amanda's eyes followed her friend's footsteps as Fiona clicked the door shut behind her.

CHAPTER SEVEN

Corinthia Zanetti sat at a table opposite the bar, waiting.

She was inside Dukes, the local college watering hole, where the circular bar sat smack in the middle of the room. Bright orange cardboard pumpkins in various sizes were taped to the walls and mirrors. Tiny spiders adorned the fake cobwebs that someone had hung on the ceiling over the bartenders serving drinks. Two of those bartenders were dressed like zombies. Almost half of the patrons were costumed, too. In the bar's semidarkness, Corinthia spied a few girls with smudged eye makeup and face paint that made them seem as if they were bleeding or suffering from some sort of decay. Others were dressed as Playboy bunnies, tufts of white cotton stitched on their butts. A fair-skinned Black girl with piercing green eyes threw her head back in wild laughter, her blond braids flying when she wailed with glee at her companions. She had on green thigh-high leather boots and little else—save for a midnight-green Eagles jersey emblazoned with the number sixty-two and the name Kelce on the back. A single line of eye black was beneath each eye.

Quite a few guys sported eye patches. Three smiled through Guy Fawkes masks. Corinthia saw six girls dressed like Elsa and Anna from *Frozen* and two like Angelina Jolie's Maleficent. In the thirty minutes she had been sitting there, she had spotted five Batmen, three Spider-Men, a Ninja Turtle, quite a few vampires, witches, ghouls, and some clowns. A Minion from *Despicable Me* was on the dance floor trying to get some girls to do a dance called the Dougie.

The speakers pulsed with pop music, pumping a rhythm of excitement through the crowd.

From behind her mask, Corinthia grinned. She was dressed head to toe as the Dark Knight, a black-and-gold Batman emblem emblazoned on the padded chest of her costume.

Tonight would be the night. She could feel it.

She sipped her beer and watched as two very pretty, inebriated blond girls ceased their twerking, whispered to each other, and began dragging the people closest to them out on the dance floor. Meanwhile, the DJ played on and the duo LMFAO and rapper Lil Jon started screaming the lyrics to their song "Shots," over and over again. All over the bar, girls acquiesced and drank while Corinthia sat there and imbibed a vibe of a different kind.

It was Corinthia's decision to help stalk their prey. After Tallulah, and because of so much media attention, the twins decided this new girl would be their last. They agreed that Ben could keep her indefinitely—and Corinthia had promised him that they would kill no more young women after Tallulah. Her death had made him furious. He had considered her the perfect prey—since she was harboring a secret as horrible as theirs.

At any rate, Ben was often too awkward when the girls were sober. He was better after they were drunk. Corinthia had picked Dukes for a reason. She'd been following Fiona for quite some time and knew that this was her favorite spot to hang out.

She was Ben's latest favorite and after Tallulah's demise, well, Corinthia felt like she owed him—for a change.

"Coeds make the best victims," Corinthia had said, and the pair spent months hunting the perfect girl. Ben, however, insisted only that they be mirror images of Corinthia.

"It's sick," she told him often. "You know that, right?"

He scoffed at her.

"Just make sure they're drunk and alone. Then I can make my move."

Corinthia made sure they were that—but when it was her turn to "pick the vic," as she liked to call it, she made certain only that their hair was as blond as her own, that they were about her height and weight, and that their eyes were blue.

When Fiona came in with a group of guys and girls, Corinthia slid her finger across her smartphone, tapped it, and pretended to take a selfie. Instead she took a photo of Fiona with Snapchat and added it to her story for Ben. He would savor it later.

Despite the booming music, Fiona and her friends were loud—so loud that Corinthia could hear their every word.

Fiona slid in beside a girl and a boy. Corinthia heard her call them Alicia and Mark. Tall, with jet-black locs and dark brown skin, Mark was dressed like Freddy Krueger in a torn red sweater with green stripes and a black fedora. He yanked fake claws off one hand and put them down on the bar before he ordered shots of ink-colored alcohol from the barkeep. Alicia's long brown Senegalese twists swayed at her full, curvy hips. The beautiful girl with the piercing stare pushed her glasses up on the bridge of her nose and smoothed her hands over her Little Red Riding Hood costume, complete with a red cape, white hosiery, and patent-leather red ankle-boots. She ordered a plain Coke. Mark pressed a tiny shot glass into Fiona's hand, then he turned toward Alicia, who fluttered her eyelashes at him.

"Ready to get this party started?" he yelled when the music jumped up a couple octaves and more drunken girls and guys raced to the dance floor for a line dance.

Corinthia was close enough to read their lips.

"Hell yeah!" Fiona shouted. Alicia sipped her soda demurely.

Mark raised his glass and clinked it with each of the girls. Fiona downed her shot of what looked to Corinthia like Jägermeister.

An hour passed, then two. Corinthia watched Fiona drum her hands on the bar and sway to the fast music, the fingers on both of her hands forming a "W" as she raised them up and down in front of her face. Mark whispered something in Alicia's ear, and she laughed.

When Mark began nuzzling Alicia's neck, Fiona frowned, shifted in her seat and folded her hands in her lap. She looked out over the dance floor, seeming to try to ignore them.

Nursing her second bottle of Stella Artois, Corinthia ticked off her mental list of how much Fiona had been drinking—eight shots, three beers.

"Enough! Enough!" Fiona squealed when Mark took his hands off Alicia to place yet another shot of the German liquor in front of Fiona.

"One more won't kill you—it's not like you're driving!" Mark howled.

The rest of the clique had now grown to six. Some new boys arrived dressed like the Three Musketeers. People cheered when the guys entered the bar and crowded around the trio. By now, however, Alicia had her back to Mark, who was pressed against her, whispering in her ear. Both ignored the thumping music and were swaying to some invisible soundtrack only the two of them could hear.

Fiona sniffed and stood. Her eyes seemed riveted to Mark. Corinthia wondered if anyone else noticed Fiona cringe.

"I'm going home," Fiona said, her voice brimmed with emotion. "Enough to drank," she slurred.

"You can't leave yet!" That was one of the Musketeers. "We just got here, and we're going to the diner later." He draped a hand over Fiona's shoulder and openly pawed at her left breast. She glared at him and slapped his hand away.

Fiona shook her head no. The music paused momentarily.

"You can get home on your own, right?" Mark asked, his gaze never leaving Alicia's backside. Alicia leaned back against Mark, and he ducked his head down to hear her whispering something in his ear.

"Wait!" Mark said. "Let us walk you out, at least." He jutted his chin toward Alicia and she nodded. Mark staggered against Alicia, who grinned.

Corinthia blinked several times. Alarmed, she shivered a moment until Fiona put her hand over Mark's.

"I don't need you to walk me!" she said in irritation, her voice indignant. "I'm not some shirking um, shrinking tulip—violet. Whatever."

The others laughed. "Besides, I'm like two minutes from here," Fiona said, waving them away. "And I gotta get some sleep. I need to wake Mandy for brunch tomorrow, and I have a feeling I'm going to be hungover."

Alicia touched Fiona's shoulder, flicking her long twists with the back of one hand. Her hood was askew.

"No, girl. Mark and I are going to walk you out, at least," she said, concerned. "I barely drink, but I can see you're totally trashed! Take that BC powder hangover cure when you get home."

Corinthia put down her half-empty bottle of beer, pulled out her phone, and headed toward the exit. The DJ had switched to a slower song by the English band Sade.

On her way out, Corinthia bumped into another Batman, whose costume was identical to her own. Both Batmen nodded at one another and walked out together; they were standing across the street in shadows when Mark, Alicia, and Fiona came outside. While watching the college students from their vantage point, one of the Caped Crusaders reached into a backpack, pulled out a jacket, pressed a smartphone into one of the pockets, and smiled. The other Batman walked away.

Face flushed and dejected, Fiona gaped at Mark, who began kissing Alicia in earnest until Alicia pushed Mark away.

"Hey, you'll be OK getting back, won't you?" Alicia asked Fiona.

Fiona nodded. "I'll be all right." Mark slapped Alicia playfully on her rear end and the pair went back inside. Fiona shrugged her jacket on, shoved her hands in her pockets, and staggered into some people trying to enter the club before thrusting her shoulders forward and walking away in the nippy, late-night air.

While the trio spoke, Ben stood across the street and ripped off his costume's hood. He shoved it into the backpack before sliding into his Sixers jacket and a matching baseball cap.

A mist that had settled over the street was thinning out when Fiona headed south toward her dorm. She tripped once and began giggling uncontrollably when someone caught her. She looked up. A young blond man with a backpack looked down at her. He knew the smile he was giving her was friendly, charming.

"Whoa! Where's the party?"

She laughed. "Behind me."

"Hey, are you OK? You shouldn't be walking around out here this late. Not by yourself."

Fiona gawked at him. He could tell she was taking note of his height from her petite perch.

"I'm OK," she said. "Lost my bearings for a few minutes. I've seen you before somewhere? Dukes?" she asked.

He nodded. "Probably." He tipped his baseball cap to her. Even in the dead of winter, he knew his smile and delicious bronze tan were dazzling.

"Wow, you smell good!" Fiona said, looking up into his blue eyes. She batted her eyelashes. "You gonna walk me home?"

"Sure," he said, extending his hand. "I'm Ben."

"Fiona," she said, shaking it. She laughed and tripped again. This time, she fell in the street, bumping her head on the curb. Hard. Blood from a cut over her eye trickled down her cheek. "Ouch!" she said, smearing blood across her forehead with the heel of her left hand.

Without a word, Ben again helped her to her feet. She wiped that hand across her sleeve, staining her jacket. "Dammit," she said, taking off the jacket and shaking it in the cold night air. She swayed when it fell on the ground. Because his grandmother raised him right, Ben picked up the jacket and handed her a clean handkerchief.

"Press this on your head. It'll stop the bleeding. Where do you live?"

She dabbed her head with it. "Just up the road a half mile."

"You're not going to make it on those rubbery legs," Ben said. "Let me drive you. It's freezing."

"Mmmm, 'kay."

Ben grabbed her by the elbow and half-dragged her toward a small silver SUV. Had it been any other night, the street may have been deserted. But because it was Halloween, a lot of people were milling about. Ben realized too late that it was the furtive glances over his shoulder that probably gave Fiona pause.

"You know what?" she blurted. "Maybe I should walk after all."

"What? You won't make it." He stopped and put his right hand over his heart and said, "It would be my extreme pleasure to make sure you got home safe. Don't worry. I'm practically a Boy Scout."

When he took off his baseball cap and threw back his head and laughed, his shoulders were cloaked by a mantle of long blond hair.

"No," Fiona said after a moment. "I think I should walk. I don't want to get into your car. I mean . . . I don't know you."

A thin young Asian man glanced at them before he walked by and darted around a corner.

Ben smiled and, without another word, punched Fiona in the stomach. When she doubled over, Ben opened the passenger door and pushed her inside.

"I'm sorry," he whispered.

Disoriented and now in pain, Fiona coughed and gasped. "No," she said faintly when he leaned over before locking the passenger door and slamming it shut. When Fiona watched Ben fling her jacket into a bunch of trees, she wailed, "My phone!"

He then slipped into the car, behind the wheel, just in time to see tears fill her scared, dazed eyes.

He told her, "I promise you I will not hit you again, but right now I need you not to scream. Forgive me?"

That's when Ben struck her hard on the head. When she slumped against the passenger side window, he drove off.

CHAPTER EIGHT

Amanda entered the apartment soon before the autumn sun would start to rise. She plopped down on the couch in the empty living room, kicked off her shoes, flexed her pinched toes and winced. It had been a long night at Joyce's.

She grabbed a comb and quickly parted her hair in four sections, massaged in some creamy moisturizer, and braided it again. "Ah," she sighed after grabbing her black satin bonnet and sliding it over her hair. She was glad none of her friends had showed up during her shift, which ended two hours later than usual at 6:00 a.m. The night had been crazy enough with what seemed like every drunk, costumed college student that ever lived showing up for cheap pancakes and eggs. Bored, she pulled out her phone and began swiping on yet another dating app.

"Ugh!" she said after a picture of a penis appeared as someone's profile photo. "I have no idea why guys do that," she said to the quiet apartment.

She put her purse on the coffee table and walked into the kitchen, opened the fridge, and grabbed the last bottle of Sprite.

Amanda sat in one of the kitchen chairs and checked her social media. Snapchat held a video of Fiona. Quite a few familiar drunken laughing faces had been at Dukes. Amanda smiled and watched it once more before it disappeared.

She peeked in their bedroom. "Fiona?" she said softly. Both beds were empty. Amanda glanced down at her phone: 6:17 a.m. Fiona had probably spent the night out or was still partying.

It was now Sunday, November 1, and Amanda's only plans that day were to drive herself and Fiona to brunch at noon.

Amanda sent Fiona a text.

Hey woman. It was their standard greeting to each other. *Lemme know if we're still doing brunch in Philly later. Remember, it's over @2 and it's your turn to wake me up in time.* Amanda was a light sleeper and she hoped their dorm mates weren't still going too crazy into the morning with noisy Halloween activities. She took off her waitress uniform, climbed into bed in a T-shirt and panties and fell asleep.

Hours later, someone knocking on the bedroom door awakened Amanda. She peeked outside the blankets. Sunshine from the half-open mini-blinds screamed its brightness in her face.

Fiona's bed was still empty.

"Come in?" Amanda said.

A fellow premed student, Grace Carbonotti, appeared. "Can I borrow your *Gray's* for a little while?"

Amanda nodded. "On the desk. Don't remove the bookmarks though, OK? What time is it?"

Grace came in, grabbed the book, and looked at the smartphone in her hand.

"1:30."

"Dammit!" Amanda said, bolting straight up. "Fiona was supposed to wake me up in time for brunch! Have you seen her?"

"Not since yesterday."

"You sure?"

"I just left the bathroom, and the kitchen and living room are empty, too. Thanks for this," she said, lugging the book. "I'll bring it back later."

"You're welcome," Amanda murmured.

She pulled the covers back over her head and picked up her phone. She groaned at the screen's brightness and scanned it for messages.

No texts from her roommate. Amanda sent Fiona another missive. No response. Fiona almost always responded right away. They often joked how people thought Fiona's phone was glued to her hand. It wasn't like Fiona to stand her up like that. If something had come up, she would have sent her a text or left a message on a social site.

Amanda went to Facebook. There hadn't been any posts or check-ins on Fiona's timeline in more than a day. She hadn't even shared a photo. The pair always checked in or posted pics to let their friends know what they were up to.

She flicked through Twitter and typed in the hashtag #Dukes. She waded through a handful of unrelated social posts until she found what

she was scrolling for—mostly a bunch of random videos and photos—
often taken without the subjects' knowledge. Lots of Halloween photos
from the night before flooded her screen. None were of Fiona. Amanda
opened her Snapchat and found no additional photos or videos there,
either. Instagram, too, was a wash.

"Hey, Siri, call Fiona," Amanda said out loud. But the call went straight
to voicemail.

"Mark," Amanda said aloud. Fiona's probably with him, she thought to
herself. Amanda's eyes flashed with anger. I can't believe she stood me up
for that womanizing twit.

She went to Mark's Facebook page and found three pictures of him and
Fiona beaming in selfies. Fiona and Mark were just friends for now, but
Fiona kept saying she wanted more. Maybe they'd finally hooked up?

"Oh." Amanda scowled when she saw photos of Mark curled up against
Alicia.

Still. Maybe they all crashed together? Amanda shot Mark a text.

Tell Fiona I said thanks for standing me up for brunch. She added the
angry emoji.

Mark didn't text back.

Amanda sighed. She got up, traded the satin bonnet for a plastic shower
cap, showered, and then dressed and fixed her hair and makeup. Satisfied,
she padded into the kitchen in stocking feet and made some oatmeal. She
went back to their room and turned on the TV. A *Law & Order: Special
Victims' Unit* marathon was on. She watched it for a few hours, napped
some more, got up to make a salad and ate it. Then she watched a few more
episodes. Finally, she nodded off again.

When she awoke this time, it was now nearly 8:00 p.m. She still hadn't
heard from Fiona. Half of her roommates were home. None of them had
seen her, either.

Now she was worried.

She sent Mark another text.

Fiona's wit U, right??

Mark texted back.

No. What R U talking abt? Haven't seen her since she left bar by herself.

What? Amanda wrote back. *We were s'pose 2 go to Philly earlier.*

Quit playing, Mark texted. *I'm still hungover!* He added the green barf emoji. *Let's wait. She's probably OK. Maybe came in and went out while you slept. Ttyl.*

Amanda was incensed. She tapped at her phone angrily.

Mark, Fiona is NOT here. Are U saying she left bar alone?

Yeah. Alone.

Are you sure?

Yes, sure. Me & Alicia walked her out, but she went back to dorm by herself. U check rest of dorm? Maybe she's getting food or jogging or something.

No, Amanda responded. *She sleeps in Sundays unless we have plans and we had plans! Her stuff's still on bed from yesterday. Roommates haven't seen her, either.*

Amanda waited as the three little dots in iMessage indicated Mark was typing a response. *Oh no!* Mark had written. *She snapped me saying she was lost right after she left. Just now seeing it.* He sent the pile of poo emoji. Then he texted: *Ugh. Getting dressed. I'm coming over.*

Amanda sent out more texts, posted question marks on Fiona's Facebook page, and waited in the living room. Fifteen minutes later, Mark knocked on the door. When Amanda opened it, he didn't bother to say hello. He pushed past her and three of their other dorm mates and sat on the couch.

He ran his hands over his locs. "I can't believe that girl got lost. I really don't think you have anything to worry about, although I haven't heard from her since then either, and I've been texting her, too."

"I don't know what to do," Amanda said. "I mean, who else were you guys out with last night?"

Mark shrugged. "The usual. Alicia, Jamal, Jack, Carter. And I spoke to them. Carter and Jack don't think it's that big of a deal, like maybe she hooked up with someone on the way home and she's probably sleeping it off. I mean, she had a lot to drink."

"We need to start looking for her," Amanda said.

He shook his head no, unconvinced. "She might get mad if we bother her."

"Maybe I'm overreacting. But I don't think so. Can we please just split up and look for her?" Amanda pleaded.

Mark groaned when he stood. "I'll start at the gym. You walk the quad and the castle."

They each went off in different directions. It was 10:00 p.m. when they returned to the dorm. Amanda was frantic. Fiona had been missing for almost twenty-four hours.

"How can she just be gone?"

Mark put his arms around Amanda. "She's . . . somewhere. We just don't know where. What are we going to do?"

"Shouldn't we get more people to help us look again? It's so dark now." Four of Amanda's roommates offered to help.

Mark shrugged. "Maybe wait till the morning? Or call the cops then?"

Amanda ignored Mark's suggestion to wait another day. She swiped on her phone and called Fiona's father through Facebook Messenger instead.

"What? When?" Mr. Kessler said it so loud everyone in the room could hear him.

Amanda held the phone in her hand as she stared at Mark and the others. "She went out to Dukes about 10:00 p.m. last night and left alone shortly after midnight. No one has seen her since. The last person to see her was our friend Mark and some other students."

Amanda paused.

"He's right here." She held out her cell phone to Mark.

"Yes, sir," Mark said into the phone. "I asked her if she wanted me to walk her home and she said, 'No, it's only a few blocks back to the dorm.' Yes, of course. Goodbye."

"What?" Grace, one of their roommates, asked.

"He said to call the police and report her missing. Right now," Mark said, dialing 911. "He's driving up from Maryland."

CHAPTER NINE

By Monday, the police, students, and dozens of volunteers were searching for Fiona on campus, in the neighboring woods and surrounding areas—all to no avail.

Fiona had vanished.

Amanda remained in the thick of the search, as she had been. She was eyeing a local TV newscaster who was speaking into a camera, on campus, a microphone up to her lips.

"Although her parents and friends were convinced the twenty-one-year-old woman had no reason to take off, it wasn't until searchers found her cell phone flung into a clump of trees not far from campus that the police suspected foul play. Her car is still parked in the student parking lot."

Within days of Mark's 911 call, police were canvassing the campus and the surrounding neighborhood, talking to people, and collecting security footage from nearby businesses and organizations.

By the end of the week, the hashtag #FindFiona was trending on social media and the hunt for Fiona had become massive. Her parents, the township and campus police, the dean of the college, and local, national, and now international media were all in attendance for an evening press conference on the progress of the search.

The last search like this had been months ago for another young woman. Her name was Tallulah Montgomery.

While TV crews filmed, the headlights from news vans cast eerie white shadows across the now pitch-black asphalt of the parking lot outside the girls' dorm.

"I've got people from Australia calling me," Dean Brookland groused to one of his assistants. He frowned. "Who in the hell called all this press?"

"I did," Amanda said, sidling up to him. "She's gone. When someone vanishes, you call everyone so they can be found. That's what you should have done the first day we reported her missing!" She glowered at him with her hands on her hips. "None of you here are doing enough to find my friend!"

He blanched. "Miss Taylor, we're doing everything we can to locate Miss Kessler."

Amanda turned her back on the dean of students and stomped off.

Web and print bloggers and writers milled among the crowd, notebooks in hand, scribbling names. They used their smartphones to record quotes from students and search teams. Printed on flyers was a photo of Fiona, her pretty blue eyes crinkled, her lips curved into a smile. Stamped across the bottom was a phone number.

Numb. That's what Amanda felt—that and an overwhelming sense of guilt, which was incomprehensible—especially to her own parents. Amanda was certain that if Fiona wasn't found she was going to fail this semester, but that was the least of her concerns.

"Why do you care about this girl so much?" her mother, Sharon, asked on the phone. She was taking a break from rounds at the hospital in New Jersey where she worked as a cardiothoracic surgeon. "She's not even family!"

Amanda could just picture her mother, twirling her shoulder-length brown braids like she did when she was anxious. "Mom, I'm hanging up now."

And she did, no doubt stunning her mother, who kept calling back. Amanda put her phone on vibrate.

Amanda couldn't imagine what she'd do if they never found Fiona. If Fiona never came back. They kept saying it wasn't Amanda's fault—that she had nothing to do with Fiona's disappearance. Yet she felt responsible.

"I should have gone with her," she kept saying under her breath. Two is better than one, she thought to herself. Whoever took her wouldn't have been able to take us both.

So Amanda stood there outside in the cold, feeling punished in its wicked sting. Ned, Fiona's father, took to the podium and addressed the crowd. By now, everyone following Fiona's disappearance knew she was a natural athlete, confident, independent, outgoing, and vivacious. They'd seen videos of her helping her dad coach a Little League baseball team; heard tales of how active she was in her church back in Maryland. How the brave young woman had fought off a purse-snatcher earlier that summer. They knew Fiona was a fighter. They knew she would not give up so easily. And so on this night, her parents addressed the searchers, thanking them profusely for their help.

Fiona's father took a deep breath. His wife, Lois, rubbed his back.

"As a parent," he said, his voice breaking, "we are now living our greatest nightmare. Deep down, I know in my heart that someone has taken our daughter. She wouldn't just up and leave or wander into the woods in the middle of the night by herself." He gulped and paused. "I know Fiona. She would call us if she could, which makes me think she's somewhere being held against her will." He took a deep breath. Amanda knew he was told by the police to speak to the kidnappers.

"I am asking the person who has taken our daughter to please just let her go. You were someone's child once. Remember that. She is a person with feelings and a family and friends that love her. Her whole life is waiting for her, and so are we."

Ned stepped away from the podium and trembled. The steam from his sobs became frosted in the cold night air.

Beneath her wool hat, Corinthia Zanetti shivered, too. She turned on her flashlight and moved deeper into the woods, falling in line behind the other searchers.

Fiona's silver bracelets jangled against each other on her left wrist.

Back in her dorm, Amanda opened her laptop and typed into the search engine: missing girl, Pennsylvania. An hour and a half later, she sat alone in her room, printouts of articles tossed across her bed. She took off her glasses and smiled.

There was blanket media coverage of Fiona's disappearance. They'd interviewed Amanda and her friends and even some of her classmates—many of whom didn't know her well. Every sound bite had been given; every possible stone unturned. While reporters noted that several girls had gone missing from the same region over the course of a decade, not one had mentioned the one similarity all of the Glastonbury girls shared.

But Amanda had—from their Facebook pages.

She picked up the phone and called Karl Karstarck, a reporter from the

Laurel Valley Dispatch. An editorial assistant told her the reporter was still on campus. She grabbed her coat and headed back outside.

Karstarck was a kind, older, ruddy man in his late sixties with graying black hair and a towering physique. Amanda liked his demeanor, his doggedness, and the way he challenged the police during interviews. He told her he had once been a cop. She stood behind his cameraman, near a group of other students and volunteers. Karstarck was taping a report for the paper's YouTube channel. His smile was wide when he saw her. He nodded in her direction and held up an index finger, signaling her to wait.

"You ready?" His "cameraman," an intern with a smartphone, asked.

Karl stamped his feet and blew on his hands in the wintry air. He tapped the small wireless microphone on his coat lapel to make sure it was on and nodded.

The intern held up all five fingers of a gloved hand and began a countdown.

"Five, four, three, two . . ."

"This is Karl Karstarck reporting from Glastonbury University, where volunteers have renewed their search for sophomore Fiona Kessler, who went missing late last month. This isn't the first time a young woman from the Glastonbury area has gone missing, however. This first happened more than four years ago with the disappearances of Cassidy Fisher, a seventeen-year-old high school student, followed by the loss of nineteen-year-old Bethany Jamison and, most recently, Tallulah Montgomery, who is twenty. All three young women disappeared in a similar fashion in and around the same region, yet parents we've spoken to have said the university mentioned nothing about these cases during the most recent freshman orientation."

Karstarck paused and nodded before raising a hand to touch the earpiece in his ear. "Meanwhile, the search for Fiona Kessler continues unabated—even as many here and around the country prepare for the Thanksgiving holiday."

"And we're clear," the cameraman said.

Quaking in the cold, Amanda approached the reporter.

He took both her hands in his and smiled. Despite the cold, genuine warmth emanated from him, washing over her like a balm. "Amanda, my dear. How are you?"

"I think I've found something," she responded.

Over the course of the last few days, Amanda kept turning to Karstarck. At first, she just wanted someone to vent to, someone outside of campus who got how very shaken she was. He was kind and a great listener, and he entertained any little clue Amanda presented him. She also liked the way he wrote about Fiona; the picture he painted of her was the same one Amanda had in her head. And as the days accumulated, she became convinced that if anyone could help find Fiona, it was Karstarck.

"What have you got?"

She took a deep breath. "More than a dozen girls have disappeared over the course of eight years—up and down the East Coast. Not just from Pennsylvania. Of those twelve, four of them had the same physical characteristics and five of them were born on the same day, September 1, which is also Fiona's birthday."

"I know."

Her mouth hung open. "You do? Why haven't you reported it? Don't you think that's important?"

He paused. "Could be. But the police asked us not to share that detail just yet."

She raised an eyebrow. "Why?"

"Amanda," he said with a great deal of patience and not a jot of exasperation, "Laurel Valley has never had a case quite like this. Cops sometimes ask the press not to share every detail they discover. That's because they may be afraid of tipping off their suspect—or spooking the public. But that's something we learned right away. I think it's important too, and we'll reveal it, but not now."

She hung her head, sighed, and nodded.

"Listen, Amanda," he continued. "Can I get you on camera for another piece I'm putting together later? It's messages for Fiona."

"Of course," she said.

Karstarck told her where to stand and his cameraman unclipped the wireless mic from the reporter's coat and moved it onto Amanda's. Then he tapped the head of a larger microphone to make sure it was connected before handing it to the reporter. When his assistant trained the camera on the duo and gave them the thumbs up, Karstarck introduced her and asked, "Did you and your friends ever take any precautions on campus? Before Fiona's disappearance?"

Amanda spoke to the camera. "Fiona and I were both taking self-defense courses. Her father insisted. He wanted her to be safe."

"Do you think she thought she was safe here?"

"We all did. I mean, we are on a university campus. The Laurel Valley Police Department is just up the road! What I can't believe is that the school never told us other girls disappeared from here."

"Do you have any words for Fiona? If she's watching?"

"We love you, Fiona. Hang in there. Help is coming."

CHAPTER TEN

A week after Fiona's disappearance and days after her father's plea, a local detective named Warren Christian asked Amanda and Mark to meet him at the police station.

"I hope they have some real clues," she told Mark on the way there.

He warned her to mind her tongue. "You know how some of these white people are."

"And?"

"And I ain't trying to go out like Freddie Gray or Eric Garner." He sucked his teeth. "That's all I'm saying."

She rolled her eyes. "Whatever, man, this ain't even that. 'Case you forgot we got an invite."

Rarely, now, did Amanda ever think before she spoke or acted—something her mother had often warned her about. "One time, when I was fifteen, I jumped out of an idling car, ran across two lanes of traffic, and dove headfirst into a lake not far from our house to save a drowning puppy." She laughed as she recounted the tale.

"My mom almost had a heart attack. My dad called me stupid. But when that dog licked my face over and over again, I didn't care. Someone recorded it and it went viral. The local papers called me a hero. I told them heroes wear capes and mine was in the cleaners."

Mark snorted as he pulled up to the station house. "I agree with your dad."

She was silent in response.

Later, as they walked in, Mark turned back to her. "The police department is small, only a dozen or so officers. Karstarck said both the sheriff and this Christian guy are new—less than a year."

The station bustled with activity. Because Amanda worked at the only twenty-four-hour eatery in town, some of the officers looked familiar. A handful sat at small desks interviewing people. Telephones rang, and cops in uniforms—guns holstered at their hips—milled about, some nursing steaming cups of coffee.

Laurel Valley was small, too. And even though the school hadn't been her first choice, it had grown on her. Glastonbury University, which overlooked the valley from its perch so high in the mountains, felt like home. The castle turrets seemed to kiss the clouds. About five thousand students were enrolled at the rural school, which prided itself on being close-knit. The student-to-teacher ratio was also among the best in the entire country. Two years ago, when she toured the campus, the student guide joked, "Unless you're hiding from the cops, everyone knows everyone in Podunk Laurel."

Amanda pouted and nodded to the mostly white officers and a few nodded back. She inhaled slowly, keenly aware after Mark's comments that she stood out—and not just because of her ever-present black combat boots or her tightly coiled hair.

Laurel Valley had few minorities.

So she was pleased when Sheriff Nick Foster greeted them with a smile and a gruff handshake. About fifty-five, fit, tall, balding, and the department's only African American male, Foster was with his new Chief of Detectives, a short redhead named Warren Christian, who, to Amanda, barely looked like he was out of college. She followed them into a conference room. Foster walked with an odd gait.

"Don't stare at him," Karstarck had warned her when she called him the night before to tell him the police had summoned them. "He shot his toe off by accident years ago. Lucky for him, he did it before YouTube."

Their footfalls were silent while they walked along plush carpeting to the lone conference room at the end of a narrow hallway.

"Just leave the door open," Foster said over his shoulder. "The radiator's busted so it gets hotter in here than it should." Before they sat down, the sheriff, who had dark circles under his eyes, pulled a small white notebook from his back pocket and flipped it open. Then he cleared his throat. Something he did each time he spoke, like he had an important announcement to make.

"Let's begin with you, Mark. Did you notice anything odd at Dukes Friday night? Say, like someone coming on to Fiona in a weird way or staring at you and your friends?"

"No," he said with a shrug. "We were just . . . talking and drinking and listening to music. There were a lot of people there, you know, it being Halloween and all. Plus, Dukes isn't really that well-lit inside most of the time."

Foster nodded and scribbled in the notebook. "Did you see Fiona talk to anyone?"

"No. When we weren't dancing, we were sitting at the bar all night. I mean, she didn't even get up to go to the bathroom. She never left my side. I didn't know she was missing until Amanda called, and I saw her text on Snapchat the next day saying she was lost."

"What time did she send that text again?" Christian asked.

Mark pulled out his phone and looked at it. "Exactly 12:31 a.m."

"Let's bring in the surveillance footage," Foster said, nodding toward Christian, who left the room.

"When did you last see Fiona, Amanda?" Foster continued.

"In our bedroom on campus. It wasn't that late. About eight or nine, I think? She was headed to Dukes. She asked me to go with her, but I couldn't. I had to study and then I had work."

When Christian returned, he placed a laptop on the table in front of them.

"With the FBI's help, we've collected surveillance footage from a number of cameras that were outside every establishment between Dukes and your campus housing," Christian said. He was looking at Amanda.

Foster continued. "We're in the process of identifying and interviewing some additional witnesses who saw Fiona after she left Dukes. We sifted through this footage we're about to show you and spliced it together in order to construct a timeline from the moment you say she left the bar, Mark, until, well, just look at this. Tell us if you see something or anyone familiar."

"Of course," Amanda said.

Mark nodded. "And from inside the bar?"

"Useless," Christian said. "Like you said, it was dark inside."

Christian opened the laptop, popped a thumb drive into it and hovered the mouse over a "play" symbol. He pressed it and blurry, soundless video began.

On the screen they watched two people dressed in identical superhero costumes bump into each other outside the bar when they left Dukes, ahead of a woman who resembled Fiona.

One in a hooded mask veered off the main path and into some trees.

Mark snapped his fingers. "Wait a minute."

Christian paused the tape.

"Batman sat directly across from us all night! He didn't say anything, just drank. I think he was alone. I wasn't paying him any attention."

"Are you sure that it was a man?" Amanda asked.

"I can't say for sure, to be honest. I mean, that Batman costume is all padding across the chest so it could have been a man or a woman under the mask."

Christian took some notes and restarted the film. "Is that Fiona, though?"

The woman on the screen wore a pair of high-top Converse sneakers, jeans, and a dark leather jacket. In the black-and-white video, her hair looked white. When she looked up at the camera, both irises held two pinpricks of white light. A time stamp in the upper right corner read 12:12 a.m.

"That's her!" Amanda and Mark said in unison. Foster and Christian looked at each other. Christian stood just behind the students, his hands on his hips, staring at the screen.

Foster, who sat opposite them, cleared his throat. "You sure?"

"I'm positive!" Mark said.

"Yeah, me too," Amanda echoed.

The video jumped like it had been spliced from additional footage. On it, a man with long blond hair wearing a dark backpack came into view. He followed Fiona. Dressed in dark pants and a dark bomber jacket, he kept his distance behind her for at least two blocks. The film stopped for a moment and then restarted, picked up at a different angle by another camera. Fiona's face was clearer. It was her, both Amanda and Mark were certain. She seemed to be looking up at the street signs before pulling out her cell phone and texting someone. She walked a bit further. It was now 12:37 a.m., according to the time stamp. Amanda and Mark watched Fiona stumble. The blond man caught her, except now he was wearing a baseball cap, pulled low over his face.

"Damn. We can't see anything," Mark said.

"Wait for it," Christian replied.

The pair on the recording exchanged words. Fiona seemed to laugh. Then she took a few uneasy steps, slipped off the curb, and fell hard into the street. Amanda cringed. It was clear Fiona was hurt. The man helped her stand. She raised her left hand and wiped the sleeve of her jacket across her forehead. Disoriented, she peeled the coat off and dropped it. The man picked it up. Fiona looked up and peered into the blond man's face. He put his hand over his heart, leaned forward slightly, said something to her, and then put his arms around her. Then he pulled off his cap, threw back his head, and laughed.

Christian paused the tape.

"We've got a clear picture here," he said. "Recognize him?"

Amanda shook her head no, but Mark nodded.

"I do. I've seen this guy before. In the bar, I think. He might go to our school, but I'm not sure."

Dubious, Amanda squinted. "He seems a little old for a college student."

"I agree," Foster said, clearing his throat again. "Did you see him in the bar the night Fiona went missing, Mark?"

Mark nodded. "I think so? I can't say for sure, though. Almost everyone was in costume. Plus, we had all been drinking."

Christian jotted something down and restarted the video, again from a different perspective. Fiona and the man had moved further down the street. The blond man flipped his smartphone in the air a couple times. Then he opened the passenger door to a silver Honda SUV. The license plates weren't visible. He looked like he was trying to convince Fiona to enter the vehicle, but she kept shaking her head no and tried to move past him. The man put his hands together in a prayer pose and then he made some animated gestures. Fiona appeared to be arguing with him. A thin dark-haired man in glasses walked past them and glanced in their direction before turning a corner. Fiona said more words to the blond before he punched her hard in the stomach.

Amanda gasped.

When Fiona doubled over, the man pushed her inside the passenger side of the car. The man cast furtive glances up and down the street before he tossed her jacket into some bushes and got in on the driver's side. The time stamped on the video was 12:43 a.m. Christian paused it again. He zoomed in on the back of the car.

"Did you see that? He hit her! Thank God you've got his license plate number," Amanda said. "You guys put out an APB. That's what you call it, right?"

Christian nodded his head. "We found the car with the plates. Both the vehicle and the tags had been stolen."

Mark and Amanda looked at each other. "So?" Mark asked.

"So, we have the car. It was found in New Jersey."

"New Jersey?" Both students said at the same time.

"Yes," Christian said. "Toll booth footage shows the man driving the car alone on the Pennsylvania Turnpike. It exited in New Jersey. Where we found it."

"We also ran his pictures through a facial recognition database."

"And?" Amanda asked.

"Nothing," Foster said.

"How is that even possible?" Mark frowned. "I mean, the guy has to be on Facebook, have a driver's license, right?"

Christian shrugged. "Or not."

"Are you saying you can't find him?" Mark asked. "What about that guy who walked by? What did he say?"

"We haven't found him yet, either. But we will," Foster interjected, standing. "We're canvassing Laurel and the surrounding counties and we're going to put the blond man's picture out there—eventually."

Flushed, Amanda smiled before narrowing her eyes at the detectives, bracing for a fight. "Why wait? Can't you just release the video now?"

"We have a little more sleuthing to do," Christian said. "Thank you both for coming in. And please, we're still investigating, so no talking to the press, Miss Taylor," he said pointedly.

He stood to show them out.

Outside in the cold, Amanda said, "Can you believe that?"

"Believe what?" Mark answered.

"They have a photo of the guy who obviously kidnapped her and they won't release it! That's crazy."

"Amanda . . ." Mark warned. "I know that look."

"Wait right here. I'm going back in to ask them some more questions."

CHAPTER ELEVEN

While Mark waited in his car, Amanda reentered the station, and a young patrolman with a nametag that read "Rothstein" greeted her. She recognized him from the diner.

"Hey! Coffee, black. Two sugars," she said, smiling.

He smiled back. "Forget something, Miss Amanda?"

"No, I just need to clear something up." She pointed toward the hallway leading to the conference room. "Are they still back there?"

Rothstein nodded and waved her through.

When she walked back down the hallway and approached the conference room door, Amanda could hear the detective and the sheriff discussing the case.

"Let's call the DA right now," Christian said. She could tell he had placed the call on speaker because she could hear someone punching a number into a phone on the conference room table when she approached the door. Neither cop noticed her standing near the doorway. Amanda watched Foster smooth his hand over his tie. She retreated against a wall out of sight and eavesdropped.

The phone rang twice before a woman answered.

"Detective Warren Christian. I need to speak to ADA Booker Aires. Tell him it's about the Kessler case."

Outside in the hallway, Amanda froze. "Just a moment," she heard a voice on the speakerphone respond. Amanda held her breath when the line went silent.

"Aires." The district attorney's voice sounded like he could sing backup for an R&B group.

"Booker," Christian said, "we've got a development. I have at least one witness who might be able to place a suspect at the bar on the night of Fiona's disappearance."

"So," Aires asked Christian, "does this guy fit the description?"

"Yes. I'd say he looks to be our perp in all eight of those disappearances we discussed," Christian told him. "Medium build and height, has long blond hair and, up until about a week ago, he was driving a silver SUV. We found the car, but it was clean of prints. We also don't have any cars fitting that description registered locally. However, we've got him on video. We know five of the girls were born on September 1 and we've been able to keep the press from revealing that—for now, because you said it might be relevant later."

"At trial, maybe," Aires confirmed. "I also don't want to cause a panic or to clue in our killer that we know he's been stalking women. Let him think we think these kidnappings are random."

Amanda looked down the hall to be sure neither Rothstein nor anyone else was watching her.

Christian interrupted him. "Right. Hey, Booker, my sheriff is here on speaker. Can you tell him what you told me earlier?"

Aires paused. "We've found the remains of at least four missing girls, hailing from here to New Jersey. Christian, I spoke to Leslie George after I talked to you. She thinks we've got a traveler."

Foster cleared his throat. "A traveling serial killer?"

Amanda could hear Aires sigh. "I told George I'd call her once you guys got a lead. She wants to speak with you."

"Leslie George, the author?" Christian asked.

"Can't hurt to have an FBI expert on hand if the worm turns, right?" Aires asked.

"Yeah," Christian said, his voice up an octave. "I love her books! *The Definitive Guide to Serial Killers, Death at a Moment's Notice,* and . . ." He snapped his fingers. "What was that other one, again?"

Aires cut him off. "Defense attorneys hate her, so it's good to have her on our side. She may not lecture or teach criminal justice anymore, but her interest in crime? That's not going anywhere. Let me see if I can patch her in. Give me a minute."

Amanda heard the phone ring once. A woman answered. She didn't say hello, just: "Booker."

"Leslie. I've got the Laurel PD on the line."

They exchanged pleasantries before George got down to business. "Gentlemen, I do believe all these cases are linked." They were silent while she explained how. Then she asked, "Have you got a suspect?"

"Yes," Christian said.

"Blond?" she asked.

Amanda heard a sharp intake of breath. Then Christian's surprised voice, "How'd you know?"

"He fits the profile I'm developing," George said. "There's some kind of connection between his appearance and that of his victims. The birth dates may be important, too. I haven't worked out why, but I strongly encourage you to suppress that detail for as long as possible."

"Certainly," Foster said.

"What nature of evidence do you have so far?"

In his deep voice, Foster explained the surveillance tape and the witnesses—two students and a passerby—who overheard Fiona say she didn't want to get into the man's car.

Amanda furrowed her brow.

"What we need to know is if we release the footage to the public and he still has her alive, will he kill her?"

George didn't respond to Foster's question for a moment, then said, "No."

Outside, in the hallway, Amanda slumped her shoulders and exhaled. She could feel the blood draining from her face.

"However," George added, "I do see extenuating circumstances that might . . ."

"Such as?" Aires asked, cutting her off.

"Well," she said, pausing for a moment. "Each killer has their own quirks, of course. But most tend to follow a pattern, a set list of rules, and rarely do they deviate from it. She's been missing, what? Less than a month? Do you have any idea how long he kept the previous victims?"

"Assuming it's the same guy?" Aires asked. "Longer than that."

"Right," George replied. "Could be he keeps them for a great deal of time—until he's finished with them. If that's the case, then he'll keep her alive for as long as he wants or is able to—even if the authorities are barging through his door. But, as you know, every unsub is different."

"Of course," Foster said. "Thank you, Leslie."

"You're welcome," she told the sheriff. "Oh, and Booker?"

"Yes?"

"Let me know when you catch him. I'd like to do the psych eval on this one. I've been following the disappearances of young women all over the country—particularly on the East Coast. I'm intrigued."

"Right."

Aires hung up with George.

"So, there you have it, gentlemen," Aires said. "Get back to me if you need warrants, OK?"

When the line went dead, Amanda crept back down the hallway, but not before she heard Foster tease Christian for being a "fanboy."

CHAPTER TWELVE

A manda was shaking when she went back outside.

"What?" Mark said.

Amanda leaned against his car in the cold air. Her tears warmed her cheeks when they slid down her face. Mark got out of the car, hugged her, and pleaded with her not to cry.

"I can't help it," she blubbered. "I feel so helpless." Her breath appeared like small puffs of smoke in the November atmosphere. She told him what she had overheard. "I mean, I can understand they're concerned for her safety. But they know what he looks like and they won't tell people! It's hard to accept!"

Mark was meditative. "Come, sit inside the car. I'll put the heat on." When they were both seated and the car doors were closed, he started the car. But before putting it in drive, he leaned over and whispered. "Can you imagine being held hostage by a serial killer?"

She shook her head no and was silent a moment. "I can't. I mean, I don't know what I'd do. Do you?"

"No, but I don't think most serial killers kidnap men and hold them hostage. I think if he wanted me dead, he'd just kill me. Girls have it harder."

Amanda nodded. "I think I could reason my way out of it."

Mark gave her a dubious look. "You mean argue."

"I mean reason. I would make him see the benefits of keeping me alive."

"How?"

"I don't know," she sighed, running her hands over her face. "I think I'm pretty cool once you talk to me; get to know me and I can be quite convincing."

They were silent for a moment. Amanda closed her eyes and let her head fall back against the car's headrest.

"You think she's alive?" Mark asked softly.

She wiped her face. "I pray to God she is. But if this guy fits the description of someone who has kidnapped and killed all these other women, shouldn't the police be able to do more? Say more? Share more, before it's too late?"

Mark shrugged. "They're the cops. I guess they need more evidence."

"They have enough! What the hell do they know? I mean, other girls could be in danger too. I can't believe Fiona might be dead. She just can't be dead, Mark!"

He patted her leg.

"I can't sit by and wait." She gulped and wiped her face again, this time smearing black eyeliner across her cheek. "That would eat me up inside if I just did nothing!"

"What else can you do?"

She looked out her window and mumbled, "I could call that reporter at the *Valley Dispatch*."

Mark turned toward her, frowning. "They explicitly told us not to say anything. Not to talk to the press. We could get into real trouble for blabbing. I mean, big trouble. I want us to find Fiona. I do. But I'm not trying to jeopardize my baseball scholarship, Amanda."

She gasped. "To hell with your scholarship! We're talking about Fiona! And for the record, Mark, I'm far from stupid. I know what obstruction of justice is. Fiona could still be out there alive and these dumb hick cops aren't doing all they can to save her. Think about it. People may know who this guy is if they could just see his face."

Mark cut her off. "Amanda, didn't you just hear an FBI expert also tell them not to release that detail?"

Amanda paused, as if contemplating that point. "Yeah, but she also told them there could be extenuating circumstances where he might keep her alive—even if the police were breaking down his door. It's a chance, Mark. All Fiona needs is a chance."

"I don't agree!"

"You're living in a fantasy, Mark," Amanda huffed. "It's always the newspapers that break these kinds of stories, that solve these kinds of cases. It's always because people like me give them these kinds of tips!"

A commotion erupted behind them and the pair craned their necks to see Christian and two cops run outside the station like they were on fire.

"Where do you think they're going?" Mark asked.

Amanda sighed. "I don't know. I don't care, either."

"They don't have any sirens on. Let's follow them," Mark said. He was never impulsive. Yet he pulled out behind them.

"Why?"

He turned to her and raised an eyebrow. "You got something better to do?"

Twenty minutes later, the pair pulled over to a hilly, wooded area not far from an apartment complex near Glastonbury's campus. They waited, watching the cops disappear through a gap in the woods and down a narrow path.

"Come on," Mark said. He snatched the keys from the ignition, got out, and slammed the door. Amanda trudged behind him.

CHAPTER THIRTEEN

The ground was frozen. A light snowfall—the winter's first—blanketed the woods, frosting everything a wraithlike white.

But Amanda would soon discover that the cold hadn't stopped a German shepherd from sniffing out the remains of a young woman. Her half-submerged hand was found beneath a clump of snow-covered leaves in a wooded area near the Walnut Knoll Village apartments, about seven minutes from Glastonbury University.

When Mark and Amanda approached unseen, the dog, whom they would later learn was named Mitzy, stood in the snow with her owner, Nico Eboma. Amanda and Mark crept up behind the police and eavesdropped while Eboma told them what happened. Mitzy wagged her tail in the bright sunshine. While a bespectacled Eboma spoke to the sheriff, Amanda spied forensic crews a few hundred feet away carefully collecting and bagging evidence near what could only be the remains. The area had been cordoned off and members of the press were beginning to appear on the opposite side of the crime scene. From behind the yellow police tape, some of them shouted questions.

Amanda bolted past Mark. "Oh no! Is it her? Is it Fiona?" she cried.

Christian whirled around. "What are you doing here?"

"We followed you," Mark said, catching up to her.

"Why?"

"I need to know what's going on!" Amanda said. "Is it her?"

Exasperated, Foster blew air through his mouth. His cheeks puffed out. Then he cleared his throat, thought better of it, and turned away from the trio.

"Handle this," he shouted to Christian over his shoulder. "Make them leave. Now, please."

"You heard him," Christian said, opening his arms wide and waving his hands in a shooing motion. "Time to go."

"That guy said you found a body," Mark spoke up. "If it's Fiona, we can identify her."

Christian paused for a moment. "We did find a young woman's body."

Amanda blinked, then stumbled. Christian caught her. "Hey, are you OK?"

"No," she said, just above a whisper. "Please tell me it's not Fiona." Her eyes were wild with fear. "I need to see!"

Christian held her tight against him, no doubt, Amanda later realized, to keep her from running over to the crime scene, contaminating it. But in that moment, Amanda didn't care. She was keenly aware that even through her coat he could feel her heart thumping fast against his chest.

A sympathetic Christian explained that the body had been discarded like trash, buried in a shallow grave and covered with leaves. Blond, dirty, and half-clothed, the killer had also stripped her of identification.

"We don't think it's her," Christian added. "She's not wearing the same clothes Fiona was last seen in, and this girl had a short peacoat thrown over her."

Foster approached again, pointing at Amanda. "Why are they still here?"

She cut him off. "Sheriff, that guy with the dog said you found a body. I'm a witness. Maybe I can help identify her."

Foster glared at her. "That's something you can do later. Not here."

Christian flipped open a notebook and pulled out a pen. He bit the top off with his teeth. "How long does the coroner say she's been out here?"

Foster shook his head from side to side and murmured his uncertainty. "Hard to tell," he said, jutting his chin toward the team collecting evidence. "We haven't gotten the forensics yet. They're bagging the body in a few."

"Can I see her?" Amanda asked again. "Please."

"No," Christian said, starting to escort her away. "She has to be taken to the morgue and we have to contact her next of kin to identify the body first."

Amada whirled to face him, her soft hair ruffling in the wind. "But I can do that! I know what she looks like! I'm her roommate, for Pete's sake, and her parents are over two hours away!"

It was clear from his tone that Christian was running out of patience. "You need to let us do our jobs."

Amanda took a step back, gawking at him. "OK," she said loud, enough for a few reporters to hear. "Now are you going to release to the press the photos and video of the man who snatched Fiona?"

He grabbed her by the elbow and pulled her out of earshot of the media. "Eventually," he snapped.

When Mark approached them, Amanda threw her hands in the air in frustration. "That's not good enough! Do it now. Don't you see? Even if that's not Fiona—what if this girl's death and Fiona's disappearance are somehow connected? I don't see how you can sit on that kind of clue— actual video and a photo of the suspect and not release it!"

"I don't see how, either," someone said from behind them. The four of them whirled around.

The man who spoke was about forty, bald, pasty, and stocky. To Amanda, he looked like he had been fit at one point before abandoning physical fitness for smoking. He took one last long drag before letting the dying butt of his cigarette fall to his feet, where it sizzled to death in the snow.

"Huntley Field. Philadelphia Bureau, FBI."

Mark leaned over to Amanda and whispered in her ear, "Is he for real?"

She looked up at Mark and, despite her apprehension, hid a small smile behind one gloved hand.

Foster paused for a moment and then the four of them advanced on the federal lawman, arms extended for handshakes.

Field repeated himself, and then added, "Release the video. Stills, too." He cupped his bare hands and blew on them before rubbing them together. "At this point, everyone in this tiny town knows you collected video. The people who gave you the footage have probably shown it to their friends and neighbors already anyway. It's only a matter of time before it winds up on Twitter. Maybe someone will recognize him—ticks and all—and turn him in. Maybe it'll make the killer make a mistake."

"Well," Foster began, "our consultant, Leslie . . ."

But Amanda stepped forward and interrupted him. "Are you taking over the investigation, Mr. Field?" she asked in a rush. "Aren't kidnapping and murder federal offenses?"

The local cops bristled at her questions.

Field grinned, but just on the left side of his mouth, and handed her his card. "Call me Huntley. And no, I'm just here to help," he said, walking toward the forensic crews. "For now."

Christian turned toward Amanda. "There's nothing you can do here."

"Take her home," he ordered Mark before stomping away. He and Foster followed Field. Amanda trembled and clenched her fists. She was still for a solid minute before removing one glove and swiping open her phone.

"What are you doing now?" Mark asked, worried.

She waited until the cops were out of earshot. "Not one, but two FBI officials have said there's no reason not to release those tapes," she said, holding up two fingers for emphasis. "As far as I'm concerned, these stupid ass cops need incentive to release that footage, so I'm going to give them some. And I don't care if they lock me up."

"Keep me out of it," Mark said.

Her fingers flew across the screen when she typed out a text: *The police have a suspect on video, but they're not releasing it to the press.*

Mark frowned. "Are you going to at least call the Kesslers?"

She nodded. "Right after I talk to someone else first." Minutes later, the phone rang. She put it to her ear. "Mr. Karstarck?" Amanda said, slipping with purpose now back toward Mark's car. "There have been some new developments. You can't quote me though."

CHAPTER FOURTEEN

Two hours later, the headlines across the web screamed their discontent with the police investigation:

Who Has Fiona Kessler? Cops Won't Say

Police Chase Theory: Serial Killer Is Among Us

Body Found: Is It Fiona or Is Missing Coed Trapped in Killer's Lair?

University Hid Pattern of Abduction from Parents, Students

In Surprise Development, Local Cops Consult Author Leslie George

Citing anonymous sources, Karstarck's paper led the charge, questioning why the Laurel County PD hadn't been more forthcoming with details of their investigation into the disappearance of Fiona Kessler. It linked her vanishing to that of eight other women—all were Fiona's same height and age. Each had come from somewhere between the tip of southern New Jersey and Central Pennsylvania. Four of them were found dead—including the latest one on the outskirts of Glastonbury's campus.

Karstarck and other journalists had interviewed the families of the other dead girls. Two were waitresses who vanished after leaving work; one was a nursing student on her way to her shift at an area hospital. The other was a student at a neighboring university who disappeared after leaving basketball practice.

Sometime just before 8:00 p.m. the next night, Amanda heard someone banging on the door to her apartment. She knew who it was—even before one of her roommates poked her head in her bedroom to tell her a Detective Warren Christian was asking for her.

"You couldn't wait to tell them about George, could you?" Christian yelled at her.

His face was scarlet and spittle had flown from his lips. Three of Amanda's other dormmates scrambled from the room.

Amanda crossed her arms and gave the detective a blank stare.

"You and Mark are the only ones who could have heard me and Aires talking to George. Mark insists it wasn't him, and I believe him."

"I don't know what you're talking about," Amanda told him.

Christian grabbed her by the elbow.

"We're going outside so I can speak to you privately." He marched her into the cold and pushed her toward a patrol car. "Get in." He shut the passenger door, got behind the wheel, and switched on the heat.

Amanda glared at him. "I didn't say anything about George!"

Christian spoke in measured tones, treating her like a toddler.

"After we showed you out, Patrolmen Rothstein told us he saw you return and go down the hallway toward our interrogation room. We're not stupid, Amanda! Now the mayor, Aires, and a lot of other people are on our case about that conversation. George is unhappy, too. I know you're upset about your friend, but if you impede my investigation again, I will lock you up for obstruction of justice."

Amanda's heart was thumping so fast she was sure Christian could see it whipping against the green and gold GU emblem on her sweatshirt. She twisted her body toward the window, shrinking away from him. "It wasn't me," she lied.

"Unbelievable! You know Karstarck isn't going to tell us his source—former cop or not! And if you didn't tell Karstarck, who did? Did you tell anyone else?"

"What difference does that make?"

He huffed and rolled his eyes. "So you did tell someone."

"I didn't say that!"

"It makes a difference, Amanda, because it hampers our investigation if the suspect knows what we're doing!" He turned toward her. "Remember, whoever has Fiona watches the news and reads all that garbage on social media, too."

"I'm sorry," she said. "But I don't understand what harm it would do to let people at least see his face. And the FBI agrees with me."

Christian inhaled and lowered his voice. "We're not even sure it's him. For all we know, that could be some random guy."

Amanda's mouth fell open. "Some random guy? He punched her in the stomach and forced her into his car!"

Christian pursed his lips. "How about you stick to your schoolwork and let us do our job?"

"How about you release that surveillance footage so people can identify the man who took my best friend before he kills her?" she shot back.

Christian got out of the patrol car, went around to the passenger door, and opened it.

"Good night, Amanda. If you think of anything else that can aid our investigation, do call the station—but not for any other reason."

CHAPTER FIFTEEN

"Later tonight on GCN—your best choice for Global Crime News—we'll bring you never-before-seen footage of a suspect in the disappearance of twenty-one-year-old college student Fiona Kessler."

Ben's jaw dropped.

The television remote he was holding clattered to his feet.

He plopped down on the sofa. His pulse increased. Blood rushed to his ears. Leaning forward, he plucked the remote off the floor and turned up the volume.

He didn't care that Fiona could probably hear it too.

"There have been new developments in the vanishing of a Glastonbury University sophomore in Central Pennsylvania," the news anchor began. When photos of a smiling Fiona flickered across the screen, Ben cringed.

"Police tonight are continuing their probe into the disappearance of Fiona Kessler on Halloween, and now they and the FBI are searching for a white male with blond hair who can be seen in this exclusive video footage forcing Fiona into a vehicle not far from a tavern where she was last seen partying with friends."

Ben stared at the screen and began to tremble. His heart palpitations intensified.

"Police say this man may hold key information about the deaths of at least three other women who are about Fiona's age. Authorities aren't calling the man a suspect—rather 'a person of interest they want to question.'"

When an enlarged, grainy photo of him appeared on screen, Ben's throat constricted. It felt like an out-of-body experience. He reached over and grabbed a pad and pencil from an end table.

"Authorities say the description of the man suspected in Fiona's kidnapping also fits that of someone wanted in the kidnapping and now murder of another young woman whose body was found not far from where Fiona went to school. They've also linked that death to the murders of three other young women whose bodies were discovered not far from this tiny community that borders Amish country. Global Crime News' Marco Garcia reports live from Laurel Valley, Pennsylvania."

A tall, handsome reporter with dark curly hair dressed in a navy wool coat appeared on the television screen. Wind ruffled his hair. He stood in front of Dukes, holding a microphone.

"Just hours ago, authorities released film of Fiona Kessler and the suspect from the early morning of November 1," Garcia began, "and witness Chris Chong, who police say may have been the last person to see Fiona that night, told GCN exclusively that he overheard a heated exchange between the man and the college coed."

A young Asian man, dressed in a light jacket despite the frigid temperature, appeared on the screen; a microphone had been shoved in his face. As he spoke, the words "Witness Chris Chong" scrolled on the screen beneath him.

Ben wrote down his name.

"I saw her talking to the guy and heard her refuse to get in his car," Chong said, smiling. It was clear he was happy to be on television. He pushed his glasses up the bridge of his pimpled nose. "But I didn't think anything of it. Figured it was just a guy and his girl arguing."

The reporter continued and a still image of Dukes flashed across the screen. Ben whipped out his smartphone.

"Fiona's disappearance is similar to those of eight women—who have all gone missing from this same area since 2006. Four of them were found dead."

On the screen appeared the photos of four blonds. Their names were under their photos and the photos shuffled until one was enlarged. Ben snapped a picture of the TV screen.

"Last night, police discovered the body of this woman—twenty-year-old waitress, Tallulah Montgomery—who went missing earlier this year. She was buried in the snow some twelve miles away from where she disappeared. Sources tell us both of her eyes had been gouged out. Again, police want to question this man, who, we should caution, may be armed and is certainly dangerous."

Ben's face flushed and he felt bile rise in his throat when his photo and that of an artist's rendering of him were shown side by side.

"As you've just heard, he fits the description of the person who was last seen with both Tallulah Montgomery and Fiona Kessler, who he forced into a vehicle that police say was later found in New Jersey. That places him with at least two of the eight missing women. Combined rewards leading to the arrest and conviction in both Montgomery's death and Fiona's disappearance now stand at one hundred seventy-five thousand dollars. Law enforcers are hopeful that leads to more tips in both cases. Laurel County Sheriff Nicholas Foster, shown here, says the police are hoping someone recognizes the suspect."

Ben wrote down the sheriff's name and watched when one of the cops limped up to a podium and took questions from reporters. The man cleared his throat and quaked a bit when he spoke.

"Solving these cases is paramount. We're talking about our beloved town versus a despicable criminal, and the more information we get, the closer we get to finding a suspect. Please keep sharing your tips—either by phone or on our social channels."

A buxom older Black woman with long blonde locs and horn-rimmed glasses appeared on screen next. Beneath her were the words: Former FBI Profiler and Author Leslie George. Ben Googled her and dozens of entries along with her pictures appeared on the small screen in the palm of his hand.

The reporter continued: "Best-selling crime author Leslie George, now a professor in Pennsylvania, says despite the similarities in all of the victims—young, blond, Caucasian, and of similar height and age—a great deal about this case remains unanswered."

George sat in front a blue screen blaring the words "EXPERT OPINION."

"Fiona and Tallulah were low-risk victims in moderate-risk areas," she said. "Both disappeared while out alone at night. But there may be more about the suspect that's recognizable. For example, pay attention to the way this man flips his phone in the surveillance footage," she said while Ben watched himself flip his phone in the air, a habit he had developed years ago. He immediately questioned if anyone else had ever commented on him doing so. His stomach lurched and he began shaking again.

"Even if you don't recognize his face, you may find his mannerisms—the way he walks and behaves—familiar."

The camera cut back to Garcia.

"Police are canvassing neighbors and businesses that have security cameras. They're asking residents in the area to again review any video footage they may have and to share it with detectives. Back to the studio for more on this developing story."

Ben shut the TV off, walked into the hall and stood in front of a mirror. He shook his head from side to side. He couldn't believe how much he looked like his sister. He closed his eyes.

"Dammit, Ben!" His eyes flew open and he flinched. Corinthia's voice was awash with anger. "You were supposed to be careful when you snatched her! What the f—"

"Don't you yell at me!" He stared at his feet. Her harsh words had startled him. But it wasn't so much what she said that wounded him, it was the way she spoke to him. Her voice was so full of vitriolic loathing he nearly stopped breathing.

"Ben, they've got you on camera!" he heard her hiss. "Your face is plastered all over the damn news. I knew this would happen! It's just a matter of time before they figure out who you are, where we are, and what we've been doing!"

Ben pushed his face into his hands, wiping the sweat from his forehead. "I'm aware of that," he muttered, his chest tightening.

"Now you can't go out at all! I have to do everything because the police are looking for you!"

"What are you talking about? You're the one who does most of the shopping and stuff anyway."

Corinthia's voice vibrated with rage. "I have to fix this. I know I promised you we wouldn't, but we've got to get rid of Fiona."

"No!" he shouted, alarmed. Down the hall Ben could hear Fiona wailing through her gag while she thrashed against her restraints.

"You promised me we wouldn't kill this one, Corinthia."

But his twin pleaded with him.

"Can't you see? They will be relentless in trying to find this girl! We cannot keep her here!"

"You promised me we would stop!" He ran a hand through his long hair. "Besides, if you kill her, where are we supposed to put her?"

"Same place as the rest of them," he heard his sister mumble.

Ben threw his hands in the air and let them slap back down against his jeans. "There's already enough bodies scattered all over the place! This is all your fault!"

"My fault?" she shouted, her voice dripping with incredulity.

"You're the one killing them, Corinthia," he said pointedly. "Not me."

"You're the one bringing them here."

"And I have been begging you for years not to kill them!"

"This shit again?"

"Just leave me alone!" Ben opened the front door and walked out into the fresh air, slamming the door behind him. He took a deep breath and paced. From within, her voice was faint.

"You really think it's smart to stand outside? Where someone might see you?"

With his chest puffed up, he turned on his heel and went back into the house, slamming the door behind him. He walked down the hall and shouted at her.

"Just drive the Pontiac from now on."

"Better get a sack of cash together in case we have to leave in a hurry, Ben," he heard her respond.

"You do it!" he told her.

"Fine! Don't forget to pack it, dweeb."

"I won't!" he shouted. Ben slammed the door and went into Fiona's room. He removed the gag from her mouth and took off her blindfold.

"I'm sorry you had to hear that."

She swallowed and stared into his eyes. "It's OK," she said, her voice measured. "I appreciate you keeping me safe."

Ben plopped down on the mattress next to her. "Really?"

She nodded her head. "Yes, really. I mean, your sister is . . . a handful."

"Tell me about it."

Fiona was quiet a moment. "Why do you listen to her?"

"Huh?"

"I mean, why do you let her tell you what to do? If you want to let me go, why not just let me go?"

Ben was pensive. "I . . . I don't know," he said after a few moments. "She . . . has only my best interests at heart, really. She loves me."

"I get that," Fiona said, her voice calm. "But, at the end of the day, like you said, you're not the one responsible for how things turn out. She is, though, right?"

Ben nodded.

"So . . . just let me go. I won't tell anyone. I'm really scared, Ben. I don't want to die here."

"I'm not going to let that happen."

"But from what I understand, you've never been able to keep that from happening. And she keeps saying she wants to get rid of me." Fiona's voice remained calm, soothing. She made perfect sense.

"You're right," Ben said. "I'll let you go. I promise, but not just now. I mean, I'm enjoying your company," he said, lying down and curling up next to her. He ran his fingers through her golden tresses. He caressed her arm and felt goosebumps pimple her warm skin. "Aren't you enjoying mine?"

Fiona nodded. "I am. But are you sure you can protect me? From her?"

Ben nodded. "I've learned my lesson. I have the only key to this room now."

She swallowed. "Well, that makes me feel somewhat safe, Ben. But I . . . have a life of my own and I'm sure my parents are really worried about me."

"Fiona, I promise you. I will not let Corinthia hurt you. At all. You have my word."

"Good," she said. "Ben, can you tell me why you have this . . . need to be with girls that look like your sister?"

Ben sighed and raised his eyebrows, surprised by the question. "I . . . don't know," he said, his voice cautious. "I mean, Corinthia is my whole world. Ever since I was little, I found comfort in just being close to her, like this," he said holding Fiona tight. "But as we got older, it became impossible for me to hold her like this, cuddle and just . . . be affectionate. She's not . . . the same warm person I knew as a child."

"Why do you think that is?"

Ben sat up then, annoyed. "You ask a lot of questions, Fiona."

She uttered a nervous laugh. "Well, I am studying to be a therapist, Ben."

"Ha!" he said. "That explains it." He sniffed and smiled. "So, what's the verdict, doc? What do you think is wrong with me?"

She licked her dry lips. "Well . . . given my situation and from what I've been able to tell, you have been carrying a lot of hurt inside you, Ben. Maybe your whole life. You are desperate for love, for affection. For some reason, you want that love from women who remind you of your sister. There's a reason why—even if you can't articulate it. And you want it so much that you are unconcerned about the consequences of your actions—even though you know she'll continue to destroy that love, that new love. There's a big part of you that knows that what you're doing is wrong and you want it to stop. But you're trapped in a cycle you refuse to break. I know that with therapy—with help you can free yourself from this hell you've put yourself in."

"Hell?"

"Ben, you don't want to do this—put women in situations where you know they're going to die. I know you love your sister, but you're too dependent on her. Way too much," Fiona lowered her voice when she added, "and she needs to be stopped."

She paused. "Have you ever thought about seeking help for this . . . impulse?"

He looked down at her and nodded his head yes. "I have, but she won't let me. And, I mean, how much could that help?"

"A lot, Ben. You and your sister are hurting innocent people. That isn't right and you know that," she said, her voice gentle, kind. "I could help you, Ben. I would go with you to . . . the authorities to . . ."

He cut her off. "No, no, no. I can't do that."

"Why not?"

"Because they'd separate us!" he wailed. "I can't live without my sister. Neither of us would survive without the other."

"But . . ."

"I gotta go," he said all of a sudden, standing up from the bed. He leaned over and replaced her gag and blindfold. He kissed her forehead.

"You're easy to talk to, Fiona. Thank you." He shut the door gently behind him.

CHAPTER SIXTEEN

Right after GCN's report, fear gripped the school, sleepy Laurel Valley, and most of Central Pennsylvania. Panicked parents descended in droves on the campus and pulled their daughters—and sons—from Glastonbury University, and neighboring colleges too.

For students who refused to leave, the university instituted a "buddy system," insisting that no student travel alone at night—from class, to the gym, to the cafeterias or restaurants and lounges off campus. As dusk neared, neighboring nightclubs and eateries and bars were nearly deserted. The college town had placed itself on lockdown and a somber, quiet mood took hold as the Thanksgiving holiday approached. If anyone recognized the mysterious blond man from the video, they didn't say. New footage of blond men shown walking near businesses and residents' homes near Glastonbury proved useless. It was as if the suspect had vanished, too. Dejected by her last encounter with Christian, Amanda hadn't bothered to call the Laurel Valley police again. She did phone Huntley Field of the FBI, but he said there were no new developments.

Depressed, Amanda cornrowed her hair instead of doing it every other day and sleepwalked her way through the next two weeks of classes. She went to football games and movies with her roommates, but nothing made her feel better. She quit her job after customers who saw her on TV began grilling her about Fiona and the case. She kept messing up their orders anyway. She walked all over campus with Mark and deep into the woods to help search crews, but that proved fruitless.

But then one night, there was a sharp and persistent knock on Amanda's bedroom door.

"My God, you look awful!" It was her mother, Sharon, with her father, David, by her side.

"Hi," Amanda responded, flopping back on her bed. She had been expecting this.

Her mother brushed by her and sat opposite her on Fiona's bed. She faced her daughter and crossed her arms.

"Pack," she said. "We've come to take you home."

"I'm not going anywhere," Amanda said, her eyes defiant, her heart pounding.

"You listen to your mother!" her father boomed.

Amanda sighed. "Forgive me, Daddy. It wasn't my intention to be disrespectful. But I'm not going anywhere until they find Fiona."

"The dean called me," her mother said. "Your grades are falling."

"What? I'm twenty! He's not supposed to do that without my permission!"

"He's concerned," her father interjected. "This school is in crisis, Amanda. You're all over the news! This is as much a liability issue for them as it is for . . ."

"Liability issue for them?" she said, cutting her father off. "You're kidding me, right?"

"Think of your grades," her mother said. "Your future."

Amanda bristled. "I might not nab any scholarships next year—but I'm not flunking out, either."

Mrs. Taylor gaped at her daughter. "It's obvious you're not sleeping and that you've lost weight. Have you considered what this is doing to your health?"

"Amanda," her father said, kneeling in front of her. "Be reasonable. You cannot stay here. It's not safe." Her parents stared while she slipped on her black combat boots and shrugged into a black leather jacket.

"I beg to differ. He's not kidnapping Black women, Dad."

"That you know of," he shot back. "You know just as well as I do only missing white women make the news." Her father's upper lip quivered: a reaction, Amanda knew, that characteristically expressed his frustration.

She took a deep breath and exhaled. "I love you both. But I'm not going anywhere with you, and you can't make me. In case you haven't noticed, I'm not a kid anymore. I'm grown."

Then she walked out and closed the door behind her, leaving her stunned parents in her room.

Still, they called after her as she marched out of the building and into the wind.

"Amanda! Amanda! For God's sake, don't walk around out there by your-self! Amanda!" her mother cried out of an open dorm window. "Come back here!"

More snow had fallen, painting Laurel Valley's rolling hills clean and new. Amanda ignored her parents and trudged to Mark's dorm in ankle-deep drifts.

He ushered her into his toasty room. "'Sup?"

She stamped slush from her combat boots on his rug. "Can I borrow your car? Mine is in the shop."

"Sure, but for what?"

Amanda silenced her phone. Her father was calling. "I need to get out of here for a little while," she said before slipping the device in her back pocket.

"Sure. OK. I get that. My brother's driving up from Temple now. We're headed to Penn State to watch the Nittany Lions play the Buckeyes tomor-row. You can keep it all weekend if you want since I'll be at State College." He threw her the keys. "Don't put a scratch on it and don't mess with my stuff in the trunk though, OK? It only looks like a mess. There's a bunch of old sporting equipment in there from travel baseball I need to clean out."

When Amanda raised an eyebrow at him, Mark winked.

"My brother keeps teasing me about keeping that stuff—especially my cracked bat from high school. I hit a walk-off grand slam with that one—memories, you know?"

Amanda smiled and slipped the key ring over her right thumb. "Sorry if I got you in trouble with Christian."

Mark smirked. "Stop apologizing. I already told you, you didn't. They kinda knew it was you." He paused then asked, "Amanda, are you OK? I mean . . . you look tired and thin."

She sat on his sofa and ran her fingers over her hair. "OK, Mom."

"I'm serious. Eat. Rest. And be careful. There's a guy out here killing girls."

"He's only killing blonds so I think I'm pretty safe. Besides, I take self-defense classes, remember?"

Mark laughed before giving her dap and a quick embrace. Moments lat-er they exchanged slight head nods before she pulled off and drove down-town to Karstarck's office.

The only true hub of activity in Laurel Valley now, aside from the many bars and restaurants ringing the campus, was the lone Walmart. It was located in a massive brand-new shopping plaza on the edge of the city not far from the university. Amanda drove past it. A zillion tiny lights winked off and on in the trees, heralding the approach of Christmas. She turned on the radio and Mariah Carey crooned "All I Want for Christmas Is You."

Amanda took a deep breath and exhaled slowly. Relaxing her shoulders, she let the music sweep over her.

Green wreaths dotted with red ribbon and holly were placed strategically on the doors of restaurants and shops. Because there was no indoor mall, bored students who weren't old enough to bar hop frequented the plaza for almost everything—clothes, shoes, groceries, and books from Barnes & Noble.

When the locals referred to downtown Laurel Valley, however, they meant Main Street, which was five miles away.

It spanned four blocks, boasting very old, stately manor homes and several red-brick office and municipal buildings, including the Laurel Valley Courthouse and the Laurel Valley Police Department. The jail was behind that and next to it was the Sure Is Tasty Café, which also fed the lockup's occasional inmates. Down the block and around the corner was a traditional Irish pub—The Dubliner—where Guinness and Tullamore Dew whiskey and live music flowed nightly for patrons, including a few cops. Each of the buildings was no taller than four stories—save for the *Laurel Valley Dispatch*, which was smack dab in the middle of Main, in between two banks. It was eight stories high and also housed the town's only clock tower, embedded in polished white granite.

Amanda parked outside, took the stairs two at a time, and threw open the glass doors to the foyer of the *Dispatch*'s building, blowing cold air in as she entered.

The building had been constructed in the 1920s. Marble floors and stone pillars lined a shiny hallway that led to the receptionist's desk. A dark-haired man of about nineteen sat there, reading *Media Circus* by Kim Goldman and Tatsha Robertson. Recognizing Amanda, he waved her in as the clock struck 8:00 p.m.

"Hey there," Karstarck said when he saw her. He removed his glasses and ran his hands over his face. "How you feeling?" He stood and offered her his chair. As she sank into it, Amanda knew Karstarck wasn't just a friendly reporter. She was his source, and anything she told him about Fiona, herself, or the case could wind up printed where both of the girls' parents would see it. But Amanda didn't mind. She needed his help.

"How's school?" he asked.

She exhaled. "Not good. My grades are falling and my parents are pissed."

"What's the mood like on campus?"

She shrugged. "For the kids that are left, they've all gone back to their lives." Karstarck whipped open a notepad and began to take notes. "But a lot of students have gone home."

"Why do you think that is?"

"Parents." She shrugged. "Some of the students jetted early for the holiday, though. Some professors are allowing them to study off campus and turn in their final work online. But most parents don't want their kids on campus near a serial killer stalking coeds."

"Do you think that's what's going on, Amanda?"

"I . . . I don't know," she stammered. "I mean, Fiona's not the only girl to disappear from near our school, and we don't know for sure if the man who took her is the killer."

He continued to scribble. "Why haven't you left?"

Amanda stiffened. "I'm not going anywhere. Fiona's like my sister and I'm not leaving until she's found. My parents are mad, but they can't make me leave. And anyway, they're not paying for my education. I'll do what I want."

Karstarck stopped writing and looked up. "They're not?"

She shrugged. "My maternal grandparents left me a small trust. I pay for most of it out of that and scholarships—or else my parents could threaten to withhold my tuition payments, but they can't." She smiled then. "I feel bad for them."

"Why?"

Should she trust him so much? "Can we go off the record?"

Karstarck put his pen down. "Of course."

"I'm their only child, and I'm living in an area they think is unsafe." She laughed wryly. "And to think this was mostly their choice—safer and better than New York or DC, they said."

The reporter smiled paternally. "I'm sure two years ago it seemed the right thing to do."

"Have the police told you anything new?" Amanda expected his answer would be the same as it was two days before.

"No," he said. "Let me get you something to drink. One of my colleagues just got back from India. He gave me some delicious cardamom tea. I'll be right back."

Amanda offered him a tepid smile and said thanks.

He patted her on the shoulder and walked toward the kitchen. The veteran reporter had regaled Amanda on more than one occasion of his days as a vice detective in Brooklyn and his part-time work at the Valley Police Department before he joined the *Dispatch* full-time.

"Believe me," he had said often, "these hicks out here don't know crime. They also wouldn't know how to run a real murder investigation if it jumped up, bit them on the booty, and said, 'Hi! Here's how you work a murder inquiry.'"

Amanda had agreed with him.

"Don't tell anyone," he had told her the last time she was there, "but I called the FBI last year when that second girl's body was found near Gettysburg. I told them I wouldn't be surprised if it was the work of a serial."

Less than a minute after Karstarck had made his way down the hallway, Amanda heard the familiar ping of an email being delivered. She glanced at his computer screen just before a dark box displaying the partial missive dissolved from her view.

The subject line read: "Possible suspect car pix."

Amanda looked up over the monitor. It was now 8:37 p.m., and the bright newsroom was empty—save for the copy desk editors on the other side of the room. She leaned forward and hovered the mouse over the message. It had come from someone named "Anonymous Copper."

A source? Karstarck said he had a lot of them. The email intrigued her.

Amanda was debating whether or not to click on it when Karstarck walked up behind her. A chill ran through her.

"I'm sorry!" she said, a sheepish look on her face. "I noticed 'Anonymous Copper' sent you an email. Look at the subject line."

Karstarck handed her the steaming mug of tea. Amanda blew on it before sipping it while he looked over her shoulder and opened the missive. It was empty save for four JPEG files.

"I don't know if you should even look at these, Amanda."

"Why not?"

The reporter took a deep breath and exhaled. "I get a ton of tips like this all the time. It may or may not be real. This 'Anonymous Copper' could be anybody. I've never gotten a tip from someone with that name before."

She was silent for a moment. "Can I see it anyway?"

He opened the files and enlarged the photos of dark-colored sedans. "They're just cars. Recognize any of these?"

"I don't know. Let me take a closer look." She scrolled through the large attachments and zoomed in on some of the vehicles.

"No, I don't think so."

"Well, let me forward them to you so you can take a closer look later. What's your email?" She told him, and he said, "It's late. Go home. Get some rest. Think about it. If you recognize anything, call me."

Amanda nodded her head yes and rose to leave.

"And be careful on the way back to school. OK?"

CHAPTER SEVENTEEN

Amanda tossed and turned that night. She sat up in the empty room and switched on the light. She had a feeling she couldn't identify at first. Then it dawned on her.

It was loneliness.

Fiona had been gone for three weeks now. Amanda's parents had begged her to come home early for the holidays, but she declined. She stared at Fiona's neat bed, hung her head, and cried. She curled up into her pillow, closed her eyes, and waited for sleep. But then she sat up and grabbed her phone and unplugged it from the charger. It was 2:00 a.m. Amanda swiped over to her email and opened the message from Karstarck. She studied the cars longer this time, drinking in the details.

"I'll be damned," she whispered. She dialed a number.

Karstarck was groggy when he answered the phone.

"I've seen one of these!" she said. "And recently, too."

"What? Who is this?"

"Amanda Taylor. I'm so sorry for calling so late, Mr. Karstarck."

"No problem," he grunted, still fighting sleep. He yawned. "OK. You've seen one of what?"

"The cars. I recognize one of the cars."

"You do?" Amanda could hear him becoming more alert. "Where have you seen it?"

"Maybe the farmer's market near campus? The dent on the back left bumper is identical to one I put on my father's Chrysler when I was in high school. I was so afraid to tell him."

"You mean the Produce Den?" Karstarck asked.

"Mmhm," she answered.

"My wife and I go to that one, too."

134

The Produce Den was on Beverly Road, not far from the university. Amanda and Fiona walked to it all the time. Minutes away from campus, it was in a squat building where almost all the students shopped.

"I remember the car because the woman driving it is Quiet Girl."

"Quiet Girl?" Karstarck queried.

Amanda could recall that her long golden hair was often tucked beneath a pink baseball cap, shielding her eyes. Sometimes she wore sunglasses, even though she often didn't need them. Her makeup, however, was flawless—something the waitstaff at the diner noticed and discussed as well. Some of them had seen her at Dukes, too. But whether she was at the bar or the diner, Quiet Girl never spoke to or met anyone.

"That's what we call her. She used to be a regular at the diner. Always alone, head in her phone, paid in cash, sat in the same section. Last semester she ate there almost every Friday morning—early."

"Did you ever wait on her?" Karstarck asked.

"Nope, she never sat in my booth," Amanda said. "But I've seen her get in and out of that car at the Produce Den. We have to tell the police. Will you go with me?"

"I'll drive you there later—but you have to let me quote you for a story on this development."

"Sure," she said.

Later that day, a little after noon, Amanda and the reporter pulled up just as Detective Warren Christian was walking out of the police station.

"Glad we caught you, Christian," Karstarck said. "We may have a lead."

Christian crossed his arms. "What is it?"

The pair stared at him outside in the freezing cold. Karstarck pulled out photocopies of the sedans. He handed the detective the printouts, which rippled in the wind. Before they could explain that Amanda had recognized one of the cars, Christian bristled.

"Where did you get these?"

"An anonymous source."

"Who's your source, Karl?"

"I have no idea. People are always emailing me stuff like this. Why? Recognize it?"

He ignored the question. "Unverifiable stuff."

Karstarck spoke slowly, "Amanda happened to be in the newsroom and saw these photos. She recognizes one of the cars."

Christian leaned forward. "You do?"

"I've seen this one before," she said, pulling off a glove and pointing to the one with the dent in it. "It's usually driven by a blond woman at the Produce Den on Beverly Road and sometimes she comes into . . ."

Christian held up one hand to stop her. "We're looking for a man."

Karstarck scolded the young detective. "Warren, you and I both know this car could be shared by the suspect and his family members. Can't hurt to investigate this."

The lawman said nothing while he stared at the reporter for a few moments.

"There are only three people who had those pictures," he said, tapping the printouts and narrowing his eyes. "Me, the sheriff, and Agent Field. I know the sheriff didn't send them to you."

"For Pete's sake, Warren! What difference does it make who sent it to me? I'm publishing them anyway," Karstarck snapped. "It's a lead, and I'm a reporter. That's my job. Do yours," he said, jabbing an index finger toward the detective's chest, "and investigate it! Or do you care if I run the photo and say despite the fact that a witness recognized a car possibly linked to the suspect in this case you did nothing?"

"Don't threaten me."

"I'm not threatening you."

Christian opened his mouth to say something but shut it.

"Maybe I'll investigate it," Amanda said.

Both men turned toward her. "No!" they said in unison.

"You're a college student—not a cop," Christian added. He sighed and ran his hands over the stubble on his chin. "There's a lot of political stuff going on with this case." He cut his eye toward Karstarck. "This is off the record. OK?"

Karstarck nodded. Christian exhaled. His breath appeared as puffs of smoke in the freezing air.

"Some parents have launched a lawsuit against the university, whose provost also heads the town council. Both he and the mayor are pressuring the force to be very careful with this investigation—to make sure we've got the right suspect so it doesn't have any bearing on the lawsuit later. This may be why, to you, it seems like we're dragging our feet. But we're not. We're working with the FBI—who also disagrees with the pace of our investigation, by the way." He paused and raked his fingers through his red hair. "I can assure you we're going to follow up on each lead, including this one. But you have to be patient."

Amanda exploded. "How can you expect me to be patient? My best friend has been missing for weeks! If there's any chance that she's still alive, you have to take it!"

Two rosy spots appeared on Christian's cheeks and he raised his hands in frustration. "There are a lot of leads, Miss Taylor. We're going to look into this," he said, snatching the photo from the reporter. "But you have to promise me you're going to let us do our job. Thanks for the heads-up. Now if you don't mind, I need to grab lunch."

The student and the reporter drove back to campus in silence. Additional printouts of the car lay crumpled in Amanda's book bag. When she opened the passenger door to get out, Karstarck put a hand on her shoulder.

"Amanda, you're not a cop. Let the police handle this. Promise me?"

She nodded, got into Mark's car, and pulled off.

She looked in the rearview mirror. She had always sucked at keeping promises.

CHAPTER EIGHTEEN

Each day for four hours—even when it snowed—the Produce Den near Glastonbury's campus was open for business. Despite the pending Christmas break, students milled about, stocking up on eggs, fruit, vegetables, flowers, homemade cookies, pies, and thick slices of cake. Crowds were a rarity. Most of the Spanish-speaking staff in the Amish-owned establishment, including the cashiers, spoke little to no English—just enough to discern what customers wanted.

Impatient, Amanda decided to run her own little stakeout. So for three days she skipped class and sat in the farmer's market parking lot, waiting for a glimpse of the dented car driven by the blond nicknamed Quiet Girl.

"Where the hell are the cops?" she said under her breath, scoping out other vehicles.

While there wasn't a cop to be found, unless they were undercover, Amanda soon discovered blond girls in Laurel Valley were a dime a dozen. They seemed to be crawling all over the market.

On day three, however, she spotted her. Quiet Girl was wearing dark sunglasses and her signature pink baseball cap, driving a classic, well-kept dark green Pontiac LeMans with New York plates.

Hmm, Amanda thought to herself. That's not the car I'm looking for.

The girl's hair was longer now, almost past her shoulders. She hadn't noticed Amanda following her and why would she? The girl was glued to her smartphone—even while driving.

When the blond pulled off from the market, Amanda did too. She followed Quiet Girl to the driveway of a large Tudor-style home. The woman got out and leaned her slender body against the LeMans, pulling out a compact and lipstick and staring at her reflection in the mirror.

It was her all right; Amanda was sure of it. She drove by nice and slow, watching in the rearview mirror when Quiet Girl, dressed in a pink track-suit, sans coat, applied a deep red stain to her lips. The woman looked up at Amanda's car and watched her drive by.

Had she been spotted?

Amanda pulled over on a side street and parked. She pulled her hood over her head and took a light jog back toward the house, a red-brick Mc-Mansion. It was one of those ostentatious, impractical homes with a kiss-my-ass winding driveway, dozens of windows that would piss off the maid staff, and a four-car just-for-the-hell-of-it garage.

"Room after room filled with furniture no one is ever allowed to sit on," Amanda said under her breath. From a distance, she could see Quiet Girl walk down the driveway toward the rear of the house, a box of produce in her hands.

Where's she going? Amanda looked over her shoulder to make sure no one was watching, waited a few minutes, and followed. She was surprised when she rounded a stand of trees and saw Quiet Girl emerge from what looked like a guesthouse. Smack dab on the edge of some woods and situated entirely behind the main house, the tiny cottage was hidden from view.

The girl was staring down at her phone. Amanda dipped unseen behind an oak tree. Quiet Girl hadn't noticed Amanda—at least she didn't think she had. Amanda held her breath when the girl walked just fifteen feet away from her. Amanda was still until she heard a car start and pull away from the property.

Blood racing, Amanda walked back to her car and drove off with every intention of coming back—with the police.

Back at her dorm, Amanda threw her coat on her bed, whipped out her smartphone and called Karstarck's number, hoping he'd go with her again to speak to Christian.

He pushed her call to voicemail.

"What the . . . ?"

He texted her a moment later. *Can't talk*, it read. *With Agent Field and FBI just outside Philadelphia chasing a clue. Chat later?*

She texted back: *Found Quiet Girl's house. Thought you'd want to know. Calling cops now.*

Good! Will follow up soonest.

Amanda called Christian's cell phone and texted him repeatedly about finding Quiet Girl. But she got zero response. She also called the tip line Fiona's parents had set up.

"Uh-huh," a woman on the other end told her after she relayed who she was and what she'd seen. The woman bit into something and chewed. Loudly.

"Got it," she said between bites. "I'll let 'em know." Then she hung up.

Amanda stared at the phone. Frustrated, she walked over to the student cafeteria, grabbed a ham and cheese sandwich, and flipped through websites for news—nothing. Then she scrolled through the random Facebook posts on her phone. She erased some texts from her folks without reading them, but responded with a "Hi I'm fine" message.

She then returned to her dorm and fell into a fitful sleep.

At 3:00 a.m., she got up and scowled at her phone. Karstarck still hadn't texted her back, and neither had Christian or Agent Field. Without thinking, she drove back to the Tudor house and shut off the engine.

Frowning, Amanda tried one more time to call the Laurel Valley Chief of Detectives.

"You're where?" Christian asked, his sleepy voice incredulous.

"I followed the blond woman to a house on Kennedy Street yesterday. Now I'm sitting in front of it."

Silence shouted down the line. "Hello? Are you there?" Amanda asked. After he had ignored her all day, she had awakened Christian on his cell phone. In her defense, he did tell her she could call his personal line "anytime day or night"—but only in the event of an emergency.

She could tell from his demeanor that this, apparently, wasn't it.

"Amanda," he said, still groggy, his voice tired and impatient. "It's the middle of the night. We found the dented sedan with the Pennsylvania plates in Gettysburg. So there's really no need for you to . . ."

She cut him off. "What? When?"

"Last night. It was set on fire. We also staked out every farmer's market from here to Harrisburg and we didn't spot any blon . . ."

He's lying, she thought, and cut him off again. "Wake up, Detective! I'm telling you I saw her and followed her. Can't you just send somebody? Anybody?"

"Amanda, we can't burst into someone's home in the middle of the night two days before Christmas without a warrant! On a 'hunch' you have that this girl might be connected to Fiona's kidnapping."

"It's not a hunch!" She snapped. "And I watch *Law & Order*! I know about probable cause. Come on!"

She could hear him seething. "I've already told you; we found the dented car. It had been set on fire."

"You know, it dawned on me, Detective, that once word got out you were looking for a dented sedan there would be no way they'd keep driving that car. Would you?"

Christian's yawn was loud. "Amanda," he said, his voice trailing off. "We are aware of that. It's just this lead . . ."

"Detective, if someone in your precinct thought enough of those photos to email them to Karstarck, they must mean something! Hell, the fact that I recognized the driver must be important," she pleaded. "You know damn well we're not even looking for the car! We're looking for the girl, and I'm 100 percent positive I've found her. I'm sure she knows something! You said to call you day or night."

After a very long pause, he sighed. "Where are you?"

She gave him the address.

"OK, Amanda," he said. "We'll send deputies over there in the morning."

"You can't wait till morning! What if I'm right and Fiona is in there?"

"We'll send someone as soon as possible."

"When's that? It's starting to snow again."

"As soon as I hang up with you," he said wearily.

"Good! Great! Thanks!"

"Amanda, go home," he said, his stern tone dripping with condescension. "Now."

"What? There's no way I'm going home!"

"This is a police matter. No civilians allowed." Then he hung up on her.

"Hello? Hello?" When she realized the line was dead, steam rose from Amanda's mouth—and not just because she had blown on her ungloved hands, trying to warm them.

The abrupt end to the conversation stung.

❧

Ten minutes passed and still no cops. Her face flushed despite the cold, Amanda clenched her fist and rapped her fingers against the steering wheel. She pursed her lips, shook her head from side to side, and swiped her phone, checking the time. Another five minutes passed. She tried to nod off, but her mind kept stirring in circles. She stared into the distance. Fat snowflakes stuck to the windshield, obscuring her view.

Amanda knew she should wait, but she couldn't help herself. And she didn't want to turn the car on, alerting whoever might be in the house to her presence. So, clad entirely in black—like some weird brown ninja, she thought—Amanda got out of the car. I'm just going to look, she told herself. There's no harm in looking, is there? She pulled her black hoodie up over her head and winced when her feet sank into the fresh snow. Her heart danced a two-step beneath her breast. Inside her gloves, her palms were sweating. Snowflakes fell around her, decorating the dark woolen coat and covering her hoodie in white flower-like patterns.

Damn, this is stupid. But she dismissed that thought with a shrug, sucked her teeth, and huffed. The snow was now coming down faster. She had just trudged across the street when a thought occurred to her. Her breath left a jagged line of smoke in the air when she ran back to the car and threw open the trunk.

Just in case.

She gripped the fat end of Mark's old cracked Louisville Slugger baseball bat and resumed her walk back to the guesthouse.

CHAPTER NINETEEN

Heart hammering, fingers frozen, Amanda used her phone's flashlight to light the way. Somewhere inside her, a small voice said repeatedly: wait for the cops.

She ignored it.

Beneath a luminous moon and fluttering snow, the rustic guesthouse with its chimney perched against the night sky looked like it had been plucked from a Christmas card painted by Norman Rockwell. The main home wasn't too far away from neighboring residences, some of which twinkled with holiday lights that had been tacked to windows or laced through shrubs. But not this house. Amanda noted how most of the homes were at least a half acre apart. An eerie calm enveloped her, numbing her in the still, wintry air.

What a perfect place to hold a hostage, Amanda thought as she crept closer. No one would hear any screams. Deep snow and the brambles from cocklebur plants obscured her way. When she tried to jerk herself free from the burs, their tiny prickly spines caught and snagged her coat, nearly shredding it and her gloves to pieces. She cursed under her breath. Over and over again, she swung the bat, and with relative ease the spindly brush—hardened by ice and cold—broke apart. Despite the freezing temperature, sweat dotted her forehead. Using the sleeve of her wool jacket, Amanda ripped dead wisteria vines away from the windowpanes on the left side of the cottage.

Through window after window, she peered into unlit rooms; seeing nothing, she moved on. After clearing frost away from a pane of glass on the back of the property, Amanda stuck the bat into some snow. She stood on her tiptoes and raised her hands to her face. She cupped them on either side of her temples and pressed them against the freezing glass. Her breath clouded the pane. She wiped it and gazed inward. It was in that moment that Amanda thought of Trayvon Martin. She prayed none of the neighbors decided to play vigilante on a hooded Black person peeping inside the window of an expensive house in the middle of the night. After looking inside yet another dark room and seeing nothing, she was moving away when she heard the telltale sound of a ringing smartphone.

A loud slap was followed by a man's voice:

"I like you. You know I do. But if you scream when I answer this phone, I will kill you."

Inside the room, a woman cried out in surprised anguish and a light came on.

Amanda crouched below the window, her heart overflowing with dread. She had caught a glimpse of someone with long blond hair. Could it be Fiona? Could it be the killer?

A chill that had little to do with the weather swept over her.

Where the hell are the police?

Shit, she thought. It dawned on her that she'd forgotten to tell the detective about the guesthouse! They're probably at the wrong house, the McMansion. Her heart was now knocking so hard against her chest she felt like she couldn't breathe.

"Do you understand me?" the voice said, interrupting her thoughts. Amanda heard a woman answer very faintly, "Yes." The ringing stopped.

"Hello," he said. "What do you mean we have to leave now?"

Movement in the room followed so Amanda waited a few minutes until it was over, stood up on her toes, and stared through the glass again. Just opposite the window and along the floor, Amanda could see a beam of light coming from what looked like a hallway. Her eyes followed and rested on the half-open door. The light illuminated the shadows in a small corner of the room. Amanda squinted, trying to comprehend what she was seeing. Moments passed before the room came sharply into focus.

Secured to a mattress on the floor by rope was a naked foot. It wriggled. All of a sudden, the light in the hallway went out, thrusting the room back into darkness—but not before Amanda noticed that along that foot's ankle was a distinctive tattoo.

Three interconnected hearts.

Outside, Amanda flung herself away from the window and up against the side of the house. Her hand flew to her mouth to stifle her gasp. In the bitter cold, her stomach churned.

Tears stung her eyes: it was Fiona.

She needed to make sure the police were coming to the right house! Terrified, she sank into the cold snow and reached in her pocket for her smartphone.

"Dammit!" For five minutes, she tried to swipe open the phone, but her fingers were so numb and wet from cold, they were like claws. The snow fell faster. She thought of asking Siri to call 911, but was afraid the home's occupants might hear her. Amanda smeared the slickened handheld device, rendering it impossible to place the call. She began to shiver.

Whether she trembled from cold or fear, she couldn't tell; nor could she make the sudden shuddering stop.

Just then, a woman's scream pierced the gloom, roiling Amanda's blood.

Everything happened so fast after that. Amanda could hear the distinctive sound of someone running barefoot across a wooden floor.

She heard slapping. Tussling.

A grunt. A moan.

It sounded like someone was being dragged.

A man cursed, and a woman begged for her life.

"No, please, you said you wouldn't hurt me," the woman pleaded from somewhere deep in the cottage.

Amanda opened her coat. She dried the phone off on her sweatshirt. In the upper right corner in small white letters were the words "No Service."

The woman within the house cried out, "I won't do it again!"

Still staring at the phone, Amanda took a step back. Thank God, one bar! She punched in 911 and the unspeakable happened.

The phone went completely dark.

The next scream made her hair stand on end.

"Don't kill me!"

Amanda stood and slid the dead phone back into her pocket. Fiona needed her now! And the police were probably close enough to at least hear the screams! Amanda smashed her way through the spiky shrubs and ran around to the front of the house.

To her surprise, the front door was ajar.

Gripping the bat, she took a deep breath and kicked it open.

Wind, icy and stiff, blew snow in and around her, ruffling the hair across her forehead. Moonlight drenched the hallway. A figure with long blond hair was hunched over a woman dressed in a T-shirt. He straddled her in the near darkness, yelling and pummeling her with his fists.

"You almost got out!" he cried. "I've been good to you! I've protected you. Kept you safe! Why are you trying to leave me?"

Beneath him, the woman whimpered.

When an Arctic blast from the open door stung his back, the blond man turned his head toward Amanda. In the faint moonlight, with snow swirling around her, Amanda could see his lips part in surprise. Shock flickered across his handsome face. He stared at her like she was an apparition.

"What in the hell?"

Without a word, Amanda took two quick strides, raised the cracked bat above her head, and brought it down across his back so hard it exploded, shattering in her hands and splintering into pieces.

He shrieked and fell over the prone figure below him. Amanda drew closer and looked into the face of the moaning, battered woman.

The recognition was immediate.

"Fiona!" Amanda exclaimed. She kicked the man repeatedly in his ribs.

"Get off of her!" she shouted. "Get off!"

The man rolled over and grabbed Amanda's ankle. He yanked it and she fell backward, banging her head hard on the wooden floor. Bruised and dazed, Amanda cried out in pain and reached up to grab the back of her head. The man crawled toward her.

He drew back his hand and punched her in the throat.

When he mounted her, Amanda gasped. She tried to curl into a fetal position.

"You little bitch!" he screamed and punched Amanda in the face. In vain, she tried to escape the blows, turning her head from left to right, causing him to box her ears.

Stunned, bloody, and in pain, Amanda cowered on the floorboards, winded and inert. When she coughed, blood spurted from her lips. It tasted like metal. Alarmed, she watched the man reach for a large remnant from the splintered bat.

"No, don't!" she implored, her voice hoarse.

"I'm so sorry," he said, his voice low. "You leave me no choice." He had beaten her ears so hard, her plea and his apology sounded muffled. Pain, sharp and intense, stabbed her back when she tried to slide away. She howled. Her eyes widened in horror when the man raised both hands high above his head to stab her.

But like a specter, Fiona rose from the floor behind him and pierced him in the back of his hand with something pointy and sharp. A primitive cry escaping her lips, Fiona pushed it so deep inside his flesh it went all the way through his hand.

To Amanda, in the bright moonlight, it looked like a pen. Their predator released a high-pitched scream. Then he dropped the bat and grasped at his hand, trying to yank out the slippery, blood-covered implement. Crumpled and bloody beneath her assailant, Amanda watched, shocked, when Fiona, clad solely in a filthy Run-DMC T-shirt, darted barefoot and nearly nude around them both and bolted through the open door and into the bitter cold. Her swollen face still pressed into the floor, Amanda panted. She reached a hand out toward the fleeing Fiona, mouthing her name.

With the moon casting a mesmerizing glow off the glittery snow, a bruised and helpless Amanda saw Fiona vanish through a mass of trees. Beaten and weak, gore from a cut on her head obscuring her vision, Amanda glanced up in time to see someone else enter the house and yank the pen out of her attacker's hand.

The police?

No, it couldn't be, because her assailant groaned in relief over the jagged, bloody hole where his flesh had been.

"She's gone!" He was frantic. "We have to get her back. Let's go get her!"

Amanda struggled to hear him straight. Through mind-numbing pain, she fought to stay awake. Curled up on the floor, she flattened her body and tried to slither away.

"Benji." To Amanda's damaged ears, the calm voice sounded faint. "We're going to leave. Right now, before the police get here."

"What are we going to do about her?" Her assailant stood and pressed a rag into his wounded hand, trying to stem the bleeding. When the one named Benji gave her a vicious kick, Amanda moaned in agony.

"There's no time to get rid of her. The police are already at the main house and it's really coming down out there."

"You know damn well we can't just leave her back here in this guesthouse."

"We'll take her with us. Good thing I parked my car two streets over."

"What! But she's nothing like the others!" His voice was sorrowful, bewildered. "She won't work!"

"She's going to have to. You don't have a choice."

Two faces with long, disheveled blond hair hovered over her, swimming out of focus just before Amanda lost consciousness.

PART THREE

For everything that is hidden will eventually be brought into the open, and every secret will be brought to light. —Mark 4:22

CHAPTER TWENTY

As the police descended on the main house, the pair grabbed Amanda's limp body and an emergency duffel bag with cash, untraceable burner phones, and other essential items, and trudged through the snow and into the woods. The car was parked on a side street a quarter mile from the property. In the heavy snow and dark, they managed to slip away from the two uniformed police officers undetected. Hours later, Ben was sprawled across a filthy mattress with his eyes closed. His bandaged hand throbbed. He could feel his sister hovering nearby. He knew she was annoyed.

Well, so was he.

It had been a day and a half since Fiona had escaped and Benjamin was forced to flee Pennsylvania with just the clothes on his back—and a new captive.

For more than three hours he had stared in the car's rearview mirror while they fled authorities across ice-slickened highways.

Like a mantra he was desperate to believe, Ben kept whispering to himself over and over, "We're not going to get caught." And he pointed the car north and drove through Pennsylvania.

"Are you crazy?" Corinthia had asked when Ben contemplated taking Interstate 78 after driving the car with care along local, icy roads.

"It's faster," he had replied, "and there are no tolls."

"So then take 95, if anything. It's snowing like crazy. We'll get stuck if we take back roads."

"Pfft! I-78 isn't a back road and 95 has tolls—and cameras."

When she cursed at him, Ben's heart quickened. "Don't be stupid, Ben. Just keep the baseball cap and the hoodie on. Look in my duffel. There's plenty of cash in there to avoid electronic tracking at the tolls. And keep the radio off. We wouldn't want to wake our guest, now, would we?"

And so he drove along Interstate 95 in the pitch black of early morning across the rolling hills of Amish country through quiet, falling snow. Somewhere ahead of them, a snow plow had cleared their path and left crystals of salt on the wet, slushy highway. Otherwise, the soft swish of the windshield wipers was the only sound made driving up the Pennsylvania Turnpike. By the time he hit New Jersey, the sun was coming up. It was there that he stopped for gas, not far from the Lincoln Tunnel. With the hoodie of his dark green sweatshirt pulled over his shoulder-length hair, he walked around the station's convenience shop, quickly grabbing hot dogs, bandages, painkillers, drinks, and snacks. He dropped them on the counter and fiddled with his wallet. The clerk, who was laughing at a video on her phone, didn't look up at him once—not even when he asked for thirty dollars' worth of gas.

She turned from her phone's tiny screen to the register. "What pump?"

"One," he said.

She swept his purchases into a bag along with his receipt, handed it to him, and wished him a good night—all without making eye contact. With Amanda still unconscious in the trunk, Ben slid behind the wheel of the car. He turned on the engine, exhaled, and relaxed his shoulders.

There wasn't a cop in sight during the entire ride.

"I can't believe we got away," he murmured.

But they had. And they had arrived undetected at their destination—a former factory—in the middle of the night. The structure, which Corinthia had purchased years ago using a fake name, was uninhabited. And, from what Ben could tell, the conversion from factory to apartments was nearly complete. Located in Union City, New Jersey, the high-rise was constructed of tan and pale red bricks, and had floor to ceiling windows and jaw-dropping views of the Big Apple. Stowed in various corners of the empty edifice were paint-splattered buckets, saws, and wooden sawhorses coated in a powdery film. It was musty. The fact that they were at the tail end of a snowstorm gave everything, including their situation, a nearly apocalyptic feel—except for an adjacent, makeshift room that had a heater, a mini fridge, a couple of chairs, and a partially finished bathroom complete with a working shower and tub.

Ben turned the knobs. "I'll be damned. The water's hot, too."

"Lucky us," Corinthia said in a sarcastic tone.

With an unconscious Amanda tied to one of the chairs, Ben curled up on a filthy narrow mattress he had found in the basement along with a working space heater. Outside, snow continued to fall, blanketing the streets and their arrival in a white cocoon of silence.

Ben was restless. Corinthia had thought of everything—including charging the untraceable cell phones that she packed during the trip. The phones were in one of many fake names she'd accumulated over the years. He swiped the burner phone open and Googled the name "Fiona Kessler." Then he gasped.

Not only was Fiona's abduction, their fight, her escape, the assault, and kidnapping of Amanda Taylor on a steady loop rerunning in his mind—it was all over the Internet, discussed in print and video.

The press was calling her escape a "Christmas Miracle."

How could Fiona just leave like that? Ben sniveled and wiped his eyes with the back of his left hand. He felt he was good to her. After all, he had tried to protect her from his wayward sister and her predilections. It was not an easy thing to do, either.

Corinthia was like his shadow sometimes, always hovering in the background, judging, criticizing, begging him to stop. Damned if you do, damned if you don't. He had no idea why this . . . compulsion drove him to seek these carbon copies of his sister. Maybe Fiona had been right. Maybe he should have gotten help—a long time ago. He sighed. Corinthia had called his need to kidnap his "baser instinct." He didn't know what that meant. But he did know Corinthia was deathly afraid of them getting caught. Much as she was afraid of their parents discovering their shenanigans when they were little kids.

So Ben kidnapped.

And Corinthia killed to cover it up.

It was always the same thing. She would plead for him to "stop it." And ask again and again: "Why can't you stop? If you love me, you'll stop."

And then there was the one question he could never answer—despite her begging, her pleading, her tears.

"Why?"

He never answered her. He couldn't answer her. And he would not stop. He needed them.

You're sick, Ben. You know that, right? he thought to himself. Yeah, he knew. He had been telling Corinthia for years he wanted to get help and she had refused. Talking to Fiona was the closest he had ever come to seeing a therapist. And what would he even say to a real one?

"Oh, hello, doctor! I have this overwhelming need to kidnap women who resemble my sister and, even though I know it's wrong to hold someone against their will, I can't help it. Let them go, you say? Why, I would if I could! But I can't because my sister keeps killing them so I won't get in trouble for kidnapping them in the first place."

Ben ran his hands over his face, scowled, and grunted in frustration. If he had taken Fiona's advice and gotten help, that would have been as disastrous as this situation. "Help" would have meant the destruction of his family—not to mention besmirching his beloved granny's memory. It would also mean a betrayal of trust—something neither of them would do to the other. And it also meant so much more—it meant he would damn his sister to a hell he could not fathom. Jail or worse—he would never see her again and that was a fate worse than death itself.

"Ugh, that ungrateful skank Fiona has told everyone who we are!" Corinthia bellowed.

Ben scowled. "She promised me she wouldn't do that." He sighed and went to fbi.gov. His heart sank.

Sought from New York City to western Pennsylvania, Benjamin and Corinthia Zanetti were now on the FBI's Ten Most Wanted Fugitives List. He, for one, suspected they would eventually get caught. Much to Ben's consternation and despite her rages, Corinthia, on the other hand, now seemed indifferent to their situation.

"I told you this would happen," Corinthia had said on the drive out of state. "For years I told you to stop bringing blond coeds home. This is your fault. If you hadn't brought them and encouraged me to help, I wouldn't have had to kill them to keep our secret safe."

"Will you please just be quiet?" he asked.

His biggest dilemma now, however, was their loss of anonymity, which had afforded him something more precious: the ability to hunt victims undetected.

By now, he was certain, the Laurel Valley police and the FBI had crawled all over their grandmother's property. Even so, when Ben had pulled up the news on his phone—which, of course, was not in either of their names—he was stunned by the intensity of the media attention.

Could Twins Be Responsible for Missing Girls' Deaths?

Murdering Twins Wanted in Disappearance of Coeds
Bodies Found on Pennsylvania Property Linked to Vanishings

Ben swiped the last article open. When he read that the authorities had unearthed remains on the property, his hands started shaking. The third paragraph of the article was most alarming:

It is, perhaps, the biggest crime scene since Gary Michael Heidnik's dungeon of dismay in Philadelphia where, in the late 1980s, Heidnik kidnapped, tortured, and raped six women while holding them hostage in a pit in his basement. Two of the women died.

One had been cooked on his stove.

Ben threw his phone on the mattress, stood, and punched a hole in the wall with his good hand.

"Stop it, you'll wake her up," Corinthia said, referencing Amanda.

"I don't care anymore! Thanks to you they've found all of my girls buried on Granny's property!" Perspiration dotted his upper lip. His heart jackhammered against his gray and burgundy sweatshirt stenciled with the words "Temple Owls Football."

"Thanks to me?"

"It's only a matter of time before the police find the other graves in the woods. You know this means lethal injection!"

"Don't effing yell at me!" Corinthia shouted back at him. "And quit punching holes in the walls! They haven't executed anyone in the state since Heidnik. So just calm your ass down."

Ben sat down and raked his fingers through his long blond hair. "That's easy for you to say! They don't have any photos of you plastered in newspapers and all over the Internet. I can't even walk down the damn street!"

"You worry too much, Benji."

"We need a plan, Corinthia."

"I have a plan."

Ben leaned forward and raised his eyebrows. "Let's hear it."

"It's simple, really. We'll just change our hair, ditch Amanda, and start fresh somewhere else."

Ben was quiet.

"You don't like my plan, little brother?"

"We can't. We don't have enough money."

"You mean aside from the few thousand in my duffel bag? Where's the rest of our emergency cash I told you to pack?" She was speaking of the tens of thousands she had socked away in case they needed to flee.

He stared at the floor. "I left the rest of it at the house."

"You did what?! You're such a stupid mother . . ."

Ben put his hand over his ears while she shouted invective at him. He waited for her to stop, his face as crimson as the tiny owl on his gray sweatshirt.

"I guess we'll have to just lay low here for a while and then make our move," she said after her tirade.

Amanda, oblivious, remained injured, blindfolded, and tied to the chair.

Ben awoke the next morning to his sister screaming.

"This is all your fault, Benji! I told you for weeks we should have killed her!"

Ben yawned. He took some strands of his shiny pale hair and slid it behind his ear. Then he covered both ears with his palms in another useless attempt to tune her out.

It didn't help, it couldn't stop the rattle in his head. She was screaming about how it was only a matter of time before the police tracked them down. They—two white people—had kidnapped a Black woman. He knew how that looked. He knew that. But he wasn't prepared to leave just yet—not with their hostage.

The dark-skinned Black woman had weathered the trip from Pennsylvania gagged and unconscious in the car. With the hood of her coat pulled over her head, Ben had half carried, half walked Amanda inside their hideout. The dark hoodie he wore had concealed his face.

He rose from the mattress and peered out one of the large windows and looked down at the snow-covered sidewalks. There wasn't a cop car in sight.

"Will you please just shut up?" he told Corinthia.

"Don't tell me what to do," he heard her respond.

Ben exhaled and took a deep breath. "Do you know how lucky we are? I can't believe we didn't get caught."

Outside, what should have been busy streets were abandoned. Some shopkeepers tried to clear the ice-covered pathways in front of their stores. Piles of snow ringed the streets from plows that had driven by hours earlier. Despite the snow, the occasional mix of Hispanic children, young whites, and a smattering of African Americans filtered through the neighborhood with its blend of hip, shiny new shops, businesses catering to immigrants, nail salons, beauty parlors, restaurants, graffiti-scarred bodegas, and several Dunkin' Donuts shops and liquor stores. Some passersby held steaming mugs of coffee in their hands while they trudged through snow to take the bus to the Port Authority in Manhattan.

"Well, this place sucks," Ben said under his breath. Sure, it wasn't old and rat-infested and it didn't reek of piss and regret, but it paled in comparison to the pristine, bucolic environment brimming with the college-town innocence that was Laurel Valley.

He sighed, guessing it could be worse—like some bad, clichéd version of the New York of old where gritty, trash-strewn streets were chock full of broken bottles and needles, crumbling tenements, and blight. At least here there were no heroin addicts twitching for a fix in the cold. Still, Ben longed for the healthy, rosy-cheeked students who frolicked in flurries and huddled at country bars fretting over their fake IDs in the snow-covered mountains of Laurel Valley—a place where it had been easy to disappear simply by staying indoors.

Ben scowled. In that moment, he desperately wanted to throttle his sister.

Looking out the window, he hadn't spied a single blond woman that would fit his needs. He shuddered at the thought of having to make do with a Black girl.

"This wouldn't have happened if you'd let me kill Fiona, Benji," Corinthia repeated.

"Please, just shut up!" Ben screamed. "Go ahead then, kill this one. Serves her right for helping Fiona escape. And when you're done, we can dump her body in the Hudson River or throw it in the bushes. I don't care. I don't even want to look at it!"

"It?" Corinthia mocked him. "Since when do you want me to kill a girl? Why is it that I'm the one that always has to do everything?"

"You didn't have a problem killing all the rest of them when I begged you not to," he barked at her. "Suddenly I'm supposed to believe you're not built for it?"

"Go to hell, Benji! I'm not killing her and you better not, either."

He was floored. "Why not?"

"Because, genius. While we did recon on the other girls, we have no idea who *this* girl is. You left the bulk of our money in a place we can never go back to. Now, if we have a serious cash flow problem, we might need to ransom her. She could be worth something."

He snorted. "I highly doubt it."

"You just want to curl up with her and play in her hair," she taunted him.

"I do not! You know she's all wrong!"

"Then find a new playmate."

"You know I can't do that either," he whined. "The police are looking for us everywhere!"

"Variety is the spice of life, Ben," his sister giggled. "Give the little Black chick a try. You might like a little soul food."

Ben's face turned red and he huffed. "That's not funny!"

Then, from inside the next room, they heard her struggling against her restraints.

"You racist assholes! I have a name! It's Amanda Taylor!"

Ben looked through the door to the room. A blindfolded Amanda was still tied to a chair. He would soon discover she was a feisty one—kicking, screaming, biting, and raging.

Where Corinthia, as the day wore on, found Amanda's willingness to fight dazzling, it exhausted and bewildered Ben. This captive wasn't like the others. She seemed at times without fear. He had often heard Black women were strong, resilient. Some had claimed it was a stereotype. But Amanda Taylor was incredible. Not once had she begged to be set free. She had, however, kept cursing at Ben—even predicting his fate.

"The electric chair."

"Hanging."

"Lethal injection."

"Firing squad." Corinthia had cracked up over the absurdity of that one.

What worried Ben, though, was how Amanda had confirmed his sister's suspicions. Amanda kept saying people were looking for her, coming for her—that they had no idea who she was or who she knew or how much trouble they were in.

Which was true. The girl was naming detectives and FBI agents. And on top of that, she was threatening the entire wrath of the Black Lives Matter movement. It was scary. Ben went through her pockets and found her driver's license and her student ID. From his phone, he glanced at her social profiles and Googled her, but didn't find anything, either. There also wasn't any mention of a reward for her like there had been with Fiona. Maybe, he reasoned, because she was Black, nobody actually cared? Shit, that didn't even make sense. Somebody was looking for her; somebody looked for all of them.

"Personally? I think she's just blowing smoke up your ass," Corinthia said.

"Go to hell."

"Right after you, Benji. Be sure to say 'Hi' to Mom for me!"

Ben muzzled Amanda. But Corinthia delighted in the girl's rages. That evening, while alone with her, she removed the gag, putting them at further risk. For Ben, it was as if Corinthia didn't care, for some reason, that someone might hear Amanda's screams—even though there wasn't another soul in the building and wouldn't be for a few days because of the weather and the Christmas holiday. But Ben was used to his sister's ire.

Amanda, though, was another story: she was driving Ben crazy. Still, no matter how many times he begged, Corinthia refused to kill her and wouldn't let him, either.

Ben sulked. "Then find me a new playmate when you get our disguises."

"No. Play with this one."

He scoffed at that. "She's just so . . . wrong. She's not even the right race!"

The next day—Christmas Eve—Corinthia wore her dark wig and went to a Family Dollar store to buy them more food and supplies, a blond wig, and two knit caps. Then she went to a novelty shop to purchase blue contact lenses. She also brought home some apples and a very pointy paring knife.

"What's this?" Ben asked, frowning after he opened another bag and a bottle of strawberry shampoo fell out.

"Your Corinthia kit," he heard her reply. Then she howled with laughter. Another screaming match between the twins ensued.

But in the middle of the night, when Ben's compulsions grew too great to ignore, he untied Amanda and ripped off her blindfold.

"Get up!" he said. He snatched her out of the chair where she had been slumped asleep and he pushed her up against the wall. She struggled against him. He pulled out the paring knife and waved it in her face.

He shoved a plastic bag into her hand. "You will wear this wig and put in these contacts."

A groggy Amanda croaked in defiance, "Oh no, I'm not either!"

Ben pressed the knife into her throat, nicking the soft flesh just above her collarbone. She dropped the bag. Her entire body vibrated. "Don't make me cut you again." Ben didn't know it at first, but her quaking wasn't with fear.

Her response was slow and resolute.

"You are going to have to cut me, Benji," she said in a voice that could slice through bone. "Because I am not wearing that fucking yellow wig or putting in blue contacts. And no matter how hard you try, asshole, you cannot make a Black girl white. I may want many things, but being white is not one of them!"

In that moment, Ben didn't care about Corinthia's edicts. Blind with an immense hatred, Ben opened his mouth to say something—something like, you little bitch—thought better of it, and instead slashed Amanda's cheek. She screamed, and he clamped a hand over her mouth.

"Shut up!"

She raised her palm to the small crescent-shaped wound on her face. Ben's face contorted when droplets of blood rolled down her wrist and onto the sleeve of her shirt. Then he wiped his forehead with the back of his hand. He couldn't believe he was being so cruel to the girl, but he was mad as hell at her for helping Fiona escape—for ruining his life.

"You sure you want to try me?"

He knew his rank breath stung her nostrils because she frowned and bowed her head away from his lips.

He trembled with a rage so fierce he could feel it reverberating down his spine. "You're the reason Fiona's gone and why I'm in this mess." He glared at her. "I will slice you up like a damn chicken."

Amanda cowered. "Please don't kill me."

"That's more like it." He snatched the bag from the floor and thrust it at her. Her fingers shook while she held it. He punched her in the guts. When she doubled over, Ben kicked her in her back. Amanda fell face first on the dusty bathroom floor. She cut her bottom lip on her teeth; a thin line of pink drool trickled down her chin.

"Don't come out of there until you're finished!"

But she took too long. Twenty minutes later, Ben burst through the bathroom, only to feel a sharp kick narrowly miss his genitals. Amanda darted around him, but Ben was faster. He stumbled when he chased her, catching her just before she got to the door. With his free hand, he jerked her around to face him. Weapon still in his bandaged hand—the same hand

Fiona had stabbed him in—the pair crashed to the floor, where the paring knife slid from his grasp and went through Amanda's right eye.

A deafening, inhuman howl of pain erupted from her chest and bounced off the walls.

He yelled at her. "Dammit! Look what you made me do!" When Ben ripped the knife from Amanda's face, her breathtaking screams made the hairs on his neck grow rigid.

"Shut up!" he screamed, alarmed. "Someone will hear you!"

A line of red liquid sprayed across her cheek and onto Ben's closed fist, leaving a pattern of droplets in varying sizes against his fair skin. When he reared back, she kicked him again. Without remorse, a furious Ben yelped when he picked her up. When she bit him, he tossed her halfway across the room where she landed on the mattress. As he approached, she skidded away from him, both hands clamped over her eye.

"Oh my God!" she wailed with incredulity. "What have you done? You stabbed me in MY EYE?" Blood seeped through her fingers. When Ben straddled her, Amanda twisted and buckled between his legs. She began to hyperventilate. Propelled by fear and pure adrenaline, she struggled with all her might beneath him and screamed for Corinthia.

"Help me! Corinthia! He's going to kill me!"

Angry and frightened, her hands still clasped over her face, Amanda whirled like a windmill, screaming and kicking at her assailant with both feet, connecting with his jaw first. Ben cried in agony when her knee caught him dead center between his legs.

"You little whore!" he roared. Ignoring the pain ricocheting through his crotch, Ben used his fist to subdue her, smashing her in both eyes. Then he bashed the top of her head over and over until she stopped moving.

When she was unconscious, a blood-covered Ben slid huffing and puffing from her body. He tossed his hair over his shoulder, snatched the bag from the floor on the other side of the room, pulled out the blonde wig and put it on her head. A stream of scarlet fluid trickled from her injured eye and onto the mattress.

With the back of a filthy sleeve, he wiped the gore away from her battered face. Eyes closed, he sniffled and apologized when he ran his sticky fingers through the wig. Her warm body in his arms, he rocked Amanda back and forth.

Murmuring his sister's name, Ben took a deep breath and buried his face into hair as soft as corn silk.

❧

The next day was Monday. It dawned bright and blustery. Corinthia woke to the sounds of car horns and people arguing outside in Spanish. She yawned, got up, and padded into the room where Amanda lay motionless.

Corinthia stood over the girl and gazed at her limp body. Amanda's bruised face was now swollen beyond recognition. "You're having a crappy Christmas," she told the young woman, who stank of dried blood. Yellow pus oozed from the girl's right eye and trickled down her cheek.

The girl twin frowned. "This is a mess, Ben. We can't stay here. Not like this. The workmen might be back tomorrow. Pretty soon they'll track us to this place, anyway."

"So can we get rid of her?" he asked.

She exhaled. "I don't think we have a choice."

Ben nodded.

"Wait!" Corinthia said, still looking down at Amanda. "I've got a better idea!"

"What?" Ben asked.

"Let's wait till it gets dark and put her in the trunk."

"Are we leaving, then?"

"Yes. I know I'm right. We shouldn't stay here, and I think I know exactly where we should go, Benji. Missouri."

Ben peered at his phone and swiped open the Waze navigation app.

"Missouri?" He was looking at highway routes.

"It's perfect," she said. "Think about it. We can't go to Canada. We'd never be able to cross the border without scrutiny," Corinthia had told him. "Upstate New York in winter by car? Not happening, little brother. But take a look at College of the Ozarks in Point Lookout, Missouri."

Ben Googled it. Surrounded by greenery, the campus looked beautiful, and the rents nearby were cheap.

"Looks like the perfect place to blend in," Corinthia pointed out. "It's also a place without connection to us. No one would dream of looking for us there."

Ben nodded and for the first time in two days, he smiled. "Let's do it."

CHAPTER TWENTY-ONE

Ben spent hours arguing with Corinthia about their disguises. Sunglasses were a given, naturally, but Corinthia told him he should dye his hair.

"No," he snorted. "I'll just trim it. You can wear one of your dark wigs since they're looking for two blonds."

When he put the scissors down, she jeered at him.

"You should have cut it more than that," she said as she stared at his handiwork in the mirror. He shrugged and glanced at his reflection.

"I'm going to cover it with a hat and a hoodie, anyway. It doesn't have to be really short, see?" He put on a ski cap and threw his hood over his head.

In the middle of the night, when the streets were quiet, Ben hit the road, opting to take main highways—which were more likely to be both plowed and faster. With Jersey in his rearview and paying for tolls in cash, Ben headed west over I-78 to I-81 before skirting Pennsylvania over that state's turnpike and winding his way through bucolic Ohio, past gigantic twenty-four-hour Pilot gas stations, some with dozens of pumps. Ben was flabbergasted. He had never seen gas stations like these. They catered to truckers and were more like hotels than rest stops. He slowed while passing one and could hear over a loudspeaker a voice announcing, "Free Showers with a Fill Up. Our bathrooms have soap and towels!"

These "travel plazas" had movie theaters and full restaurants inside them—Denny's, Wendy's, and Starbucks coffee shops. Row upon row of service bays teemed with travelers—and not just truckers, either. There were families with children dressed in coats, hats, and mittens guarding against the cold weather. Some folks who had been traveling for hours stepped out of their hot cars and into the frigid air where they hurriedly filled their tanks before rushing inside for a bite or to bathe.

As the afternoon wore on, Ben could see that outside, some of the stations' mechanics worked in garages repairing vehicles. When he stopped for gas again, a nervous Ben kept a firm grip on the pump in his hand and watched some truck drivers get down from their eighteen-wheelers to grab food or take showers or climb in their sleeper berths to rest. When he was done, he hit the road and kept driving.

Hours passed. "How much further?" He heard his sister sigh.

"We're in some tiny town—Rushville, Indiana." The sun was setting. "We should hit Missouri by early tomorrow, I think," he told Corinthia. "I need to make a pit stop."

The drive up to that point had been uneventful. Ben took off his sunglasses. He had grown uncomfortable in the warm car, and so he had pulled off his hat and hoodie too.

He wasn't thinking when he hopped out of the car and ran inside the first gas station he found in Rushville—population 6,341, according to a green-and-white highway marker. He had to veer off the main road down a narrow dirt road to reach it. It was a restored Mobil gas station, complete with two antique red-and-white pumps. Between them was an old-fashioned sealed gas can that someone had affixed to a white cement block. To the right was a phone booth with a rotary phone.

Ben had never seen one before.

He passed an antique fire truck that had also been restored. Clearly for tourists, the station was functional, but deserted—save for a pimply faced teenager who jabbed her finger over her shoulder when Ben strolled inside and asked where the bathroom was.

He stood in front of the urinal in the small room and relieved himself. He tilted his head from side to side and pulled his shoulders back until he heard and felt a satisfying crack. Ben stood on his toes. He hadn't stretched his legs in hours. He had the bathroom door handle in his hand and was about to yank it open when he glanced at the back of the door and froze.

Ben stared in disbelief at his photo.

Beneath his picture on the flyer were the words, "Wanted for Murder and Kidnapping."

He furrowed his brow and squinted, his upper lip rising to expose his teeth. He read and reread about his misdeeds for a full minute before he ripped the leaflet off the door and shoved it in his pocket. Then he opened the door and walked out.

Be cool. Be calm.

He could feel the clerk's gaze following him around the small station, which had just three racks of snacks and one cooler filled with cold beverages—none of them alcoholic.

Had she taped up the flyer?

He took his time picking out a couple bottles of Pepsi, three cans of Red Bull, a small bag of Oreos, and a bag of Cheetos. He walked up to the register and asked the sallow-skinned girl for thirty-two dollars on pump number two. She rang up the gas and his purchases.

"Sophia" was the name on the tag attached to her drab gray shirt. She was a curvy teenager with long, stringy red hair and bright green eyes that were enlarged thanks to her owlish horn-rimmed glasses. The lenses were smeared with her fingerprints. She ogled him mindlessly while popping a great big wad of pale purple bubblegum. When she noticed he was staring back, she looked at the floor and smoothed her blue smock down over her ample gut.

He couldn't help it. "What are you looking at?"

She shrugged. "Nothing."

He handed her three twenty-dollar bills and told her to keep the change.

"You have a nice day, Miss Sophia," he called out when he walked out the door. Although it was freezing, sweat trickled down Ben's brow. He wiped it away with the back of his right hand, grabbed his bag, and left the station. His recently trimmed hair billowed in the wind.

"Something's wrong, isn't it?" Corinthia said when he got back to the car.

"No. It's fine."

"Let me drive," she said.

Ben nodded and Corinthia took over. She turned on the radio and fiddled with the dials until she found a station that played rap music—even though she knew Ben hated it. She drummed her fingers on the steering wheel as the latest Drake song, "Hotline Bling," played.

Now avoiding highways when possible, they traversed long dirt roads. Her eyelids heavy, Corinthia pulled off a winding country road to find a deserted street so she could take a catnap. She awoke a few hours later in pitch darkness to find Ben asleep, too. After she stopped at a KFC to grab a bite, Ben took over.

Pointing the car west, Ben tuned in to NPR.

". . . and although police say they have a description of the suspects' car based on video surveillance from toll booths along the New Jersey turnpike, they are no closer to catching the twin killers."

Ben twisted the radio knob and found an old U2 song from *The Joshua Tree* album, "I Still Haven't Found What I'm Looking For." He smiled and puffed his chest out, bouncing, almost dancing in his seat while he drove and crooned to the music.

"Ugh! My ears!" Ben heard his twin laugh and he laughed, too.

Forty-five minutes later, Ben could hear the faint sound of sirens in the distance. He nearly jumped out of his skin when, from the cornfields that dotted the highway, the bright lights of a helicopter rose up from behind his vehicle like a spaceship. He felt a sizable lump in his throat. He glanced in the rearview mirror and watched the black road behind him become illuminated by beams so bright they mimicked daylight.

"That damn redhead in the gas station." He slammed a hand onto the steering wheel. "I knew it!"

From inside the car, Ben saw his sister open her mouth, cock her head sideways, squint, and look up at the brilliant night sky, now awash with floodlights. The sounds from the whirring of the chopper's blades almost drowned out Ben's next words.

"I love you, Corinthia," he shouted at her above the din.

"I love you too, Ben," he heard her say.

The sound of sirens grew louder. Flashing red and blue lights approached. Ben glanced into his rearview mirror. Without vacillating, he put his right signal on and pulled the late model sedan he was driving over to the side of the highway.

Ben swallowed bile. In the rearview mirror, he watched a dozen or so police cars surround his vehicle. More troopers were careening down both sides of the highway toward him. Two Rushville Police cars slid in front of his. Troopers exited their automobiles, guns drawn, and advanced on the car. One of them raised his left shoulder and yelled into a tiny black box atop it. His eyes never left the driver's side of Ben's sedan while he approached.

"Benjamin Zanetti?"

"Yes."

"Hands where I can see them!"

Ben raised his hands slowly, pushing them up toward his ears. He gazed lovingly at his sister.

The Indiana State Trooper stood outside the driver's side of the car and aimed his big black gun at Ben's head.

"Driver!" His voice was authoritative, curt. "Remove the keys from the ignition! Open the door and get out real slow!"

The sound of helicopter blades slicing the air grew louder when Ben exited the car, leaving the door wide open. His brow was creased when he stepped into a lagoon of white light. The aircraft's floodlights ensnared him. His blond hair blew wild in the wind from the commotion from the chopper hovering above.

"Get on the ground!"

Ben's car keys fell from his grasp. He laced his hands behind his head and sank to his knees in the cold, grimy slush coating the road. Despite the wet snow seeping through his jeans, he began to sweat.

Eleven weapons were trained on him.

One of the dozen cops surrounding him picked up the keys to the car and placed Ben in handcuffs.

"Where's your sister?"

"In the passenger seat."

The Rushville Police officer glanced at the car and snorted at him. "OK, asshole. Let's try this again. Where is Corinthia Zanetti?"

Ben gave him a blank stare. From the front seat, Ben saw Corinthia crane her head and look back at him. He saw her smile. He smiled back.

He stammered, "She's . . . right there."

Lifting the handcuffs from the center, the cop pocketed the car keys and hauled Ben to his feet. Above them, the chopper took off, leaving the road's illumination to police cars—including the arresting cop's vehicle. A trooper opened the back door of the hot patrol car, placed his hand on the top of Ben's head, and pushed him inside. A gust of cold air blew in from the open window. Ben found he needed it. His heart bounced furiously within his chest. He felt the first stirrings of a new and odd sensation: apprehension. While he stared at the officers advancing on his car, he felt a sharp pain jab the base of his neck.

For one fleeting moment, Ben closed his eyes and pictured his sister just like she was when she was seven. On a swing. Pigtails flying, head thrown back in laughter. He wanted nothing more than to remember her that way. To keep her frozen in a time of innocence—to protect her from what was to come.

Heart pounding, he feared he would never see his sister again.

"Don't hurt her!" he screamed, drool running down the left side of his mouth. Ben started kicking the back seat of the car with such a vicious intensity that all of the cops turned to stare at him. He lowered his head and winced. From somewhere deep within him, wiry wings of doubt fluttered against his lucidity.

"What's he talking about?" one of them asked, approaching the back of the vehicle.

Ben leaned forward. He writhed against the restraints, trying without success to wriggle out of his handcuffs. When someone else knelt down and spoke to him from outside the car, he jumped, startled. His heart was now slamming so hard beneath his jacket it felt like it would break free.

A man in a black hat introduced himself.

"I'm Huntley Field. I'm with the FBI. Ben, where is your sister?"

Ben gawked at the lawman. "She's in the car."

The police car's headlights cast a preternatural glow.

"Where's Amanda Taylor?"

Ben was silent.

"We know you took her in Pennsylvania, Ben," Field said, blowing on his hands and stamping snow off his wingtips. "We found her cell phone. And the car she was driving was parked in front of your house."

"I don't know where Amanda is," he shrugged. "But Corinthia's in the car."

Field sniffed and shook his head from side to side. Ben watched the FBI man walk toward the other officers standing nearby.

Field stuck his right index finger in the air and waved it in a circle.

"Open the trunk."

Beneath the moonlight, lawmen trained their guns on the back of the vehicle. One of the officers used Ben's keys to open the trunk. When they popped it open, the officers standing near it looked at each other in surprise.

It was empty.

"Clear," one of them said.

"Open the passenger door," Field said. His words frosted the cold air white.

Eight officers, guns drawn, moved toward the passenger side of the car. One of them yanked the door open. Three of them clicked on flashlights.

Ben watched one of them recoil. "My God! What's that smell?" Another slapped a hand over her mouth and nose. The stench, Ben knew, was like a thousand musty dead rats. It came from a medium-sized canvas bag on the front seat.

"There's a bag here, sir," the female officer said.

"Don't touch it!" Field barked. Ben watched the FBI agent pull on blue latex gloves. He saw him lean forward to yank on the bag's zipper and pull it apart.

An officer just behind Field's shoulder gasped.

Ben sank his head into his hands, imagining what they were seeing.

Inside the duffel bag was a wad of cash and a gun, burner phones, a pink purse, and the remains of a child's body. The corpse, aged, rotted, and covered with earth, looked as if it were mummified.

"It must be at least twenty years old!" Ben overheard one of them exclaim in disbelief.

The rancid, tattered old dress hugging the carcass had faded yellow flowers on it. The back of the skull, caved in from time or catastrophe, still possessed wisps of long blond hair.

Two large blue topazes sat inside the ruined eye sockets.

Ben watched one of the officers turn and dry heave on the side of the highway.

Over ice and snow, Field stomped back toward the patrol car. He yanked the cruiser's door open, sat in the passenger seat, and slammed the door shut behind him.

He huffed, paused for a moment, whirled around, and gave Ben Zanetti a sharp look.

"Whose body is in the bag, Ben?"

"That's Corinthia," Ben said, and then he smiled.

CHAPTER TWENTY-TWO

On a clear sunny day five months later, Ben sat on a low, polished wooden bench outside a Pennsylvania courtroom and stared at the courthouse floor. His throat was dry like sandpaper. He swallowed and fixed his gaze on the white marble tile beneath his feet. He clasped his hands together in a botched attempt to keep them from trembling.

He blinked. From the hard bench he sat on, he had tried to count the tiles leading from his seat to the large wooden courtroom door, but their imperfections kept distracting him. The old marble floor was streaked with ribbons of gray. One tile a few feet away had black scuffmarks; another had a long dark scratch. It looked like someone had crawled on their knees and dragged a key along its surface. Pieces of it had been chipped away. While most of the tiles in the long corridor had been polished to a high gloss, where he sat someone had spilled coffee earlier in the day. Dried brown dime-sized splotches peeked out between his brand-new black leather shoes.

Minutes before, two heavy pine doors behind him had closed on a phalanx of reporters who weren't on the list to enter the building. They had shouted questions at him when deputies grabbed him by the elbow and perp-walked him inside. His hands were cuffed behind his back so tightly they dug into his wrists.

One of the jailers unclipped a small silver ring of keys from his belt and unlocked his wrists and the thin silver shackles on his ankles.

"Wait here," the jailer said to another guard. "And watch him." The second guard nodded and hovered over Ben.

Ben had wanted to wear one of his many expensive suits, but his lawyer had opted for a more nondescript look. And so he was dressed in a pair of tan khakis and a plain button-down white shirt. His feet were squeezed into new black penny loafers from Johnston & Murphy from the mall in King of Prussia.

He sighed, massaged his aching wrists, and winced in relief. Upon his attorney's suggestion, and for the first time in his life, his long blond locks had been shorn to a buzz cut.

His lawyer had also given him a pair of nonprescription eyeglasses.

"Wear them," he'd said. "Juries tend to be more sympathetic."

Ben's trial was about to begin.

Out front while in the prison transport van, Ben had passed a horde of journalists, some doing live feeds for their newscasts, others aiming still and video cameras at the mass of protestors, death penalty advocates, whack jobs, and just plain angry folks who wanted his head on a stick. Through the slats in the back of the vehicle that had transported him from the jail to the courthouse, he had read various homemade signs.

On one large white sign, painted in red letters was #StabTheBastard! It included a knife dripping with blood. Others read #JusticeForTallulah, #BurnInHell!, and #FindAmandaNOW!

A gaggle of students from Glastonbury stood on the sidewalk wearing T-shirts stenciled with the words, "Find Amanda NOW" and "Black Lives Matter." A chant arose among them that other people picked up and a call-and-response began:

"When I say 'Black Lives,' you say, 'Matter.'"

"Black Lives!"

"Matter!"

"Black Lives!"

"Matter."

Others shouted, "Say her name!"

"Amanda Taylor!"

"Say her name!"

"Amanda Taylor!"

From the back of the van at a stoplight, Ben caught snippets of one newscaster's live report above the fading din: ". . . and Black Lives Matter activists say they are outraged police have given up the search for Zanetti's only Black victim, Amanda Taylor, whose whereabouts are still a mystery. They claim more attention isn't being paid to her, when she could still be alive. And they worry that, given the trial, the focus may shift to the deceased white victims whose bodies have all been recovered. A modern-day hero,

Taylor was kidnapped by Zanetti after she rescued her roommate, Fiona Kessler, from his unspeakable house of horrors."

People shouted and jockeyed for a glimpse of Ben as he arrived. The mob pressed so close to the orange-and-white wooden barricades lining the curbs leading up to the courthouse, they had shifted into the street. To avoid the pandemonium outside the building, the van had turned into a restricted parking lot and Ben had been brought in handcuffs through a door reserved for court officers and high-profile offenders. The reporters' questions still rang in his ears.

"Ben, why did you kill all those women?"

"Where's Amanda Taylor?"

Inside the courthouse, he saw a striking Black woman with flowing brown braids. She didn't say anything, but she held up a photo of Amanda. Tears rolled down her pretty cheeks. As a shackled Ben hobbled closer, the woman began to shudder. It was like she was standing in front of a blast of cold air.

"Where is my daughter?" she had asked, her voice scarcely above a whisper. The dark-skinned man scowling next to her towered above them both. He was dressed in a navy suit, crisp striped shirt, a matching tie, and gleaming black wing tips. Hair graying at his temples, his bushy eyebrows creased in grief, he seemed somehow . . . familiar. He looks like Amanda, Ben thought. Ben assumed both were Amanda's parents. Amanda's father tugged on his wife's jacket. But she flinched from him and screamed at Ben, "Just tell us if she's still alive!"

Ben called out to her over his shoulder as deputies led him down the hall. "I'm sorry." His voice was filled with anguish. "I wish I could tell you!"

A guard had approached the couple, spoken a few words to them, and led them down a long hallway further away from Ben. He'd heard the woman's sobs when deputies led him to the bench where he now sat just outside the courtroom.

It had only taken a week for Ben to be extradited back to Pennsylvania from where he'd been caught in Indiana. Psychologists took weeks to find him competent to stand trial. Now, after months in custody, his Pennsylvania court date had arrived.

It was Friday, May 20, 2016, and Ben was pleading not guilty by reason of insanity.

"Stand." Ben looked up, terrified, when an officer addressed him. The bailiff uncuffed him, opened the door, and led him roughly by the elbow into the courtroom. When the doors swung open and Ben walked in, all small talk within the room ceased. With his free hand, he pushed his glasses up the bridge of his nose and smoothed his hand down over the front of his button-down long-sleeve shirt. Then he rubbed his sweaty palms across the front of his slacks.

In silence, the bailiff led him down a short pathway toward the front of a large wood-paneled room. A graying, bespectacled female judge dressed in a jet-black robe with a white lace collar eyed him over the rim of her glasses when he made his way toward her. The name on the nameplate in front of her read: Grace A. Murphy. Beneath her name was a single word in all caps: JUDGE. Her hair was pulled back into a severe bun. Judge Murphy sat above the court on an elevated dais beneath a large circular sign that read "Seal of the State of Pennsylvania," inside of which was an eagle perched above a colonial ship at sea, a plow, and bright green sheaves of wheat.

To her right, a furled United States flag sat atop a gleaming gold pole. To her left was the elevated witness box and beside that was the flag of the Commonwealth of Pennsylvania, a navy field embroidered with the state coat of arms. Beneath a black-and-white eagle and a pair of black draft horses was the state's motto embossed on a red scroll: Virtue, Liberty, and Independence.

Ben could hear soft whispers from the gallery. It brimmed with court watchers who had been waiting to enter since the wee hours of the morning. Many who had vied for a seat had held a vigil for the dearly departed.

There were officials, cops, and family members of the deceased, as well as a carefully selected group of reporters and some TV personalities from the local and national press who scribbled in notebooks. Cameras weren't allowed in Pennsylvania courtrooms, but that hadn't stopped the many courtroom sketch artists who sat with colored pencils and large pads of paper on their laps, sketching the scene. Ringed around the room were bailiffs and other unarmed officers. Ben's breath caught in his lungs.

He had never seen so many cops in one place.

His attorney, Norris Jenson, was dressed in a solid charcoal suit with a cream-colored shirt and coordinating gray-and-tan tie. He wore designer oxfords on his feet. Jenson stood when he noticed Ben's gaze and clapped him on the shoulder.

"They're here for your protection, Ben," his lawyer told him in his deep baritone. "You know, because of all the death threats we've both received."

Ben swallowed hard. Before he sat in the tan, upholstered leather swivel chair at the defense table, another officer "harrumphed" at the comment. But Ben didn't care. He was lost in his thoughts when the court proceeded to inform him that he was on trial for kidnapping, assault, and murder in the deaths of twelve women—and in the kidnapping, beating, and disappearance of Amanda Taylor. He was also charged with murder in the deaths of Jane Winters and his sister, as well as the abuse of his sister's corpse. As the charges were read, victims of the deceased wept openly. Gasps and murmurs grew louder before the judge banged her gavel and demanded order. Silence followed, but only for a moment. From the gallery, a woman stood and pointed her index finger at Judge Murphy.

"I'm from Philly, Judge Judy, and you can't tell me how to act 'cause this sack of shit killed my family!"

People applauded.

"Bailiffs!" Murphy's complexion reddened. "Remove that woman from my courtroom right now!" When the woman was escorted out, the judge took a deep breath.

"I know these are trying times for the families of the victims," she said, "but this is not the way we behave in court. You will keep quiet during these proceedings, or you will be removed from my courtroom and you may be found in criminal contempt. I don't care who you are!"

Silence blanketed the room.

The media had dubbed Ben "The Coed Killer 2.0." Some talking heads had commented on how handsome he was, how clean-cut he seemed, and how that—combined with his wealth—had likely made it easier for him to lure his prey. Some had likened him to Robert Chambers, New York City's long-ago Preppy Killer. Ben leaned over and whispered into his attorney's ear. The lawyer nodded and smiled.

Slight, yet muscular, Jenson had swaggered into the courtroom just moments before Ben. His bald head held high, he gazed neither left nor right before easing into his seat at the defense table.

He crossed his legs and leaned back in his chair; his fingers steepled together beneath the coarse beard on his chin. Both men sat still while the prosecution set forth its case against Ben.

"Ladies and gentlemen," assistant prosecutor Stephanie Patel, a woman of Indian descent, began, after rising from her seat and standing midway between the judge and the jury box.

"From the time he was fourteen years old, Benjamin Zanetti's principal focus has been to murder young women. It is literally all he has ever done with any consistency." She paused. "His immense wealth, thanks to an inheritance, afforded him the ability to do little else. His money allowed him to hide in plain sight, living on the fringe of society in a wealthy Pennsylvania enclave near a sprawling university.

"He is not like you or me, however. He has never even held a job."

Ben was rapt as she spoke. Rail thin and dressed in a black pencil skirt and matching Dior jacket, Patel had a slight accent that appealed to Ben as something sexy. She stood so close to the jurors, Ben was sure they could smell her fancy French perfume. It wafted through the air when she walked, arms gesturing, her slightly accented voice rising and falling for emphasis. Soft dark curls framed her bronze face. On her stocking-clad feet, she wore a tiny pair of black Manolo Blahnik halter pumps from the previous season. But still, Ben mused, she was not Corinthia.

When she began speaking, a projector opposite the jury box whirred to life and a white screen unfurled from the ceiling. Someone coughed. The lights went out. Projected before everyone were photos of the victims, and except for Amanda Taylor, all were blond. Reporters, scattered throughout the courtroom, squinted at their notebooks while they took notes in the dimmed light. Every now and then the prosecutor was interrupted by wails and gasps of horror from victims' families whenever a young woman's photo flashed across the screen.

When Patel told them Ben's first victim—by his own admission in interviews with the police and court-appointed psychologists—had most likely been his twin sister, Ben frowned.

"This young girl died under mysterious circumstances when she fell from a tree house on September 1, 1998, when they were just seven," Patel said. "It was her remains that were found in a duffel bag in the defendant's car when he was captured."

A photo of Corinthia Zanetti, about age six, appeared on screen. To Ben, she seemed larger than life. Her long blond pigtails fell far below her shoulders. She beamed at the jurors. Her left front tooth was missing.

As Patel laid out the murder charge in connection with his sister's death, Ben gasped. He felt a dozen pairs of eyes swivel toward him, but he didn't care. He smacked his hand on the table; it shook when he grasped his attorney's forearm. His nails dug into the lawyer's suit. He leaned in close and hissed, "Where did they get that photo? That belonged to my grandmother! They can't have that here, can they? And I did not kill my sister!" he said, his voice wavering. "It was an accident."

His attorney patted his shoulder and whispered, "Calm down. The jury's watching." Ben's face turned red. He swallowed hard and his eyes watered. Blood churning, he glared at the prosecutor. Patel continued.

"The evidence will show that after he killed his neighbor, Jane Winters, a girl of sixteen," Patel said when her photo appeared on the screen, "Ben fled. But not before he dug up his sister's body and carted it off to his grandmother's house. And even while he worshipped his sister's corpse, adorning it with jewels, he fashioned a plan to keep killing young women—all of whom bore a striking resemblance to his dead twin."

Patel cleared her throat and repeated the names and ages of his victims.

"Fourteen young women in all," she said. One by one their photos appeared before them.

"Think about that," Patel said, moving toward the jury box. "These women—young wives, mothers, sisters, and daughters—were living their lives, attending school or working near universities. Planning their days, surviving, thriving—never realizing a predator stalked them day and night before deciding to play God with their fate.

"But one woman caught on to him." Amanda's image flashed across the screen. She was seated atop a cobblestone wall beneath a Glastonbury University banner. Her thick hair was wind swept. Her head was thrown back and she was grinning. "Amanda Taylor discovered Ben's whereabouts, went to his house, and found him beating the only one of his victims to escape—Fiona Kessler. Miss Kessler will testify that because Amanda rushed in with a baseball bat to defend her, she was able to stab this prolific serial killer in the hand. She ran away—but not before Fiona saw Amanda overpowered by Mr. Zanetti, who then beat and kidnapped her.

"Amanda is a hero. She has yet to be found, because the defendant refuses to say where she is or even if she's still alive. Her fate remains unknown."

Ben turned his head and looked over his shoulder when he heard a familiar wail pierce the silence. The lone, anguished cry could only come from one person.

Fiona.

She wept, oblivious to context. Like her heart was broken. A chill went down Ben's spine. He forced his hands in his lap and hung his head, staring at the floor. As if on cue, Patel paused and all the lights came back on.

"Over the course of more than a dozen years," she said as the wailing died down, "Benjamin Zanetti kidnapped, terrorized, strangled, gouged, dismembered, stabbed, and beat many of these women to death. All while his sister's remains were not far from his grasp."

There were audible exhales and babbling from the courtroom gallery. The judge cast a silent but stony gaze over her glasses. Silence in the room resumed.

"But I didn't kill them!" Ben stood up, quaking from head to toe.

"Mr. Zanetti!" the judge scolded. "We will not have any additional outbursts from you in this courtroom. Do I make myself clear?" Her voice was full of nails and venom. His attorney pulled on his sleeve, coaxing him into his seat.

"Our apologies, Your Honor," Jenson boomed. The judge glared at them both. Ben sat, and Patel, whose voice faltered just a little when she spoke, continued.

"These women did not lay down and take their torture. You'll hear from the state's forensics experts how many of them fought back, as evidenced by their autopsies. When police captured the defendant, his jaw was swollen, most likely from an altercation with one of his last victims, Amanda Taylor. Most of the victims' broken, battered bodies were found without clothing and undergarments. These women were held captive and beaten before they were killed. The suspect's DNA was found beneath their fingernails and on other parts of their remains."

Over and over the prosecutor outlined a triple play for jurors—describing when each victim vanished from their neighborhoods, how their remains were found on Ben's property, and how each died by Ben's own hands.

"The medical examiner will testify," Patel said, "that most of their causes of death were by strangulation or asphyxiation—but others met a much more horrific and brutal end. At least one victim had her eyes gouged out—while she was alive. Three others had been set ablaze.

"The State will prove beyond a reasonable doubt that Benjamin Zanetti is indeed the so-called new Coed Killer. We know because one of his victims escaped. Held prisoner for months, you will hear testimony from Fiona

Kessler—the subject of a much-publicized search and the only victim to escape Ben's reign of terror."

Patel continued to develop her case, telling the jurors, "The defendant intentionally kidnapped and killed many, many women. This we know not just because Fiona identified him, but because we found her blood and saliva on his clothing, on his mattress, and all over his property," she said, pointing her index finger at Ben. "He kidnapped and tortured Amanda Taylor on purpose. Both Fiona and Amanda's blood were found at his home, and Amanda's blood was also found at an apartment building police tracked him to just outside New York City. He didn't just kidnap these women for his own nefarious reasons. He deliberately killed them because he enjoys killing.

"Unfortunately, you are in for a frightening and disturbing nightmare, ladies and gentlemen. One that will leave an indelible imprint, because the evidence is incontrovertible and will show far beyond a shadow of a doubt that Benjamin Zanetti—and Benjamin Zanetti alone—is guilty of these horrific crimes and more. Let's not forget—one victim, Amanda Taylor, remains unaccounted for."

Patel then turned on her fashionable heel and returned to her seat, ending her opening statement.

The judge looked at the defense table and said:

"Does the defendant wish to present an opening statement at this time?"

"Yes, Your Honor," Jenson said. When he stood, his chair clattered against the polished floor. He cleared his throat, smoothed his tie, and approached the jurors, sauntering toward them like the entire courtroom was his and his alone. His smile was friendly, charismatic.

"Despite what you've just heard," Jenson began, in a voice so deep and clear it cut the cool air like a blade, "Benjamin Zanetti is, in fact, a victim.

"He has spent his entire life trapped in a state of his own delusions, unable and unwilling to accept the death of his twin sister, Corinthia, who died in a tragic accident when they were children. You will hear from an expert who will show you that Ben is mentally ill and suffers from, among other things, something called Dissociative Identity Disorder, or DID. That, ladies and gentlemen, is when the mind splits into multiple personalities. It caused Ben to actually believe he was his sister, Corinthia. And it is, in fact, his alternative personality—an alter named after his sister, Corinthia—who is guilty of these horrific crimes.

"Benjamin Zanetti did not possess intent, under the law, to kill any of these women!" Jenson bellowed. "He wanted only to care for them, to pamper them in ways a loving brother would treat his sister. His alter, Corinthia, however, did aim to kill them. She used and manipulated him into doing so.

"Ben's condition—his mental illness—began to manifest itself in his childhood. It was exacerbated after Corinthia's death when his mother beat and tortured him and made him behave as if he were his dead twin.

"You will hear how his own father witnessed young Benjamin being forced to dress up as his sister—to wear the clothing of little girls—and yet did nothing to stop it. Ben's mother, in fact, forbade Ben to leave the house dressed as a boy and, once he matured, she made Ben wear padded bras and girls' panties. She even once threatened to cut off his manhood."

Jenson stood very still as he addressed the jurors, his determination never wavering.

"Even when his voice deepened—as a boy's voice tends to do," the defense attorney continued, "Ben's mother forced him to speak in a falsetto, to mimic his sister's voice. He was a teenage boy when he began to rebel. He ran away—to live with his grandmother. But the damage, ladies and gentlemen, was done.

"Now, certainly, not every person living with DID turns into a murdering psychopath. I'm not arguing that. But experts will tell you that being forced to live and behave as if he were his sister caused irreparable psychological damage because Benjamin was already suffering from a mental illness. In fact, this specific type of abuse made that illness worse," Jenson said.

"Experts will also tell you that there were times when Ben could simultaneously be himself and his twin sister."

Ben's defense attorney held up his hand and counted up with three fingers for emphasis while he told jurors, "He would converse, reason, and even argue with the Corinthia persona. She often intimidated him. And she pretended to be remorseful over the deaths of these women." Jenson paused before continuing.

"Not only did Ben dress as her, he went out and about in public, carrying on his days, living as Corinthia. And as the dominant personality, the Corinthia alter completely took over—for years. Leaving Ben at her mercy." Jenson walked over to his client.

"Not only did Ben use his own voice to speak for Corinthia," he said, gesturing toward Ben, "he often deferred to her judgment, turning over large portions of his life to her, letting her decide how and where they traveled and how they lived. She even made the decision to commit these murders—independent of my client. In fact, Benjamin begged her again and again to stop. But you won't have to take our word for it. This was something witnessed by Fiona Kessler," Jenson said. "She told police that despite being blindfolded most of the time, she overheard two people arguing. Overheard Ben trying to protect her—that there were two kidnappers: Benjamin and his sister, Corinthia." He walked toward the jury box. Ben could see Jenson imploring the jurors with his eyes before he pointed toward him.

"Here sits before you a very, very sick man who not only believed his sister was carrying out these crimes—fueled by her own rage over what she perceived as his complicity in her death, an unfortunate accident that occurred when she fell from a tree and broke her neck when they were both just seven years old. No, not only that—he, in fact, tried to stop her. You will hear what it was like living with a mother who tortured him emotionally, physically, and mentally—so much that it broke the little boy inside and caused the man to grow into a monster.

"Even the prosecutor has alluded to Ben's grief," Jenson continued. "You will see, and the defense will show, that Ben was so upset over the death of his sister that he dug her body up from her final resting place and carried her remains with him his entire adult life. That is, in fact, why the FBI found her corpse with him when he was captured.

"Benjamin Zanetti is no killer. It was never his intention to kill these women. In fact, he fought hard to save them. The killer lives inside him in the personage of his alternative personality—his alter, if you will—Corinthia.

"He is insane and therefore he deserves mercy, not the death penalty."

When Jenson returned to his seat, the judge banged her gavel.

The day's events had come to a close.

CHAPTER TWENTY-THREE

Weeks passed as the prosecution trotted out its witnesses. Many spoke fondly of victims. Others of how, in retrospect, their encounters with Ben and Corinthia seemed steeped in weirdness.

Tom Antzakas, a plump twenty-year-old with shoulder-length black hair, sat on the witness stand, running his hands through his thick, dark curls. He had been a waiter at a diner near campus where Amanda Taylor had also worked. While Tom recalled his encounters with Corinthia, Ben sat at the defense table and pressed his palm into his cheek. Tom told the court Corinthia had frequented the eatery often, dressed in a series of pink and black tracksuits, dark glasses, and a pink baseball cap.

Tom testified the restaurant staff had no idea Corinthia was a man. In fact, few did. Many Laurel Valley denizens had seen her at the mall and in shops and restaurants and bars. She always wore a tracksuit and was never without her hot pink hat. A parade of witnesses told the court over and over that they had no idea Corinthia wasn't a woman.

"Why couldn't you tell?" Patel asked Antzakas.

"He, um, I mean she, was always polite, soft-spoken. Wore lipstick. Women's clothes. But we never talked to her, I mean him," Antzakas said, rubbing his hands together. He then smoothed his left hand over his red tie and dark blue shirt, staining them with his sweat before he continued.

"She always had on headphones. Never once looked at the menu. Ordered the same thing all the time—a cheese omelet, rye toast, and coffee— and always paid in cash. I served that guy coffee every Friday morning for like a year. And I never knew she was a guy." Antzakas sighed and looked up at the ceiling, flustered. He took a deep breath and tried again. "I mean, her hair was nice beneath that baseball cap and was always down her back in a ponytail or out loose across her shoulders."

Patel pursed her lips and nodded. She walked over toward the jury box, her tan, patent-leather heels clicking across the marble floor. They matched the tan wrap dress she was wearing. She folded one arm and pressed the other hand under her chin.

"Tell us, Mr. Antzakas, about Mr. Zanetti's demeanor. And you can refer to him as the defendant if that helps."

"We didn't get a lot of people in that time of morning—5:00 a.m.," he began. "But I remember one time a lady came in and she, um, the defendant, kept staring at her. That was the one and only time he took off those sunglasses."

"And you remember this why?"

"Well, I knew the customer he was staring at, and because Corinthia, I mean, the defendant, beckoned me over and offered me one hundred dollars for that customer's signed receipt."

"And what did you do?"

The witness hung his head. "I'm not proud of it, but a hundred dollars is a hundred dollars. So I told the defendant he could look at it—but he couldn't keep it." Antzakas turned to face the judge and said, "I mean, we keep the signed credit card receipts."

"And what was on the receipt?" Patel asked.

"A name, a signature."

"Permission to approach the witness with exhibit 118e, Your Honor, a copy of the aforementioned receipt obtained from Joyce's, a diner located in Laurel Valley, Pennsylvania."

The judge nodded her assent.

Ben's defense attorney shuffled papers to find his copy of the exhibit. When Patel approached the witness box, Ben sat up and leaned forward. "Mr. Antzakas," she asked, "does this look like the receipt you gave Mr. Zanetti that day?" She handed it to him.

He nodded.

"And can you read the highlighted portion?"

"Fiona Kessler."

"Thank you," Patel said. "No further questions."

"Your witness, Mr. Jenson," the judge said.

"No questions, Your Honor."

After the exit of Antzakas from the stand and a brief break, Patel again rose.

"The prosecution would like to call its next witness, Your Honor," Patel said. The judge directed her to proceed. The prosecutor called Dr. Sameer Hamid, the county medical examiner, to the stand. He testified about the collection of DNA evidence.

"Dr. Hamid," Patel began, "was foreign DNA found on the body of Tallulah Montgomery when she was discovered in a shallow grave not far from Glastonbury University?"

Hamid, who wore a rumpled gray sport coat, leaned forward. "Yes."

"How were you able to find DNA on her after she had been in the ground for so long?"

Hamid raised a fist to his mouth and coughed. "Miss Montgomery was found in the snow. She'd been there for months. The cold preserved some of the DNA."

"How's that possible?" Patel asked.

"There wasn't complete decomposition of her flesh. There are many cases documented in forensics literature demonstrating how human DNA can be extracted from bugs found in and around a decaying corpse for months after a death. And that was the situation in this case."

"How long had Tallulah Montgomery been in the ground before you found her in November?"

"About six months," he said, crossing his legs, revealing the bottoms of his scuffed gray oxfords.

"And did the DNA you found on her body belong to anyone in this courtroom?"

"Yes," Hamid said.

"Who?"

"The defendant."

Hamid testified for most of the next morning as well about how DNA found on victim after victim could only belong to one person—Benjamin Zanetti.

∽

After being sworn in later that day, FBI Agent Huntley Field took the stand. He was wearing a dark blazer, crisp white shirt, and a blue tie with tiny red squares. His worn, dark brown wing tips had been polished to a high gloss.

"Agent Field," Patel said when the lawman sat down, "can you explain to the court why the DNA evidence the coroner testified to earlier is so important? Can you put it in context for us?"

"Sure. In some of the victims we unearthed, we found traces of DNA linking the subject, the defendant, Ben Zanetti, to the crime. Semen leaves its own DNA fingerprint. But DNA, as we heard earlier, can be found in saliva, in sweat, in tears, and in hair. One of the victims, Miss Kessler, told us the defendant wept in her hair—often for hours."

"Hair? Why else is that important here?"

"Because we also found follicular DNA in Tallulah Montgomery's hand. Apparently, she had ripped some strands of hair from her killer."

"And whose DNA was that?" Patel asked.

"Benjamin Zanetti's," Field answered.

"No more questions, Your Honor."

The judge glanced at the defense attorney.

"Any cross-examination?" she asked.

"Yes, Your Honor," Jenson said. For the first time, he had decided to question a prosecution witness.

He kept his seat and fiddled with some paperwork in front of him while Ben looked on.

"So, Agent Field," Jenson began, "when you captured my client in Indiana, you were under the impression that he committed these crimes alone?"

"Objection, Your Honor!" Patel said.

"I'll allow it," the judge responded.

"No," Field said.

"Why?"

"Because one of his victims, Fiona Kessler, told us two people had held her hostage."

"Two, huh?" Jenson asked. "And who was the other suspect?"

"A woman named Corinthia who we believed was Benjamin Zanetti's sister."

"And you also thought that because Miss Kessler told you Corinthia was the one she was afraid of, that Corinthia was the executioner, wasn't she?"

"Objection," Patel said.

"Overruled," the judge replied.

"Yes," Field continued. "The victim, Miss Kessler, said she'd been kidnapped and held against her will by a man and a woman who argued with each other about whether or not to kill her."

"And isn't it true Miss Kessler frequently heard Ben beg Corinthia to let her live, and Ben also promised to protect her from Corinthia?"

"Yes."

Jenson paused and shuffled more papers. He cleared his throat. "Now, although Miss Kessler overheard them bickering, she never saw Corinthia. Isn't that right, Agent Field?"

"Correct," Field said. "The defendant, Ben Zanetti, kept Miss Kessler blindfolded when he wasn't in her presence."

"Isn't it also true, Agent Field," Jenson continued, "that you believed up to that point— because of Miss Kessler's statements—that Ben Zanetti was not your only suspect?"

"Objection, Your Honor. Asked and answered." Patel said.

"Sustained. Move on, counselor," the judge said to Jenson.

Jenson did not miss a beat. "Agent Field, when you and the other officers caught Benjamin and you asked about Corinthia's whereabouts, isn't it true my client told you she was in the car?"

"Yes."

"And was she?"

"Yes."

"Did Ben say . . ." Jenson paused to read from a police report. "'She's right there'?"

"Yes."

"Did you see anyone sitting in the car?"

"No."

"Yet he told you she was in the car so you decided to check anyway?"

"Yes."

"Why?"

"Well, we weren't sure if she was hiding in the back seat or the trunk."

"And was she in the car?"

Field paused on the stand.

"Special Agent Fields?"

"It's Field."

Jenson smiled. "I stand corrected."

"Yes, she was."

"She was what, Agent Field?"

"Corinthia, the sister, was in the car."

"And what was her condition?"

"Objection, Your Honor," Patel said. "Goes to speculation."

Jenson put his hand on his hip. "Really, Your Honor?" Ben heard him say under his breath. The judge raised an eyebrow and said, "I'll allow it."

"Her condition?" Jenson repeated in a louder voice.

"She was dead and had been dead for some time," Field responded. "Her corpse was found in the front seat in an old duffel bag."

"And how do you know it was her?"

"The defendant told us it was his sister. DNA testing later proved that the corpse was indeed his twin."

"And didn't you find that odd—that my client behaved as though his dead sister was alive?"

"Yes," Field said, nodding.

"No further questions, Your Honor."

"Redirect?" the judge asked Patel.

Patel stood. "Yes, Your Honor."

"Agent Field, is the person who assaulted, beat, gouged, mutilated, and strangled these women to death seated in this courtroom?"

"Yes."

"And who is that?"

"Benjamin Zanetti."

"Nothing further from this witness, Your Honor," she said.

The judge turned to Patel. "Well then, the State may call its next witness."

"The State calls Dr. Leslie George."

CHAPTER TWENTY-FOUR

Most of the gallery in the front of the room could hear her heels click across the courtroom floor before they saw her make her way toward the witness box. George wore nude patent-leather Christian Louboutins on her feet. Her flowing dress—made of tan and brown kente cloth—was covered by a dark brown jacket. Her delicate blond Sisterlocks hung to the middle of her back. On her carefully made-up medium-brown face was a pair of tiny black Tom Ford spectacles.

After George was sworn in, Patel asked about her background. George's many wooden bangles shook when she brushed a tiny stray blond Sisterlock from her shoulder.

In a clear, confident voice, she established her bona fides: "I am a practicing doctor of psychology and professor at the University of Pennsylvania, Altoona Campus, where I lecture and teach criminal justice. I am also a former FBI profiler specializing in serial killers. I've written several best-selling books on them, including my latest, *Death at a Moment's Notice*."

"Dr. George, you examined Mr. Zanetti at length after his arrest, is that right?"

"Yes, that's right."

"And you led a team of medical professionals who all gave their expert opinion that Ben Zanetti is now competent to stand trial?"

George coughed into a closed fist. "Yes, he is—even though he has been diagnosed with Dissociative Identity Disorder."

"Doctor," Patel said, nodding, "please explain for the jury your understanding of what DID is."

"Certainly," George said.

In the jury box, several jurors began scribbling in notepads.

"We have, in the past, called DID multiple personality disorder, and it has been the subject of fascination in pop culture and the topic of books and films for decades," she said, gesturing with her arms, her bangles rattling.

"Briefly, it's a mental disorder categorized by at least two separate personality terrains." She placed her hands side by side and moved them up and down. "Think of it as multiple people—or in this case, twins—sharing one body.

"People who suffer with DID," she continued, "frequently cannot remember certain events or how they behaved, and they may blame that on absentmindedness when, in reality, it could be that one individual personality may be . . . awake—while the other is asleep.

"However, the ways in which DID presents itself vary. One alternative personality, or alter, as we call them, may speak with an accent, while others do not. Another may have allergies or asthma, while the others may not. They will have different dispositions. One will have experiences or engage in activities that the others will be unaware of. For example, one may set fire to their bed and the other will put it out—never realizing they set it in the first place. The contrasts between alternate identities can be as dramatic as they are distinctive. While this condition of the mind is rare, it is very real and, in many ways, absolutely yet unbelievably incredible."

"Unbelievable?" Patel asked.

"Yes. It's . . . hard for any person—trained medical professional or not—to comprehend." She smiled. "And when we come across people with DID, we repeatedly come to a realization that we will never ever fully understand how the mind functions. Or how a person's left hand, so to speak, literally cannot know what their right hand is doing."

"Dr. George," Patel snorted, "let us assume this isn't a far-fetched defense. Isn't it true that the Corinthia personality begged Benjamin many times to stop kidnapping young women?"

"Objection. Leading," Jenson said.

"Sustained," Judge Murphy said. "Rephrase, counselor."

"Is there evidence that the Corinthia personality begged Benjamin many times to stop kidnapping young women?"

"Yes. And the victim Fiona Kessler has stated she heard as much," George answered, pushing her glasses up the bridge of her nose.

"And he kept kidnapping them anyway, knowing full well what fate would befall them, isn't that right?" Patel asked.

"Objection, Your Honor," Jenson huffed. "Counsel is still leading the witness."

"Sustained. Rephrase, Ms. Patel," the judge ordered.

Patel pursed her lips. "Did he continue to assault them?"

"Yes," George said.

"According to your interviews with Mr. Zanetti, what did the defendant say would befall his victims if he continued kidnapping young women?"

"Well, he knew they would be killed."

"Dr. George, in your professional opinion, can you tell us if Zanetti knew what he was doing when these crimes were committed?"

"Yes, he did."

"And why is that?"

Dr. George licked her lips.

"There is a cognitive distortion in the way Benjamin processes his thoughts—in the way he thinks, if you will. He's well aware that what he is doing is wrong, but he does not know why he engages in the behaviors that he does, and he is incapable of stopping himself."

"Nothing further," Patel said.

The judge beckoned from her perch. "Your witness, Mr. Jenson."

Jenson stood and folded his arms across his indigo Ralph Lauren double windowpane suit.

"So, you know a thing or two about serial killers?" He smiled as he addressed George. She smiled back.

"A thing," she said, "or two."

"Dr. George, who killed these women?"

"The defendant did," George said.

Jenson smiled again and looked down at his notes, glancing at his dark Gucci loafers. He paused between questions.

"Isn't it true that it is the alter, Corinthia, who killed these women?"

"Well," George said, gently shifting in her chair. She paused for a long ten seconds before answering. "Technically, yes."

An audible din of murmurs erupted in the courtroom. The judge banged her gavel and the noise stopped.

"Objection, Your Honor!" Patel said. "Calls for speculation."

"Overruled," the judge said. "Her opinion is in the report and was entered into evidence, was it not?"

Patel opened her mouth, then shut it.

"Yes, Your Honor," Jenson answered.

"Go on," the judge said.

"So, Doctor. In your professional opinion as a psychologist, can you tell this court in detail why you think Corinthia was the author and architect of these killings? Like you wrote it here in your report?"

George squirmed in her seat. She stole a glance at the prosecutor that seemed to Ben to say, Oh, crap.

He smiled.

"I beg to differ with you, counselor," she said sharply. "It is not phrased just like that in my report. Not at all," she protested.

"The way I read it here, it is pretty clear," Jenson said, thumbing through some typewritten pages. "Your examination does indeed show that Ben wasn't always in control of himself. You spoke to his alter Corinthia at length, did you not?"

Ben noticed Patel opened her mouth to object, but didn't.

Dr. George blinked rapidly. "Yes."

"Uh-huh, and didn't the alternative identity known as Corinthia tell you that she was, in fact, in control of Ben for much of Ben's adult life? Isn't that true, Doctor?"

Dr. George sighed. She seemed to choose her next words with care.

"Upon my examination of Mr. Zanetti, I was indeed able to converse with both him and the identity he calls Corinthia," George said.

Whispers in the courtroom began again.

The judge banged her gavel.

George continued. "Yes, the Corinthia personality was in control of Ben for much of his adulthood. It began to present itself in him when he was seven years old, shortly after the death of the real Corinthia. As children, both were close. His mind fractured in response to her death."

Jenson seized on that point and he interrupted her. "As a coping mechanism?"

She nodded. "That would be fair to say."

"In other words, isn't it true that his torturous childhood impacted his mind?"

George jutted out her chin, as if in contemplation. "His disorder was not aided by the abuse he suffered at the hands of his mother."

"Objection, Your Honor—speculation."

The judge frowned. She leaned forward, pausing for a moment before speaking. "I'll allow this, continue."

The jurors, too, seemed to hang onto George's every word.

"While it is true," Jenson said, now abandoning his scribbles on the legal pad, "that the Corinthia personality told you she begged Ben to stop kidnapping young women, Benjamin also begged Corinthia not to kill them, didn't he?"

"Yes, that's true."

Jenson paused. "Doctor, you told us earlier that you spoke with both Benjamin and Corinthia and that alternative personalities can differ wildly in behaviors and memories, is that true?"

George nodded yes.

"Let the record reflect the witness nodded in the affirmative," the judge said to the bespectacled court stenographer, who bobbed his own head up and down.

"Doctor, please speak your answers aloud for the record," the judge added.

"Certainly, Your Honor," George replied.

Jenson continued. "You also wrote," he paused as he again flipped through some typewritten pages, "that alternative personalities will have different dispositions. So how does your diagnosis of Ben differ from that of the Corinthia identity?"

George cleared her throat. "Both suffer from antisocial personality disorder, and there are many similarities. However, while they have different things wrong with them, the degree of their violent predilections differ based on their individual psychoses."

Jenson cut her off again. "Can you describe for the court in detail exactly what that means? In layman's terms?"

"While Ben suffers from DID, he is also schizophrenic and has sociopathic tendencies. He is often delusional and hallucinates. He sometimes hears and sees things and people that aren't there. However, because he's considered attractive and can appear charming, even magnanimous at times, he has an ability to captivate people when he wants to. And that's what drew many of his victims to him like a magnet. That, coupled with his wealth—the way he dressed, his cars, the money he lavished to impress some of these women—that made it very easy for him to manipulate his victims into doing whatever he wanted."

"Such as?"

"Such as getting into cars with him or meeting him places alone where he could trap them. After all, it's not typical that we equate wealth with fear. But I digress. As a result of his pathology, he lacks a conscience and is incapable of shame or remorse. Even though Miss Kessler reported he made her feel like he was going to release her, he wouldn't have. He only wanted her to think that."

"Objection, Your Honor," the prosecutor said. "Calls for speculation."

Jenson responded, "Again, Your Honor, Ms. George is an expert testifying to her diagnosis of the defendant's condition, which is in the report! She is responding in that capacity."

"I'll allow it," Judge Murphy said. "Go on, Dr. George."

George continued, "Benjamin is entirely egocentric and incapable of love; he also exercises poor judgment. He has no friends and doesn't find that odd or troubling."

"Dr. George, you write here," Jenson said, flipping through his notes, "that Ben is also a carrier of the 'warrior gene.' Can you explain what that gene variant is, please?"

"Certainly," she said, crossing her legs. "Numerous studies reveal that more than a third of white males are born with MAO-A 3R, the so-called 'warrior gene,' which can make them antisocial. And although researchers have linked that gene to psychopathy, most men don't wind up like Ben."

"And is there a connection to this gene and abuse?"

She nodded. "There are studies that show that adult men with MAO-A 3R who may have faced abuse as boys are more apt to be violent and engage in criminal misdeeds—especially if they've been isolated in childhood by a parent—as Ben was by his mother. Or provoked, as the Corinthia personality perceived she was by the repeated kidnappings. They are more aggressive, impulsive, and prone to take risks—as both the dominant and nondominant personalities here were. When it comes to Ben specifically, he also has a deep and abiding longing for the past and an overwhelming sense of guilt caused by his sister's death. That, coupled with his condition, led him to want to recreate past happier experiences with his twin. He didn't think he was hurting these women, because in his mind they were simply manifestations of the real Corinthia."

"The Corinthia alter, on the other hand, has narcissistic personality disorder. She's also a psychopath who showed no . . ."

"A psychopath?" Jenson asked loudly, cutting her off. He glanced at the jury, as if answering his own question. "A psychopath! The Corinthia personality that overtook much of Benjamin's life is psychotic. Can you explain for the court, Dr. George, exactly what that means?"

The judge banged her gavel several times to silence the gallery. "We can do without theatrics, counselor."

George blinked several times and continued. "While Ben could easily inflict pain, for example, they weren't both homicidal. But Corinthia is. She is bold, calculating, cold-blooded, incredibly jealous, devious, and utterly devoid of regret, empathy, or guilt. But I need to point out that just because you're a psychopath doesn't automatically mean you are a killer. After all, studies have shown that a small percentage of CEOs display psychopathic characteristics."

Jenson smiled wryly and nodded his head. "Dr. George, would you say it is very easy for an untreated psychotic person to commit murder?"

"Objection," Patel demanded.

"Overruled. Continue with your line of questioning."

George frowned at the defense attorney and crossed her arms. "Yes," she said, "current research establishes that it is relatively easy for an untreated psychotic person to commit murder."

"How easy was it for the psychotic Corinthia personality, who you just testified controlled my client for much of his adulthood, to kill someone?" Jenson asked.

"She could kill someone just before lunch and then go make a sandwich ten minutes later, blood still covering her hands—something she confessed to me."

"Objection, Your Honor!" Patel again interjected.

"Overruled."

Jenson continued. "In your report, you said the Corinthia personality was willing to take risks. What kind of risks, specifically?"

"Huge risks, like forcing Ben to hide out in a place where they could have been discovered. And she did it on purpose. She took great pains to make that so. According to the police I spoke with, she made Ben drive to an area where she knew it was unlikely for him to find victims that fit his particular proclivities—in an effort to manipulate him into . . ."

"Objection, Your Honor," Patel said, interrupting. "Hearsay. The witness cannot testify to what the police report reveals."

"Sustained."

"Doctor, in your professional opinion, Ben knew full well Corinthia was killing young women, didn't he?" Jenson asked.

"Definitely," George said.

"But because of his mental disorder, he was powerless to stop her, wasn't he?"

George shifted in her seat again. She played with the bangles on her wrist a moment before answering. The sound was the only one in the room until she spoke. "Yes."

"So he was powerless because he wasn't fully in control of himself?"

"Objection, Your Honor!" Patel said.

"Sustained. Rephrase."

Jenson continued. "My client could not have kept the Corinthia identity from killing young women—even if he wanted to, isn't that right?"

George cast another small glance at the prosecutor. She exhaled. "Yes."

"Please explain to the court, in your professional opinion, based upon your examination of my client, exactly why that is."

"The Corinthia personality, whom I have interviewed at length, has at many times throughout Ben's life been the dominant personality—even 'pretending' to be him, rather than the other way around. She acquiesced to her brother's desires to kidnap young women who bore a striking resemblance to her as a child because she wanted to kill them. Her sole goal was to snuff out life," George said. "Just as the real Corinthia did as a child. Indeed. On many occasions, as part of her tendency to manipulate, she appeared to beg Benjamin to stop kidnapping young women. She even showed remorse to some extent after their deaths, knowing full well he wouldn't stop abducting these girls, thereby giving her the continued opportunity to commit murder."

"And how do their personalities—their behaviors, if you will—differ, Dr. George?"

"In addition to what I said earlier, Corinthia hates criticism, craves attention, and is boisterous, narcissistic, controlling, entitled, malicious, and cruel. She enjoyed arguing with Ben, taunting and belittling him. Ben, on the other hand, is more timid, submissive, easily manipulated, and, toward his sister, more generous."

"How so?"

"He let her lead. She made many of the decisions in their lives—where to live, where to shop, what to eat—even where to hide from the authorities. He lent her his voice, which became a kind of high falsetto when he spoke as her. So distinctive are their personalities that people overhearing them thought there were two people talking to or bickering with one another."

"Objection, Your Honor. Speculation."

"Sustained. Strike from the record and continue."

Jenson honed in on that point. "Did the Corinthia personality that had control over my client live for the thrill of the kill?"

George shrugged. "You could say that in many ways, the childlike behavior Ben witnessed from the real Corinthia toward murder never changed in the alternative personality. It never wavered from the impulses she had when she was seven—when she and her brother spent a summer trying to kill small animals."

"Objection, Your Honor," Patel said.

"On what grounds?" the judge asked.

"Speculation. That was not in the report."

"Sustained."

"Let me put that another way," Jenson said. "The defendant told you his early childhood behavior included killing animals, didn't he?"

"Yes."

"It's true, isn't it, Dr. George, that you don't believe Benjamin Zanetti is responsible for the deaths of these women?"

"No, I do not."

"Objection, Your Honor. Speculation," Patel said.

"Overruled."

"Who do you think killed these women?"

"The personality who calls herself Corinthia," George said.

"No more questions, Your Honor," Jenson said.

"Redirect?" the judge asked the prosecutor.

A determined Patel stood, ran her hand over her wavy brown hair, and approached George in the witness box.

With her palms folded in front of her, she said, "Dr. George, in your professional opinion, is the person physically responsible for the kidnapping and murdering of coeds in this case in this room?"

"Yes."

"Can you point to that person?"

George pointed to Ben. The judge said, "Let the record show the witness pointed to the defendant."

"No further questions, Your Honor," Patel said.

The judge banged her gavel. "Are you going to have any further witnesses?"

"Yes, Your Honor. Fiona Kessler."

"All right," Judge Murphy said. "We will adjourn until Monday morning at 9:00 a.m."

The bailiff shouted, "All rise."

The judge left and people began to mill about.

A tall, aging bailiff placed Ben in handcuffs again and led him from the courtroom.

CHAPTER TWENTY-FIVE

B en's weekend in solitary confinement tick-tocked slowly, the seconds advancing like drops of water. But by Monday morning, back in the courthouse, his impatience was even worse. His face was bright pink and his mouth had become dry from talking so much. Still, he couldn't think straight.

The last time he'd seen Fiona, she had sprinted away from him out the door of his home and into the falling snow. It was all he could think about. He was having a hard time concentrating on the matter at hand: his own testimony.

Two hours had passed, and he was still sitting across from his lawyer at a square table in a tiny room arguing about whether he should take the stand.

While Jenson was against it, Ben's mind was made up.

"Look," Ben said, leaning forward, "lots of defendants take the stand. The Menendez brothers did in their defense. They pleaded guilty by reason of insanity, too."

Jenson raised an eyebrow. "No, they pleaded self-defense, and they were both found guilty of first-degree murder and conspiracy. Ben, that was so long ago and under completely different circumstances and, not to mention, in a different jurisdiction."

Ben's hands shook and his pulse quickened. He crinkled his brow, his gaze steady. "All I know is if I don't take the stand, I can't tell my side," he said, sitting back. "I can't make the jury see how this has destroyed my whole life. I just want to have my say."

Jenson nodded. "I understand that, and while you are on the witness list, I need you to understand something. If you do this, the cross-examination will be brutal. Patel's not all that savvy, but she's still good. You also have to tell the truth—all of it, in its entirety."

"Of course. I don't want to have any regrets."

"Anything can happen once you take the stand. You know that, right? What if your sister makes an appearance?"

"Even better!" Ben said.

Jenson was dubious. He looked into Ben's eyes. "How is that better?"

"Because Corinthia knows I'm innocent!"

His attorney paused. "What if she implicates you in other crimes, Ben? Other illegal activity you don't know about?"

"I'm willing to take my chances," Ben answered. He ran his hands over his clean-shaven face and through his short, cropped hair. He was un-shackled, but a guard stood nearby.

Jenson sighed and looked at his Patek Philippe watch. "Let's get you pre-pared."

"Your Honor, the prosecution calls Fiona Kessler."

Patel stood and all heads swiveled toward the college coed. She made her way down the aisle and toward the stand.

Fiona was wearing a pale yellow scoop-necked blouse beneath a camel-colored pantsuit; her long blond hair cascaded across her shoulders and flowed down her back, kissing her heart-shaped derriere. On her feet were tan Tory Burch ballerina flats. After she was sworn in, she fixed her gaze out toward the packed courtroom, refusing to make eye contact with Ben.

Ben was very still, sitting up straight, prepared to hang on her every word. His eyes never left her face when she cleared her throat and was sworn in.

"You may be seated," the judge murmured.

"Miss Kessler," the prosecution began, "can you tell us how you first en-countered the defendant?"

Ben gawked at Fiona and ran his tongue over his lips. He clenched and unclenched his sweaty fists.

"I . . . he helped me up after I'd fallen on my way home from Dukes on Halloween," she said, her voice a hair above a whisper.

"Miss Kessler, please speak up," the judge said. "Use the microphone," she said, pointing to the mic affixed to the edge of the witness box.

Fiona pulled the thin metal mic toward her. She cleared her throat. "I'd fallen in the street on my way back to my dorm last Halloween and he helped me up and offered to drive me home."

"And did you agree?"

She nodded. "Yeah, I . . . yes," she stammered. "He was nice at first. But he seemed odd so I changed my mind." She paused and took a deep breath.

"Take your time," Patel said, her voice gentle.

Fiona continued. "When he grabbed me by my elbow and started dragging me to his car, I knew something was . . . off."

Fiona locked eyes with Ben then. When he smiled at her, she dissolved into tears.

"I . . . I can't do this," she whispered. "Dad?" She turned her head, her eyes searching the gallery for her father.

In the back of the courtroom, her father stood, uncertain what to do next. He remained rooted to the spot.

Fiona began to dry heave before she began trembling. Her pink lips quivered and her face crumpled. Tears slid down both cheeks. She gasped for breath and began to sob.

Patel spoke up. "Your Honor. If it pleases the court, may we have a brief recess?"

Fiona turned toward the judge. "I can't do this," she implored, her eyes never leaving the judge's face.

Judge Murphy nodded. "You don't have to," she told Fiona.

"Counselors, I believe we have Miss Kessler's deposition. We can read that into the record." Both lawyers nodded. "Let the record reflect their assent." She turned toward the jury.

"Jurors, Miss Kessler has been previously deposed and a transcript of her deposition will be read into the record."

"Miss Kessler, you are dismissed," the judge told her. "You may step down."

Ben watched Fiona run into her father's arms.

"Ms. Patel, you may call your next witness."

"We have no further witnesses, Your Honor," Patel said. "The People rest."

"In that case, Mr. Jenson, you may call your first witness."

Jenson mopped his brow with a light gray handkerchief he removed from the breast pocket of his dark gray suit. It was now mid-June and a heat wave had gripped the Valley. Despite the air-conditioning, the wood-paneled courtroom was stifling. Everyone—from the judge, attorneys, and bailiffs to those in the gallery—seemed to be covered in a fine sheen of perspiration.

Jenson exhaled, flipped his tie away from his shirt, and whispered something to Ben before placing his hand on his client's right shoulder and squeezing it. Jenson stared for a moment at his dark blue wing tips. Then he stood and in a clear, loud voice said:

"Your Honor, the defense calls Benjamin Zanetti to the stand."

Murmuring in the courtroom grew louder when Ben stepped into the witness box and stood in front of the state's furled navy blue flag before taking his seat.

Dressed in a white blouse and dark slacks beneath her black robes, the judge banged her gavel and silence resumed. She brushed a strand of gray hair back into her damp bun and cleared her throat. For the first time, Ben could see the courtroom watchers who had been sitting behind him for weeks. He held his breath for a moment. There were at least two hundred and fifty people in the large gallery, including the marshals and bailiffs that ringed the walls. Many people, male and female, sat fanning themselves in the oppressive heat. Ben could feel sweat dripping down his back, no doubt staining the back of his light blue button-down shirt.

"Mr. Zanetti, you understand that you're a defendant in this case?" the judge asked.

"Yes," Ben said, turning to face her. He wiped his palms across the front of his black dress pants.

"You understand that it is the government's burden to prove the charges against you beyond a reasonable doubt?"

"Yes," he said, folding his hands in front of him. Ben glanced up at her. She seemed to be sizing him up over her glasses.

"You understand that you do not have to testify in this case?"

Ben nodded and said yes.

"You understand that if you choose to testify, what you say can and will be used against you?"

Ben responded he did.

"You're aware that you're going to be cross-examined?"

"Yes."

"But you've agreed to take the stand?"

Ben swallowed. "Yes, ma'am."

"And you've had an opportunity to consult with your lawyer and you still want to take the stand?"

He nodded again and adjusted his glasses. "Yes, Your Honor."

"OK, well, I'm going to put you under oath, and you understand you're going to have to tell the truth?"

Ben said yes, and the judge swore him in. She then addressed Jenson. "You can begin questioning your witness."

Ben took his seat in the witness box. His heart was hammering so hard beneath his shirt he was sure everyone in the courtroom could see it.

Jenson stood and addressed his client. "Ben, are you medicated right now?"

Ben swallowed and nodded his head yes. He took a tissue from his pocket and began twisting it in his hands. He was trying to remember what to say and how, just as they had practiced. His voice faltered as he stared at his attorney.

"Yes. I'm taking antidepressants, antipsychotics, and mood stabilizers. They—it's helped me be more in control of myself."

"What else are the doctors doing for you?"

"I'm also undergoing electroconvulsive therapy and psychotherapy for depression and my . . . my psychoses."

"Benjamin, can you tell us what they are, exactly?"

Ben looked out over the gallery. Some jurors shifted in their seats while others jotted down notes. He was trying to focus on what he and Jenson had rehearsed. He repeated what his lawyer told him to say: "The doctors tell me I have Dissociative Identity Disorder, paranoid schizophrenia, and I have sociopathic tendencies. I also have a borderline personality disorder." He stammered, "I . . . I did not know any of that before."

"Ben, how did your sister die?"

Ben sat very still on the witness stand. He mopped his forehead with the tissue, closed his eyes for a moment, and opened them.

"We were playing in our yard in our tree house. But before that we'd been . . . killing things, animals, all summer. She wanted to see if they'd come back."

"Come back?"

"To life," Ben said. "She didn't believe they were really dead."

"Why didn't Corinthia believe they were dead? Why did you do this?"

Ben swallowed hard and whispered, "Because of my father."

"Mr. Zanetti, speak up, please," the judge said.

Ben leaned in toward the microphone atop the witness stand.

"My father," he said so loud the microphone crackled. "He killed someone in front of us when we were seven. We helped him get rid of the body."

"Objection, Your Honor," the prosecutor said.

The judge sat up and looked down her glasses at the lawyers. "Overruled."

"Thank you, Your Honor," Jenson said. "Ben, can you tell us what happened?"

Ben cleared his throat. "When my sister and I were seven, we watched our father beat someone named Lenny to death with a pipe. It was after Lenny admitted he didn't have Daddy's money. I had never seen so much blood," Ben said, his voice shaking. "We helped him wrap the body in an old piece of tarp."

"Ben, what happened after your father beat a man to death in front of you when you were just a child, a second grader?"

"Objection, Your Honor!"

"Overruled."

Ben continued. "I remember being scared. My sister and I helped our father drag the body out to the Schuylkill River. We watched him push it into the water. Only, Corinthia didn't believe Lenny was dead."

"Your Honor, will you permit me to approach the witness with exhibit 257c? It is a newspaper clipping from the year Mr. Zanetti was seven years old, detailing the discovery of a body found floating in the river near Boathouse Row in Philadelphia."

"Proceed."

The lawyer approached Ben and handed him the article.

"Ben, can you please read the portions that have been underlined?".

Ben looked down at the paper and read the headline first, "'Body Found in Schuylkill Identified. Police have identified a badly decomposed body near Boathouse Row along Kelly Drive as that of Leonardo Bianchi. The medical examiner revealed the cause of death was severe trauma to the head.'"

"Does that sound familiar?"

Ben nodded. "Yeah, we talked about it after seeing it on TV. Corinthia didn't think it was him. She thought he came back to life and swam away. But I knew better."

"Why?"

Ben licked his lips. "I knew he was dead because Daddy threatened to kill me that night if I told anybody we saw him kill someone."

"Objection. Hearsay, Your Honor."

"Overruled."

"Ben, have you ever told anyone this?"

Ben shook his head. "No. Not until today."

"And then what, Ben?"

"Objection, Your Honor," Patel said. "Mr. Jenson is leading the witness."

"Sustained."

Jenson smiled. He nodded at Ben, their signal to take a deep breath before answering the next question.

"What happened later that summer after you and your twin sister, Corinthia, saw your father kill a man and forced you to help him get rid of the body?"

Ben sat up straighter. He reached up to his left earlobe and adjusted the spectacles on his face.

"Corinthia and I killed a lot of small animals—but none of them came back to life. So she wanted us to kill something bigger, something . . . human."

"Who did she want you to kill, Benji?"

"Luke," Ben said, sniffling. "She wanted us to kill our little brother, Luke."

"And did you kill your brother Luke?"

"Objection, Your Honor, the defendant is not on trial for killing his brother."

"Overruled. The defendant can answer the question."

"No!" he shouted into the crackling microphone. "I stopped her. I had . . . to stop her," he stammered. "She tried to get Luke to climb into the tree house so she could push him out. But I said no. The two of us were high up in the tree and she was hanging upside down from a branch. I jumped up and down on the branch she was hanging on. I jumped on it hard and . . . and she fell."

Tears stinging his eyes, Ben wept in the silent courtroom.

"What happened next, Ben?" Jenson softly asked.

Ben's voice cracked. "She broke her neck and she died."

"What did you and your family tell the police after that?"

"Nothing." He sniffed. "We didn't call the police. Daddy wouldn't let us. She was dead anyway. Momma screamed and begged him to let us call them—anyone—for help. But he said no. He just . . . beat me. My mother, well, she was never the same."

"Benjamin, what happened after your sister died in that tragic accident?"

"My parents argued for hours, and then they waited until the middle of the night and they buried my sister in our backyard." Ben sniffed then and began trembling, tears rolling down his cheeks. "Momma made me contrite."

"Contrite?" his lawyer asked. "Can you tell us what that means, exactly?"

"It was her way of saying I had to repent," Ben explained. "She said I took her little girl away so I had to give her a little girl back." His voice went up a bit. "So, I . . . became Corinthia."

"Became Corinthia? How?"

"I had to pray for forgiveness and wear Corinthia's clothes. I had to wear her shoes. At first, my mother only made me dress up like Corinthia when Daddy wasn't home. And then it was all the time. They didn't want anyone to know Corinthia was dead. My mother didn't know about Lenny, and I found out later my father was afraid I'd tell the police I'd seen him kill someone. And it was easy for us to keep Corinthia's death a secret. We never saw family or anyone else and our mother homeschooled us. We weren't allowed to play outside anymore. So I wore her clothes to church and to the mall until my mother stopped letting me go out." He sniffled.

"My parents argued a lot. Daddy ignored us—both of us—my mother and me. He would stay gone for days. He just . . . gave up and he let her do that to me." Ben swallowed, his voice breaking. He wiped his silent tears on the back of his sleeve.

"She wouldn't let me cut my hair, and when I got older, she shaved my face and made me wear bras and panties and dresses. Always dresses. Dad got mad, and one day he left with Luke."

Ben was silent for a moment. "He just . . . left me there. With her, alone."

Jenson paused. "Ben, when did you start talking to Corinthia?"

Ben squirmed in his seat. "The day she died."

"Were you ever aware that when you were speaking for her, you were, in fact, talking to yourself?"

"Sometimes at first." He shook his head from side to side. "But not all the time, no."

"Did you think that odd, Ben?"

"No. You have to understand. We talked all the time. We did everything together. We were inseparable. We slept in the same room—even in the same crib when we were babies. My mother said as an infant I would curl my fingers in her hair to soothe myself when I was troubled or unhappy. She . . . I loved my sister, and I was devastated by her death. More than my mother—more than anyone else." He sat up straighter. His eyes brimmed with tears. "I loved her best. I couldn't be apart from her, and I guess, me being sick the way I am, talking to her helped me be . . . close to her."

Ben cast a sideways glance at the jurors. He ran his tongue over his dry lips again. When he saw one of the jurors pull out a tissue and dab at her eyes, he used his tissue to wipe his, too.

Patel jotted notes.

"Ben, did you know that your sister was dead?" Jenson continued in his deep booming voice.

"Of course."

"Did you know she wasn't really there?"

"Yes."

"Were you pretending that she was there?"

Ben gave his lawyer a quizzical look. Then he remembered what Jenson told him to say the day before.

"Pretending? No. It doesn't work like that," he scoffed. "Sometimes I am me and sometimes I am her. Sometimes we argue with one another."

"Ben, were there times when you were not yourself, but Corinthia took over?"

"Objection, Your Honor. Leading."

"Sustained."

"I'll rephrase that question, Your Honor. Ben, who were you during those times when you were not yourself?"

"Corinthia."

"Was that a regular occurrence?"

"It was often. Yes."

"What was the longest length of time you were not yourself?"

"Four years," he said, his voice faint. "One day I woke up and it was four years later."

"Benjamin, are you yourself today?"

Ben gave him a small smile. "Yes. I am."

"Ben, did you kill any of these women?"

"No. I did not," he said in a bold voice, furrowing his brow. "My alternative personality, Corinthia, killed them."

"He's such a liar," someone in the gallery said a little too loudly. The judge banged her gavel.

"This is a dignified place. Please refrain from outbursts like that."

"Thank you, Benjamin. Nothing further." Jenson sat down.

"Cross-examination, Ms. Patel?" the judge asked.

"Yes, Your Honor, but perhaps we could break for lunch?"

"Good idea. We're adjourned for an hour, ladies and gentlemen."

A little more than an hour later, Patel stood in front of Ben. She was dressed today in pointy black Balenciaga heels and a black Elie Tahari pencil skirt suit over a white satin blouse with a lavalier cravat.

"Hello, Mr. Zanetti." She smiled at him. "How are you today?"

Ben grinned back. "I'm fine, Ms. Patel. You can call me Ben. That's a lovely perfume you're wearing, by the way. But you really should try a fruitier scent. It would suit you."

Patel's laugh was dry. "Ben," the prosecutor began. "May I call you Ben? Or should I call you Corinthia?" She smiled.

He frowned and shook his head no. "It's Ben."

"Ben," she said, her voice growing chillier. "The entire time you were murdering people—you were just pretending to be Corinthia, weren't you?"

Jenson shot up from his chair. "Objection, Your Honor! The defendant has already stated he wasn't pretending."

"Sustained."

"Ben, why did you kill these women?"

"I did not kill them. Someone else did."

"Someone else?"

"My sister, Corinthia, killed them."

"Your sister. The one whose body was found . . ."

"You sick, lying son of a bitch!" a muscular young man screamed before Patel could finish. Stunning everyone, the man sprang from his seat behind Jenson, jumped over the low wooden railing and lunged toward Ben in an attempt to drag him from the witness box. The judge scooted back away from the commotion. Five bailiffs tackled the assailant and wrestled the man to the ground.

Ben sat astonished while authorities pushed the man's cheek to the floor.

"Stay down! Don't resist," an officer yelled. "Put your hands behind your back! Don't fight us. Calm down!"

"It's not right!" the man kept shouting. Officers cuffed him and dragged him to his feet. "All I need is two minutes alone with you, you heartless bastard!" he screamed at Ben. "You killed my sister, you sorry son of a bitch, and you're sitting up there, smiling, flirting, and pretending like you didn't do it!"

People in the gallery applauded.

"Order in the court! Bailiffs, remove that man. We will have order in my courtroom!" the judge screeched. Bailiffs picked up chairs and righted tables.

"Well, your sister's not dead, is she, lady?" the muscular man tossed over his shoulder as authorities led him out. The judge banged her gavel.

"Ladies and gentlemen. We're adjourning for today. We'll resume tomorrow."

"All rise," a bailiff said. Those seated stood. The judge left the courtroom from a door just behind her chair. Ben's attorney approached him as he was being handcuffed and taken back into custody.

"You OK?"

Ben nodded. "What now?"

"We come back at it tomorrow. Don't worry. You did good."

When deputies led him into the hallway, Ben glanced down a corridor and glimpsed Patel. She was rushing past a band of reporters who had descended on her with microphones and digital recorders, shouting questions. Her head down, she ignored them. Her steps were brisk, her high heels clicking against the marble floor so fast it sounded like she was tap-dancing.

"Come on, Zanetti," a bailiff said, pushing him toward an exit. Two officers led him out a side door to a waiting inmate transport van.

CHAPTER TWENTY-SIX

Back inside his six-by-eight-foot concrete jail cell, Ben paced in the tight space that included a shiny metal toilet and sink. Against one corner was a small table and a stool. The heavy door, painted white, had a small window. Beneath that was a slot where guards could pass trays of food. Today, the room, which saw few inmates because crime was so low in the Valley, reeked faintly of lemon pine cleaner.

Hours earlier, Ben had flipped through paperwork detailing his defense strategy. But he couldn't concentrate. The bed was secured to the wall by bolts. Hey lay across the narrow mattress and stared up at the ceiling.

His heart was racing so fast he could scarcely breathe. He closed his eyes. Ben had never had anyone come for him like that man in the courtroom did—not even while he was in a psych ward at Harrisburg Hospital. He'd been moved to the Laurel County Jail until the end of his trial. If they found him guilty, Ben would likely spend the rest of his life at Graterford Prison, just outside Philadelphia.

"Corinthia," he whispered. "What have I done?"

She whispered back. "You know exactly what you did! I told you to stop."

Ben's eyes snapped open in the empty cell. "You're not leaving me, are you?" he whispered, his voice fearful.

"I haven't so far, have I, even though I'm all in your head?" he heard Corinthia whisper.

"You killed those girls, Benji."

"I didn't," he whispered.

"You did. Just like you killed me."

"That was an accident."

"Was it?"

Ben crawled out of the bed and sank to the hard concrete floor, where he curled into a fetal position. He put his hands over his ears and, in silence, began swaying. Over and over, he whispered to himself, "Our Father which art in heaven, hallowed be thy name . . ."

Much later, he heard someone else call his name from the other side of the door.

"Zanetti! If you don't eat and take these pills now, you won't get anything till morning!"

Ben was quiet, still. In his mind, he could see Corinthia falling through leaves.

"Suit yourself!" the guard said, snatching his dinner tray back through a slot in the heavy steel door. Hours passed. He could hear guards speaking in low whispers.

"Look at him," one said before asking if Ben was on suicide watch. Another guard answered no.

Ben didn't move at first. Then he began to rock again.

"I am not a killer. I'm not," he whimpered.

Corinthia whispered in his ear. "Oh yes, you are, Ben. Yes, you are!"

When he moaned, he heard her tell him, "But I forgive you, little brother. I don't know if they will."

Night came and the overheard florescent lights went out, pitching the cell into darkness. Ben's eyes were wide open. His mind had gone blank.

Well after the lights were back on, a just-woken Ben heard Jenson admonishing a guard on the other side of his cell door. "How long has he been like this?"

"Twelve hours? Ben! Get up! Get dressed! We're due in court soon!"

A groggy Ben could hear keys jingling and the door being wrenched open. Jenson, dressed today in a bespoke black suit and tie and white dress shirt, crouched on the floor next to him.

"Ben. Can you hear me?"

"Yeah," Ben said, staring at Jenson's expensive dark loafers.

"You have to get up! Get dressed. For Pete's sake," Jenson yelled. "Have you taken your medication?" Ben sat up and winced when he stood. The side he had slept on was tender, sore.

"No."

"Come on," Jenson said. "Snap out of it! Stand up. That's right."

A guard pressed a small paper cup with three pills into Ben's hand.

Jenson handed him another small cup of water.

Ben tossed his head back and washed the medication down.

"You'll just have to wear what you had on yesterday. Hurry up, let's go!" Jenson yelled to the guards once a rumpled Ben was ready.

A transport van was idling when the pair walked outside, but the few swallows of fresh air seemed to revive Ben. "Where are we going again?"

"To court," the guard said. "Your lawyer will meet us there."

While they stood at the side entrance to the courtroom ten minutes later, Jenson pressed a bagel into Ben's hand.

"We've got a few minutes. Eat this and sip some of this coffee." Jenson then pressed the fake eyeglasses into Ben's hands. "Put these on."

Ben put on the glasses, wolfed down the bagel, and took three large sips of the lukewarm coffee. He shuddered. Like clockwork, his skin began to crawl. It always did just before the meds kicked in.

"They're going to find you guilty, little brother." He flinched.

"You OK?" Jenson frowned at him.

Ben smiled and nodded. "Sure."

But he heard her voice again. "You're going away forever."

When the doors opened, Ben's attorney put his hand on his shoulder and pushed him toward his seat at the defense table. They spoke briefly before Ben was ushered back to the witness box and sworn in. Gazing out over the gallery, Ben was surprised by the increased police presence in the room. Several state police officers were now sitting on the front row.

All were armed.

"Let me be clear," said the judge. "What occurred yesterday cannot happen again. I understand your frustrations," she told the packed courtroom. "But you will not behave like that. This is a court of law, and we will have order. You will be quiet, or I will clear these proceedings and charge any troublemakers with contempt. That means you will go to jail."

Not a peep was uttered.

Judge Murphy turned to Patel. "Now, counselor, continue your cross."

Patel nodded and stood before the defendant. She folded her arms in front of her chocolate-brown pantsuit. Beneath it, she sported a black satin blouse and brown patent-leather Prada pumps. Her hair had been swept into a bun at the base of her neck. Two tendrils hung on either side of her round tan face. Fastened to her ears was a pair of tiny pearl studs.

Ben inhaled. Her perfume today was an intoxicating strawberry scent—his favorite. She pursed her lips together for a moment before speaking.

"Ben," she said, staring him in the eye, "you testified yesterday that you did not kill these women. That the alternative personality doctors identify as Corinthia committed these heinous crimes and you were, what? Just a bystander?"

Ben responded, his voice flat, "I was not fully in control of myself, no."

"What were you then?" she asked, her voice dripping with sarcasm. "Asleep?"

"Yes!" Ben exclaimed. "Exactly! It's like being asleep. I had no knowledge whatsoever of what Corinthia had done . . . When I did, I begged her to stop."

"Why didn't you ever call for help?"

"I . . . it never occurred to me to call the police, um, on myself or my sister. But Fiona counseled me more than once—and she's becoming a therapist."

"I see. Ben, do you feel guilty?"

"Objection!"

"Overruled. Defendant may answer the question."

"Why would I feel guilty?"

Patel smirked. "Because more than a dozen women were murdered, Ben. Even if, under your theory, someone else did it and you knew about it, at the very least that's conspiracy to commit murder."

He sighed into the microphone in front of him. "Again, I didn't kill anyone."

Jenson objected. "Your Honor, my client isn't on trial for conspiracy."

"Sustained. Strike the question and answer from the record."

Patel continued. "Mr. Zanetti, most people who witness violent crimes try to stop them—call for help. You did neither. You harbor no guilt for crimes you knew were committed. That's because you did it, Ben, and you're going away for life. You might as well tell the truth! We all know you killed these women! Will you stop placing the blame on your dead sister?"

"Objection!" Jenson roared. "This is witness harassment."

The judge gripped her gavel. "Overruled. Mr. Zanetti, answer the question."

Ben leveled his gaze at Patel. "I didn't do it! It wasn't me! Corinthia killed all of them!"

Patel put her hands on her hips and glowered at him. "Ben, don't you find blaming an 'alternative personality,'" she said, using air quotes, "as your defense is a little like saying the dog ate my homework? Or a ghost ate the cookies from the cookie jar?"

"It would be if it wasn't true."

"If you didn't kill these women, Mr. Zanetti," she asked, preparing to hammer on each point, "then why is your DNA all over every crime scene? On each and every victim? Why was it in the apartment in New Jersey? Why was your DNA the only DNA found all over Fiona Kessler? Why did Fiona state in her deposition that it was you who attacked her and Amanda Taylor? Why was the body of a long-dead little girl found in your duffel bag on the front seat of a stolen car you were apprehended in?"

Ben stared, and in a soft voice said, "I . . . because I was there."

She sneered at him. "You were there, all right! You were there because you killed these women, Ben! You killed them because you wanted to—not because some fake personality led you to do it! Or pretended to be you while you did it! Just admit it!"

Jenson rose. "Objection, Your Honor! Counsel continues to badger the witness!"

"Overruled."

"Ben, it was you who beat Amanda Taylor at your grandmother's house, wasn't it?"

"Yes, I did. But I am very sorry for that."

"Why did you attack Amanda?"

"Because she was trying to take away Fiona—my special Corinthia."

"Your 'special' Corinthia?"

"Yes. They were all special. It was the only way we could be together."

"The only way you and who could be together?"

"Me and my sister. Physically." He took a deep breath and struggled to remember Jenson's counsel. "I needed to be able to hold Corinthia, to touch her, to run my fingers through her hair like I did when we were kids. I know it sounds . . . odd, but it's what I needed." His eyes were huge, his voice imploring.

Patel paused and grimaced. "That's funny, Ben, because wasn't Corinthia physically with you? After all, the police found her body in a duffel bag when they arrested you, didn't they?"

"It . . . yes, but it wasn't like that. She was alone and I didn't want her to be. I couldn't just leave her cold and by herself."

"You couldn't leave her where, Ben? Dead? Isn't it true you hauled your sister's corpse around because you felt guilty about killing her?"

"No! It was an accident."

"An accident, yes, that's right." She regarded him with contempt and disbelief. "So, if she died when she was seven, how is it now that you're blaming her for killing these women, when your DNA was the only one left at each crime scene?"

Ben glared at her. In the muggy courtroom, he could feel his blood pressure rising. His face grew flush, his palms sweaty. He used the light blue handkerchief his lawyer had given him to mop his brow. His mouth was dry. He swallowed and took a deep breath.

"Corinthia is dead, but my alternative personality, which bears the same name, is very much alive," he said, slowing to enunciate each word. "In my mind, Corinthia was there. I could talk to her. Have conversations with her. It's hard to explain. I could . . . feel her hugs, her kisses—even her breath on the back of my neck. But over time, she wouldn't always let me touch her. And I needed to . . . feel her in a way I could with those girls. They were my special versions of Corinthia. I would never have killed them! I never even had sex with them because I treated each of them as if they were my own sister!"

He knitted his brow, trying to appeal to the jurors with his gaze.

"I wanted to keep them alive, and I fought for that! Every day I fought for that. It was Corinthia who did all those other things."

"All of those 'other things'?" The prosecutor repeated, giving him a dirty look. "Did she make you strip those women and fondle them?"

Ben exploded. "What? No! I was not fondling them! It . . . I just told you it wasn't sexual." Ben's voice rose. "I just wanted them to be the way I remembered my sister. Soft, warm, beautiful, alive."

"She just made you kill those women then, right?"

"I didn't kill them!" he yelled. "Corinthia did it to protect me, to protect us!

"We fought all the time about her killing them! She begged me not to bring them home because she knew we'd get in trouble if anyone found out I'd taken them. If you don't believe me, just remember Fiona was there. She knows that because she heard us. Corinthia was the one who killed them!"

"But Fiona's sworn testimony also shows Corinthia enjoyed killing them," said Patel.

Ben swallowed. "She did. I . . . she's sick," he said, his voice soft, pleading. "She needs help."

"She needs help," Patel repeated, emphasizing the word "she." Then the prosecutor sneered. "But Corinthia wasn't there, Ben, you yourself just said so. You just now testified that you needed these other women to be there because Corinthia wasn't real, and you knew Corinthia wasn't real, and you knew if you didn't kill these women, they would tell everyone that it was you who kidnapped them and molested them. And held them against their will. Isn't that the truth?"

"Objection! Asked and answered."

"Sustained."

Patel paused to sweep her eyes over the jury box.

"Ben, where is Amanda Taylor?"

It was so quiet in the courtroom Ben could only hear his ragged breathing. "I don't know."

"When was the last time you saw her?"

Ben sat up and ran his hands over his face. He then fidgeted and straightened his tie. "In New Jersey, before Corinthia said we should put her in the trunk."

"Ben, there was no evidence, not one trace, that Amanda Taylor had ever been in the trunk of the car you were apprehended in. Are you lying?"

"No! Corinthia suggested it. I don't know what happened after that."

The prosecutor changed tactics. "Ben, when your father left your mother, what happened to Luke?"

"He . . . he took Luke with him."

"And when was that?"

"When I was twelve."

"Sure you didn't kill him, too?"

"Objection, Your Honor!"

"Sustained. Counselor, stay on point."

"Yes, Your Honor," Patel said, turning back to Ben. "Isn't it true that you're a murdering psychopath who killed Tallulah Montgomery, Amelia Marks, Julia Byrne, Bethany Jamieson . . ."

One by one Patel named each victim and each time Ben shook his head no.

"You put your hands around each of their throats and strangled them. You tortured, stabbed, and killed all of these young women with your bare hands, didn't you, Ben?" she shouted. "You're not even sorry, are you? Are you!"

"Objection! Your Honor?" Jenson stood and gave the judge an incredulous look.

"Sustained. Counselor," the judge told Patel, "do not forget this is a court of law. Proceed in a reasonable tone, and do not badger. The defendant may answer the question."

From his seat in the witness box, Ben began trembling. The sweat under his arms stained his rumpled shirt. He placed his hands on either side of his head and stared at the floor.

"No," he said, trying to mask his rising panic. "I am not sorry because I did not kill anyone!"

Her hands crossed behind her back, Patel shook her head from side to side. A derisive laugh fell from her lips. "In addition to the dozen women you're on trial for murdering, you killed your twin sister, Corinthia, too, didn't you, Ben?"

His left leg began to shake up and down. "I did not kill my sister! I was seven years old. It was an accident."

"You told this court earlier Corinthia was going to kill your four-year-old brother. You couldn't let her murder little Luke, could you? So you jumped up and down on that branch on purpose, knowing she would fall. Knowing it would kill her. You killed her on purpose, didn't you, Ben?"

"Objection!"

"Overruled."

The room was silent while they waited for Ben to answer.

But Ben could no longer hear them. What he did hear was a faint yet familiar ringing in his ears. His vision blurred and his heart sank. Bile rose in his throat and what little control he had slipped away. He blinked several times and his whole body began tiny convulsions, like he was very cold in the broiling courtroom. He closed his eyes. With his left hand trembling, he built a small visor over his brow by holding his forehead between his thumb and index finger, which he squeezed very hard before bowing his head toward his feet.

Then he opened his eyes.

Good Lord, Corinthia thought. These shoes are hideous!

When the witness spoke, the voice that erupted in anger was at a much higher octave. "Yes, God help me. I did it. I killed all of those girls!"

There was a collective, sharp intake of breath from several people in the gallery and in the jurors' box.

Jenson stood up, feigning alarm. "Objection! Your Honor! We need a brief recess."

"On what grounds?" The judge said.

Corinthia interrupted in a loud voice, "Because Benji's lawyer doesn't want me to say anything bad about his precious client." She crossed her legs and studied her fingernails. "Ugh," she scowled. "I'm in desperate need of a manicure. And clearly a better wardrobe. What the hell have you people let him dress me in?"

Both lawyers and the judge looked at Ben in surprise. So, too, did jurors. Menace was etched in Patel's voice. "Will you state your full name for the record?"

"Objection, Your Honor! Counsel knows full well who's on the stand!"

"No, Your Honor. I'm not sure I do."

The judge frowned at the defendant and studied him closely for a few moments.

"I'll allow it."

Patel repeated the question. Ben blinked several times and shook his head from side to side, like he was clearing cobwebs from his thoughts. He yawned wide and sneered before smiling. "My name is . . ." His normal speaking voice faltered for a moment, but a split second later he resumed the loud falsetto. "Corrrrrinthia Zanetti, and I promise to tell the truth and nothing but the truth, so help me God!" she yelled, yanking off the eyeglasses. "Because I want you all to know that I killed every single last one of them because I had to. Ben left me no choice."

Her voice was confident.

"Objection, Your Honor," Jenson said without enthusiasm. "Corinthia is not on any witness list. Again, I request a recess."

"Oh, yes she is!" Patel interrupted him and held up a sheet of paper.

"Overruled." The judge raised her hand to stop the bickering. Both lawyers fell silent.

"The court has held an in-camera hearing concerning Mr. Zanetti's testimony," the judge began. "Or have you both forgotten? Although Mr. Zanetti has been deemed mentally fit to stand trial, due to the nature of his condition, I'm going to give the jury a limiting instruction regarding the remainder of his testimony," she said, while Corinthia ran both hands down her shirt before crossing her arms.

Judge Murphy addressed the jurors. "The law allows that even if a mentally ill person is under guardianship or under compulsory hospitalization, it does not mean he cannot testify on his own behalf under certain circumstances. The law relates to the mentally ill the exact same way it does to individuals who have a disability. Mr. Zanetti has a right to have his say in court."

The judge pushed her glasses up her nose. "Further, the court, accordingly, has taken into account the possibility that Mr. Zanetti's alternative personality might appear on the witness stand, which she has. Consequently, I am advising the jury that it is up to them to discern whether anything the defendant says is intentional." Then she nodded toward the lawyers.

"Your Honor, I reserve the right to cross-examine Corinthia Zanetti," Patel said.

"And," Jenson interjected, "for the potential to redirect."

"Agreed. In the interest of justice, I'll allow both."

Both attorneys nodded.

"Can you tell us," Patel began, "how you know Benjamin Zanetti?"

Corinthia cocked her head and gave the attorney a confused look. "Why, I'm Ben's big sister, Corinthia," she purred. Then she licked her lips and batted her eyelashes.

"Do you understand why you're here?"

She seemed contemplative at first, measuring her words carefully before waving a hand down in a feminine gesture. "Of course! Ben's on trial for murdering those poor girls." Her voice dripped with regret. "I begged him not to bring those girls home. I told him if he continued to, we'd get caught. Looks like we did," she sighed, gazing around the courtroom. "Guess I'll have to be honest and tell you the truth."

"What's the truth, Corinthia?"

"That I did it." Her tone was matter of fact. "I killed them; I didn't want to, but Ben wouldn't listen." She stared at the floor. Before Patel could ask another question, Corinthia looked up and posed one of her own.

"I don't remember all of their names. How many girls did you say there were?"

"Twelve women," Patel answered. "Fourteen, if you include his sister and Jane Winters."

Corinthia sighed. "There's a whole lot more than that." She recrossed her legs.

"How many?"

"Objection!" Jenson said. "Failure to state or ask a question."

"I'll try again, Your Honor," Patel said. "Corinthia, how many more people did you kill?"

"I'm sure I don't know," Corinthia shrugged. "More than fourteen, that's for sure."

"Objection, Your Honor! Defendant is not on trial for killing additional women beyond those he has been charged with," Jenson argued.

"Sustained. Jury will disregard that answer. Miss Patel, you are skating on very thin ice."

Patel nodded. "My apologies, Your Honor," the prosecutor said, turning back toward the defendant.

"So you and your brother were responsible for the deaths of each of these women he has been charged with killing?"

"No," she said, biting her nails like she did when she was a child. "I am. Ben is not.

"He left me no other option. Killing them was the only way to keep us from getting caught."

"You expect this court to believe murder was your only solution?" Patel asked.

"Why, yes," Corinthia said, puzzled. "After all, it took you years to find him, didn't it? And at least one of them deserved it," she added. "Tallulah killed a little girl with her car last February."

Patel continued, unabated. "Ben," she asked, "are you confessing to these murders?"

"Please, don't call me that. My. Name. Is. Not. Ben," she said, clapping after each word. "It's Corinthia. That's C-O-R-I-N-T-H-I-A." She leaned toward the court stenographer. "Got that?"

There was faint chatter from courtroom watchers. Reporters wrote furiously in their notepads. Two of them leapt up and ran from the room. "Yeah, run and Tweet that!" Corinthia howled after them.

"Order in the court." The judge banged her gavel. "Mr. Zanetti—er, Miss Zanetti. Please refrain from any more outbursts," she scolded. "Limit your responses to questions only from the attorneys or myself."

"Of course, Your Honor," Corinthia said, pressing a hand to her throat as if clutching her pearls. "I know I hate being interrupted." She raised a hand to her hair and gasped. "Oh no!" she wailed. "He let you cut my hair?" Her eyes filled with tears.

Patel ignored her. "Corinthia, are you confessing to these crimes—yes or no?"

"Objection, Your Honor. Asked and answered."

"Sustained."

Corinthia raised both index fingers to the bridge of her nostrils and wiped out and upward. She brushed at her wet lashes with the sides of her fingers several times as if to keep her nonexistent mascara from running. She put the glasses back on.

"Let me make this clear," she sniffled, her eyes falling on the stone-faced jurors.

"I did it. I killed them." Her voice grew soft, remorseful. "But I also cannot lie. While it made me sick to my stomach sometimes, I enjoyed it. I'm just . . . wired that way. Ben knows that. And he knows that, toward the end, he realized that making me stop would have been almost as impossible as getting him to quit bringing them home."

"Why, Corinthia?" Patel asked. "Why did you kill them?"

She sucked her teeth. "You know what?" Corinthia continued, waving her hand dismissively. "What difference does it make, now? Whatever reason I give you won't satisfy or make any sense to you, anyway. It also won't bring any of those girls back."

"Corinthia, you killed Amanda too, didn't you?"

"Nope," she said, shifting in her seat.

"Did Ben?"

"Not that I know of."

"Where is she?"

Corinthia smiled, raised her chin and darted her eyes up to her left. "I have no idea."

"Ben said you put her in the trunk of a car."

"Did he?" Corinthia leaned forward, removed the glasses, and squinted at the prosecutor. She pressed her index fingers together. "How do you know he wasn't lying?"

"How do we know you're not lying?"

"How do you know Ben has been the one testifying all this time? Hmmm?" A tiny smile graced her lips.

When both attorneys looked at each other, Corinthia chuckled.

"Look, I've already confessed to killing a dozen or more people, genius. Why would I lie about one more? The last time I saw Amanda was in New Jersey. And she was very much alive."

Corinthia held the back of one hand up to the side of her mouth before whispering into the microphone. "Ben tortured her, though."

Ben's deep voice returned, but with a childlike inflection: "Corinthia! Shut up! What are you doing? You promised you'd never tell!"

The Corinthia voice resumed: "Did I?"

Ben: "Shut up or we'll go to jail forever!"

Corinthia: "No, you shut up! You let them cut my hair!"

The judge banged her gavel and shouted for order, but the fierce bickering continued unabated.

Ben: "That's not fair! You're hurting my feelings! You know I don't have any control over anything!"

Corinthia: "Always with the excuses! You make me sick, Benji!"

Ben: "Go see a damn doctor!"

Corinthia: "I will! And while I'm at it, I'll schedule an appointment for your feelings!"

The judge banged her gavel over and over again until both voices stopped their childlike argument. For a brief moment, Judge Murphy gaped at the defendant. The entire court did.

"Defendant will refrain from being argumentative with . . . himself and answer the attorneys' questions only. Again, jurors, you are responsible for determining whether the statements made during this testimony were intentionally uttered by the defendant."

Corinthia was quiet. So was Ben.

"Corinthia," Patel continued, "you helped Benjamin torture Amanda, didn't you?"

Corinthia shook her head from side to side. "When we got to Jersey, Ben beat her because he was angry she helped Fiona get away. He wanted her to wear a blond wig and put on blue contact lenses. Which was ridiculous, considering she's not white. And when she attacked him, they got into a fight and he stabbed her in the face. But he didn't kill her."

Corinthia paused when she heard soft sobbing from somewhere in the gallery. "Anyway, neither did I. I liked Amanda. She was the only one of those girls who fought back, cussed us out, too.

"Knowing me, however, I would have killed her eventually. But Ben insisted we leave Jersey. He was afraid the cops were closing in on us."

"Isn't it true you know exactly where she is and you're just lying, Corinthia?"

Corinthia faked Patel's slight Indian accent and mimicked her speech pattern.

"No, it is not true. I have no idea where she is because I didn't put her in any trunk. I also did not take her anywhere."

A frustrated Patel pivoted to a new line of questioning. "Who killed Ben's sister, Corinthia?"

Corinthia bristled. "No one. We were children. It was an accident."

"Why have you incriminated yourself today?"

She studied her fingernails again. "Have I? After all, you've implied that I'm just a figment of Ben's imagination, didn't you? If anyone goes to jail or gets sentenced to death, it's him, and he deserves to die."

"Why does Ben deserve to die?"

"Because he killed our mother."

The Ben voice gasped at his sister: "You told me to do that!"

"Objection! Defendant is not on trial for matricide," Jenson interrupted.

"Sustained," the judge ruled. "The jury will disregard that statement because the defendant is not on trial for killing his mother. That testimony is irrelevant."

Patel narrowed her eyes at Corinthia.

"No further questions, Your Honor."

"Redirection?" the judge asked Jenson.

"Yes," Jenson said, huffing. "Corinthia, may I speak to Benjamin?"

Corinthia gave him a blank glance before sucking her teeth and turning her lips upward. "Nope."

"Why not?"

"Because Benji is sleeping. Besides, I think he's said enough. Don't you?" She offered Jenson a sly smile.

"Did your brother Benjamin murder any of the women he's on trial for killing?"

"Well, since he and I are the same person, I guess you can say he did. Can't you?"

While she stared at him, Jenson opened his mouth to pose another question, thought better of it, and closed it.

"I'm just kidding," she said. "Ben didn't kill any of those girls. I did!"

"Nothing further, Your Honor," Jenson said, his voice terse. "We rest our case."

CHAPTER TWENTY-SEVEN

Groggy, Ben opened his eyes a short time later to find himself seated in the back of the prison transport van, which was driving away from the courthouse.

"What happened?" he said aloud. The driver and his partner disregarded him. With his hands cuffed behind his back, Ben peered through the vehicle's barred but open windows, watching trees and cars whiz by. He inhaled. It smelled like fresh cut grass.

Then he remembered.

Corinthia.

They had argued on the witness stand. In front of all those people! Ben groaned. Well, at least she had confessed. When the van pulled up in front of the jail, his lawyer was standing in the hallway outside his cell, waiting for him.

Before Ben could ask him anything, Jenson said, "Corinthia's appearance may have helped our case."

"Really?" Ben said, eyes wide, his jaw slack.

"Yeah, really." The guard opened the door and the lawyer sat at the small round table against the wall. The heavy metal door clanged shut behind him. The sound of the guard's footfalls dissipated when he walked away.

"The Corinthia alter's confession and your arguing on the stand, in front of the jury, was pretty spectacular," Jenson grinned. "I was watching the jury during my closing argument. If they weren't convinced of your illness today, I don't know what would sway them."

Ben nodded. "How long will it take for them to reach a verdict?"

Jenson shrugged. "These things are never easy to predict. Could be hours, days, weeks. We're never really sure." He stood. "Get some rest—and take your medication, OK?" Jenson started for the door.

Ben nodded. "Norris," he said. Jenson turned to face him. "Thank you. For everything."

"Of course," the lawyer said. When the guard unlocked the door to his cell, Ben plopped down on the bed, which rattled. He put his hands behind his head and slept.

A few hours later, he heard a guard shout at him, "Wake up, killer! Jury's back."

Ben sat up; his heart quickened beneath his thin T-shirt.

"What time is it?" He didn't get a response. He removed his rumpled clothes and changed into a plain white button-down shirt and fresh khakis. Then he slipped on the black designer loafers Jenson had given him before walking handcuffed into the sunshine toward the waiting van.

In the end, it took just a little over three hours for the jury to find Ben guilty.

Standing next to Jenson, Ben pressed his hands into his face and whispered "no" over and over. His mind was reeling. His protests of disbelief grew louder.

"But I didn't do it!"

Jenson told him to calm down. The jury had convicted him on thirteen counts of first-degree murder, one count of kidnapping, and one count of abuse of a corpse. At least they hadn't found him guilty of killing his sister. The victims' families wept; some court watchers applauded, others punched the air and cried out in victory.

Sweat poured down Ben's back, staining his shirt. He swallowed down his queasiness and the vomit trying to claw its way out of his gullet. His life was over. His insanity defense had failed.

"What if they sentence me to death?"

Jenson's brows furrowed. "There's always a long appeals process."

Ben fainted. Bailiffs rushed forward, helping him to his feet. Moments later someone pressed a cup of orange juice into his shaking hands.

Three weeks later, Ben stood before the court, shell-shocked and listless while the same judge presided over his sentencing. His head hung in defeat. The sentencing deliberations had only taken forty-five minutes. Ashen and dour, one by one those same jurors who had snatched his freedom from him shuffled into the dark-paneled courtroom. At least two of them made eye contact with Ben. One female juror appeared red-eyed from crying. His head down, staring at the tips of polished black shoes, Ben felt a sudden, small sliver of hope. Heart aquiver, he forced himself to smile. His grin was so hard his jaw hurt.

But then he heard his sister whisper: "You're not getting away with this, Benji." Ben's grin turned into a scowl.

"What say you?" Judge Murphy asked. With tears in her eyes, an older Hispanic juror handed the bailiff a slip of paper. The judge took it, read it, and thanked the jurors.

When Judge Murphy cleared her throat, Ben closed his eyes.

"Benjamin Zanetti, this jury sentences you to death by lethal injection."

Ben swooned. He opened his eyes and saw double. Lightheaded, he gripped the desk in front of him to keep from falling.

"Mr. Zanetti," the judge continued. "You have been found guilty and convicted of taking the lives of thirteen people, and you refuse to tell us the whereabouts of the fourteenth victim, Amanda Taylor. You have not expressed any remorse for your evil acts; rather, you've laid the blame for your crimes on the 'alter' of your long-deceased twin. There is no doubt—by the sheer depravity of these actions—that you are indeed quite ill. You need help. That's clear. And taxpayers will fund the treatments for your mental illness until the moment you die.

"Yet how blessed you are, Mr. Zanetti, that our Constitution forbids cruel and unusual punishment. If it did not, I would otherwise force you to suffer in the same manner your victims suffered. In fact, I would let legions impose on you the same emotional, mental, and physical horrors you inflicted on each of those young women who were in the prime of their lives—lives you snatched away without a second thought—simply because, to you, they bore some perceived resemblance to your dead sister. Or because, in the case of Amanda Taylor, they tried to help one victim escape. While the court recognizes your illnesses, it is indisputable that these women—no matter the reasons why—did die by your hands. Who controlled those hands is of no consequence to the deceased or their families. As per the jury's verdict, your sentence is death.

"May Almighty God have mercy on your soul. Until that time, you will be remanded to Graterford State Prison in Schwenksville."

A guard grabbed at Ben's shoulders and pulled his arms behind his back before slapping the cuffs on him.

"We're going to appeal, Ben. Don't you worry," Jenson was telling him while Ben nodded through his tears, stumbling and blubbering as the guards escorted him to a secure waiting facility in the courthouse basement. Minutes later, before his transfer to Graterford, Ben gaped in surprise at the TV mounted on a wall opposite the holding cell where he was in custody. Guards stood beneath the TV, riveted. Ben's lawyer was on the screen addressing what seemed like an army of reporters:

"My client is devastated by the verdict. This conviction is a tragedy. It's wrong! Everyone in that courtroom who saw Corinthia's appearance on that stand during the trial could clearly see that my client suffers from a mental illness that made him snap. Yes, those women were killed. We were never refuting that or my client's involvement. We just wanted to prove—and I believe we did—that Benjamin Zanetti is a very, very sick man who needs treatment, not punishment or retribution."

Jenson was standing outside in the blistering heat before a long makeshift podium that captured row upon row of microphones. Dozens of reporters shouted questions at him while sunlight gleamed off his bald head. Camera lenses flashed and beeped while he spoke.

"Benjamin Zanetti should be committed to a mental institution where he can get the proper treatment he needs—not some bastardized version of that in a prison as he awaits being put to death."

Karl Karstarck shouted above the fray. "Does that mean you're going to appeal?"

"Absolutely," Jenson said. He held up a hand to silence the crowd. "No further questions!"

Days later, in an infirmary deep in the bowels of the prison, Ben choked back sobs.

Weary and delirious and dressed in an orange prison jumpsuit, he collapsed onto a thin mattress and closed his eyes. A guard sat in a room nearby, alternating between reading the *Philadelphia Daily News* sports section and glancing at a surveillance camera, which allowed her to observe Ben and two other inmates on cots in adjacent cells. Ben was now on suicide watch. He had refused to take his medication two days earlier.

Somewhere deep within him, Ben knew Corinthia had died when she fell from that tree so very long ago. He had felt her spirit exhale and depart—leaving him to fight the world on his own.

And he had been filled with dread ever since.

When he had been younger, he believed he had killed his sister on purpose. Over the years though, he had wavered between guilt and justification.

While the wind had blown the leaves in that strong oak tree, when he could stand her taunts no longer, Ben had wanted to kill his sister. He knew it was his fault and his mother did, too.

She had told him so every waking moment after her daughter's death.

And that hadn't even been the worst part. What was worse was that Luke had witnessed it. Their little brother had heard their argument and he had watched through the leaves as Ben jumped angrily up and down on the branch that held their sister.

Ben closed his eyes and was lost in his memories.

The last time Ben had seen Corinthia was, of course, on the day she had died.

Ben's parents had carried her tiny broken body in from under the tree house and, after they had prayed for her, they had left her alone beneath a sheet in the twins' bedroom. While they had argued downstairs over whether or not they should call the police, Benjamin had crept in and pulled the sheet back.

With his small right hand, Ben had turned Corinthia's face toward his. Her eyes had been closed and her neck moved almost too easily. An ugly black bruise had appeared on the spot where it had broken. Stifling his sobs, Ben had caressed her cooling cheek. For the very last time, he had twirled his fingers lovingly through her very soft, sun-colored hair.

Later that night, Ben had hidden under his bed when he heard his father coming up the stairs. He remembered quaking and peeing his pants when he watched his father wrap his twin sister's body in the thin sheet from her bed. She was still wearing the pink-and-white dress with yellow flowers her mother had made her put on earlier that day. After Jason had carried her from the room, Ben tiptoed to the hall window just in time to see his father lower his dead sister's body into a shallow grave beneath the tree house in their backyard.

Luke stood next to Ben. The boys had stared at each other in the darkened hallway, the moon their only light. Luke looked up at his big brother.

"'Rinthia's gone?"

With tears in his eyes, Ben nodded.

Luke grabbed Ben's trembling hand and squeezed it.

"Don't cry, Benji," he had said in his small voice. "I'll never leave you."

When Jason started shoveling dirt over Corinthia, Ben puked down the front of his Mickey Mouse T-shirt. In the end, though, it didn't really even matter because Corinthia hadn't left. She had always just . . . been there. Talking to Ben, taunting him, goading him, scolding him, bickering with him. She had risen from the grave of his mind to make demands and bully him and tell him what to do.

Just like when they were kids.

The entire time Ben's mother had forced him to wear Corinthia's clothes and pretend to be her dead daughter, Corinthia had spoken to him, had controlled him.

And she hadn't always been nice.

"You owe me," she had told him again and again. It had been Corinthia who had ordered him to dig up her body, kill their mother, and put the deranged woman in Corinthia's place.

From the bed in his cell, Benjamin rolled over and stared at the wall. His cheeks were streaked with tears. He had a lump in his throat. It hurt from crying so much.

Ben swallowed. "Why?" he whispered to her.

"The same reason I killed those girls," she whispered back. "Even though I really didn't want to." Her voice from his lips sounded hoarse. "You needed them to replace me to drown out your guilt. To cover up in your little mind what you did to me. We both know you killed me on purpose, Benji," Corinthia said in a very low voice. "And you never paid for it."

His exhalation was soft, resigned. She was right, of course. And until the day he died he would always owe Corinthia—of that he was certain. But there was one thing he just had to know. One thing he hoped she would tell him—even though now it didn't really matter.

Not because he cared but because, well, he was just . . . so damn curious.

"What did you do with Amanda?" Ben whispered.

From his lips, low and slow, he heard Corinthia chuckle.

Her tone was as cold as the ground her father had buried her in so very long ago.

"I'll give you one good guess."

EPILOGUE
Three Weeks After Ben's Trial

Ye have heard that it hath been said, an eye for an eye . . .
                                                  —Matthew 5:38

How appropriate, Amanda thought when she closed the Bible, one of a handful of books strewn about the sparse cottage where for the past five months she had been held against her will.

She had taken a break from attempting to remove the thick iron bracelet on her ankle, which had been bound to a long heavy chain. Amanda sighed and adjusted the black satin eye patch over her right eye and returned to her delicate work. She winced when the rusty fork she had found beneath the kitchen's old stove poked the bruised skin on her ankle yet again.

"Dammit!" Amanda had been trying, without success, to pry the shackle from the chain.

That's when she heard a car pulling onto the gravel just outside the remote home.

With her good eye, Amanda looked up and froze. Startled, her heart leapt beneath her breast like a fish on a hook. The last thing she wanted was to get caught attempting to escape.

The approaching car could only mean one thing: the man keeping her captive was back. Amanda shoved the implement into a hole she had torn beneath the worn couch. It may have been pitch dark outside, but inside, every light was on.

Amanda's long hair was braided in thin, shoulder-length cornrows she did herself. It had grown since her captor had taken her away from Corinthia and made her his prisoner. The long chain attached to her ankle was embedded into a block of concrete in a pit in a corner of the floor. The door was locked and the windows were boarded—save for two slats that allowed a little sunlight and fresh air to slip in every now and then.

Amanda never realized how much she hated small spaces until she was held prisoner in one. In the repressive July heat, she found the stifling three-room shack downright claustrophobic. It was sweltering, musty, and now rancid from months of her sweat. Because she often had to beat at a mouse or two with an old broom, she put any leftover food her captor brought into the refrigerator—the only thing new in the entire home. When the heat was too unbearable, she cooled off by standing in front of the fridge, the door wide open.

The building was so old the floorboards creaked and dust rose from them when she walked, dragging the chain from room to room. She slept on the only surface suitable for reclining—a blue lumpy sofa worn from years of wear. Two ancient, faded brown and yellow curtains hung from the windows, but they were more like rags now. When there was nothing on the small black-and-white television, she would sit on the edge of the couch, fanning herself in front of the lone window, and peek through the slats. She liked inhaling the scent of wildflowers. Amanda grew envious of the rabbits, squirrels, chipmunks, and other woodland creatures that chased each other in the vivid green grass beneath the broiling sun.

Sometimes, in addition to pizza, soda, and junk food, the man holding her hostage would bring her haircare products and toiletries she had asked for, as well as fashion magazines or catalogues to read. Once, early in her captivity, she had asked for books. Two days later, he arrived with an armload of Harlequin romance novels, which she had devoured over and over again. She read the Bible, but that often left her morose and in tears—yet another thing she hated.

He would not catch her crying.

From the television, Amanda had watched the news with a religious fervor during Ben's trial. She allowed tears to drop whenever she glimpsed her parents, worn out and haggard, in interviews.

The makeshift prison was where he had brought her after that lunatic Ben had stabbed her in the eye and beaten her face. When Ben was pounding her head in, she didn't know which was worse: the fact that she was powerless and couldn't make him stop or the pain that radiated from her damaged eye and traveled throughout her entire body, racking it with a vicious intensity.

"He owes me a favor," her new captor had whispered in Amanda's ear right after they left New Jersey. She had been lying, bruised, bloody, and helpless, on some anonymous doctor's sofa.

"Don't worry. You'll be as right as rain when he's finished."

"Who are you?" she had managed to whisper, her tongue dry, thick.

"I'm your savior," he had whispered back before lighting a cigarette. The doctor made her count backward from ten. Then she blacked out.

When Amanda came to much later in this hot, godforsaken hellhole, her entire face, save for her mouth and nose, was swaddled in bandages. Her "savior" treated her gingerly, calling her beautiful, sitting by her side, feeding her soup and medication. But he refused to let her leave.

Days and weeks blended into one another while she drifted in and out of consciousness, begging for her mother. Despite her initial fear, his voice and gentle reassurances often soothed her back to a restless sleep. As a result, she was never scared. Not like she was with Ben, although at the time she tried not to show it.

One morning, Amanda awoke to the sounds of jazz and to find that most of the gauze on her face was gone. When she reached up with her hand, her fingers traced the tiny stitches around the corners of her eye. Her right eyelid was swollen shut. She made a face when she touched it; a thick, gum-like crust kept her from opening that eye entirely. When she did, she could see nothing out of it but darkness.

"The doctor said those stitches will fall out," Amanda's captor told her. "We have to make sure you finish this round of antibiotics." Her vision in her left eye was so bad that, at first, the man appeared as a tall, thin, chain-smoking shadow.

"What is that?" she croaked.

"What? The music?" She heard his voice go up an octave. "It's called 'Grazing in the Grass,' by Hugh Masekala. It's old. You wouldn't have heard of it before."

Amanda was too weak to ask anything else, so she nodded. He pressed a pill in one hand and a bottle of water in the other.

As time wore on, the deep cuts and purple and black bruises on her face faded, leaving a faint trace of Ben's handiwork. But that was before Amanda realized the darkness in her right eye meant she'd lost her vision—hence the eye patch.

And she was mad as hell about that.

It was then that she made up her mind not to say or even think her captor's name once she had learned it. He took great pains to be amiable, and while he didn't say anything about her not addressing him, Amanda could tell it unnerved him. She would not humanize him. Amanda sensed he found her indifference attractive; from time to time she would catch him stealing glances before averting his gaze. After months of imprisonment, Amanda grew stronger and became accustomed to having only one eye. He removed the last of the bandages and apologized about her partial blindness.

Then he put chains on her left ankle. As a Black woman, she was keenly aware of the horror of being shackled—like some slave. It left her equal parts appalled and enraged.

Prisoner. Captive. Kidnap victim. Survivor. These were the terms Amanda thought of when she thought of herself. One day she'd add another:

Escapee.

He never touched her. After she had healed, however, she found him sizing her up with washed-out blue eyes that held a surprising and cunning intellect. While he was tight-lipped and wary at first, she did everything short of using his name to get him to open up about his game plan. Cussing him out and threatening him proved fruitless. But she noticed her wit, crass humor, and even her biting sarcasm would elicit an occasional smile, putting him at ease.

When he was relaxed like that, she was stunned to find him a good debater—especially on politics or '90s rap lyrics. And despite the awfulness of her situation, he often made Amanda laugh. At first, her captor, who seemed about Amanda's age, kept saying the only reason he wouldn't let her go was because he couldn't trust her not to tell anyone that he had been helping Ben for months.

Other times, when her protestations for freedom incensed him, he would get up and walk out.

Though stubborn, her captor would often return apologetic, saying he couldn't let her leave just yet, that she should behave like this was normal.

As if an eye patch and chains were ordinary.

A key rattled in the lock. The door swung open. An attractive young man with shoulder-length blond hair, her self-proclaimed savior, strolled in. At six foot one, he had the physique of a high school linebacker: pale skin, high cheekbones, and a strong jaw covered with stubble. The weird thing was, under different circumstances, they might have dated. But to Amanda, of course, he was the selfish, manipulative prick holding her prisoner. He was shrewd, too. Often, his blue eyes seemed to bore right through her, measuring the depths of her anguish and her willingness to submit to his control. Now and again, those eyes radiated kindness, which Amanda considered odd, given he was the source of her torment.

Today, the familiar scent of Bleu de Chanel tickled her nostrils when he entered dressed in an expensive tailored suit, Ferragamo leather lace-up shoes, a striped blue and gray shirt, and a gray tie with a Windsor knot. Her winter clothes long gone, Amanda had been relegated to an ill-fitting, threadbare green sundress with faded brown and yellow sunflowers. Clad in a towel, she often washed it in the bathroom sink. It dried in no time in the brutal heat.

"Good evening, captor," she said, her voice brimming with contempt. She frowned at him from the center of the room, both hands on her curvy hips. He looked like he was returning from a long hard day of being a master of the universe, not coming home to a hostage.

"Hello, Amanda." He grinned and placed a bag of what smelled like Chinese takeout on the kitchen table. Amanda ignored her snarling stomach. He left the door ajar to let in the cool night air, which he did every night when he came to check on her. Sometimes he played her music from his smartphone. Mostly jazz. Tonight's first selection: "Take Five" by Dave Brubeck.

Although he towered over his diminutive brown prisoner, Amanda didn't hesitate to argue with him or scold him for keeping her locked up. He wavered between being civil and being guarded. While she was healing, he seemed earnest in his vow to release her, yet closed-mouthed about when he would do so. The fact that he paid a doctor to mend her led her to believe he wasn't going to kill her. He needed her for some reason. She had no idea why. Amanda wanted only to get well so she could figure out how to flee.

She'd searched everywhere for a key to unlock the manacle, or a sharp object to pick it. The place had only plastic utensils, plates, and cups. After weeks of searching while he was gone during the day, the rusty old fork was the only thing she had found. But it wasn't working.

"I'm so sorry again that Ben did this to you," he blurted after he began unpacking the takeout. "You know, I tried to stop him."

Amanda licked her lips and leaned against the peeling Formica table where she was seated in the kitchen, her chin resting in her hand.

"Really? Why don't you tell me how you tried to stop him?" Maybe if she could get him to talk to her at length, he would slip up.

"In all honesty, I had no idea Ben was that sick until . . ."

"Until what?"

A shadow crossed his face. "Until I buried Tallulah," he said in one breath. "I had never seen so much blood."

Amanda intentionally hid her disgust. She ran her hand over her braids, took a deep breath, and exhaled. "Why don't you start from the beginning?"

He stared at her a moment before taking a seat opposite her. She tapped her bare foot on the floor. He parted his lips a few times to say something, seemed to think better of it, and then closed his mouth.

Why was he so reticent?

"I'm not going anywhere," Amanda huffed after a few minutes.

He took a deep breath but remained silent.

Throughout her captivity, she refused to acknowledge his humanity— after all, no decent human being keeps another human prisoner. She reasoned, however, that engaging him now, as if a friend, might make him more forthcoming.

What was that old saying? You can catch more flies with honey than vinegar.

"Luke," she said, her voice whisper-soft, inviting.

He gave her a disbelieving look. "You said my name."

What an asshole. "Well, maybe it's time for us to be on a first-name basis." When she grinned sweetly, he blushed and beamed.

"Say my name again."

"Luke Zanetti."

His pleasure was wide and deep. When Ben's little brother began speaking, it dawned on Amanda that stroking his ego might get her released. She'd have to keep her propensity for angry outbursts in check.

Luke took off his jacket, whirled around in his seat, and placed it on the back of his chair.

"You know, we weren't always little monsters when we were kids. We had a loving home. My mom and dad took good care of us. But from the time he was a teenager, Dad had a bad drug problem that he managed to keep somewhat at bay until after Corinthia died."

Amanda cut him off, yet tried to knit her voice with genuine concern. "I know all that, what happened later?"

He reached inside his jacket, tapped out a Marlboro and lit it. He took a long drag before blowing the smoke out all in one breath.

"Well, when Mom snapped, Dad and I went to live with his mother." Luke looked off into the distance, just beyond Amanda's shoulder. For a moment, he seemed lost in his recollections. A gentle breeze from the open door stirred the catalogues on the table inside the dilapidated wooden house. The moth-eaten, gingham-checked curtains billowed against the windows. Amanda inhaled, grateful for the refreshing air, even if it mixed with the poison of Luke's burning cigarette. She welcomed the sounds of crickets, croaking frogs, and the occasional hoot of an owl. Their night music flitted in between the spaces of their conversation.

But she was impatient. "And then what?"

"We were there for nearly six months and things were great, until she caught him stealing from her. That's when she . . ."

"Wait. Did your grandmother know about Corinthia?"

Luke dissolved into a coughing fit. He shook his head no, stabbed out his cigarette, and folded his hands in his lap. His hair billowed slightly from the draft. "Dad made me promise not to tell Grandma that Corinthia was dead. He said it would kill her."

Amanda wrinkled her brow. "That's crazy."

Luke nodded, coughing again when he stood. With one hand, he grabbed a plastic cup from the cupboard over the sink and filled it with water. He drank the entire contents, lit a fresh Marlboro, puffed on it, and blew smoke over her head before flicking the ashes into the cup. "I mean, I was nine. I'd seen a lot of batshit-crazy crap at our house after my sister died. Anyway, Grandma threw him out for stealing. She begged him to leave me there with her, but he refused."

While Luke sat and chain-smoked and told her his Dad taught him how to swindle and sell drugs, Amanda wondered again how she might get him to let her go. Begging and pleading hadn't worked. Neither had fighting. She knew damn well he wanted more than just a promise that she wouldn't go to the cops. When he paused, Amanda pretended she'd been hanging on his every word.

"That's horrible," she said.

"Wherever we went, Dad used me to help him make money. We'd con people—mostly women, off and on—but that got old, and it was hard on me too. My dad didn't care, but to this day I cannot stand to see a woman cry."

"Then why won't you let me go? I cry every day, Luke."

He smirked. "I have never seen you cry, Amanda. Not once."

Amanda folded her arms across her chest and returned his smirk with an icy glare.

"Why don't you just tell me what you want from me?"

Luke sighed. "I'm getting to that."

"Hello?" Amanda said, rattling the chains. "Get there faster."

He smiled. "Do you know what it's like to live on the streets when you're sixteen? Probably not. When Dad got locked up, I kept doing the same things I'd learned from him over the years: selling drugs, identity theft, making my own fake IDs. Enjoying life without a dependent parent. Living off the grid was just how we survived."

"How could you grow up living like that?" Amanda asked with a straight face.

He shrugged. "It wasn't that bad."

"Your father was a drug addict and a con man who got locked up and you were a teenager living on the streets alone. Without food. Without money."

"Well, we weren't poor, like poor-people poor."

Oh, she thought ruefully, he meant he was white-people poor. Big difference. "So, you mean like there was money somewhere?"

"Yeah, but we couldn't get to it," he snorted.

"I don't understand," she said, her voice genuine this time. "Explain it to me."

"Dad had always called his father a miserable miser and his mom a penny-pincher, which made him furious because he said they didn't have to be. Dad resented them, that was for sure. Anyway, after a few years, I went back to my grandmother's because I needed money, and I figured she must have some. And maybe she'd take pity on me. Imagine my surprise when I found Ben living there."

"How long had it been since you'd seen him?"

He scrunched up his face and shrugged his left shoulder. "At least eleven years?"

"Uh-huh."

Luke fidgeted a moment, taking the ring off his middle finger and shoving it in his pocket. John Coltrane's "My Favorite Things" began to play.

"Ben didn't recognize me at first, and when I grabbed him for a hug he stiffened. 'Ben! It's me!' I shook him a little bit. 'Luke!' But Ben stared right through me. I mean, I looked into his eyes and repeated myself until something inside him seemed to click. He said my name and told me he thought I was dead. Then he lunged at me right there in the doorway, clinging to me for dear life, and he cried. He told me our mother took off and he went to stay with our grandmother until she died. My heart just went out to him."

"Mmhm," Amanda interjected. "When did you realize he was deranged?"

"Immediately. Ben told me to sit and went to get drinks. When he came back not fifteen minutes later, he was dressed like a girl and his voice went up a couple notches. He sounded just like our sister, Corinthia."

"Wow," Amanda interjected. "That must have freaked you out."

Luke nodded. "It was surreal. I knew our mother made him pretend to be Corinthia, but I didn't know it drove him insane. He's my only family, Amanda. And since Dad died in prison, there's no one left." Luke paused and let his head hang.

Amanda was silent. She wanted to scream at him, to tell him to spare her the fake distress and to reveal the real reason he was holding her hostage. She let him continue his con, because surely that's what this was. She reasoned that maybe she needed to show some compassion.

Without warning, Amanda reached out and caressed his wet cheek. Luke seemed surprised when she looked into his eyes and said, "I'm so sorry. I can't imagine not having any family to talk to about this. Was it hard?"

And there it was, she noted, just the tiniest smirk crossed his face again.

Amanda blinked, pretending not to notice. I might have only one eye, she thought, but I'm not completely blind.

"I'm talking too much," Luke said all of a sudden. He stood, grabbed his jacket, and moved toward the door.

She had to get him back. "If you leave now, Luke," she cooed, "I may refuse whatever it is you're angling for. And I know you don't want that, babe."

That stopped him. He turned around real slow and gave her a megawatt smile. Luke's blush touched the roots of his hair. "Babe?"

"Luke," she said, gesturing to the kitchen chair with a flourish. "Sit and tell me why you're not getting to the point. What do you really want from me?" Her heart skipped a few beats when he returned to his seat and leaned forward. Their knees were almost touching.

"You asked," he said, smiling. "I want you to understand what happened. And I need you to trust me."

"Yes, you've said that before, but after all this," she said, pointing to her eye patch and the chains, "why should I?"

"Nothing is ever black and white, Amanda."

"My freedom is a hundred percent black and white to me, Luke. You're not in chains. You haven't lost an eye!" she said, her hand slamming down on the table.

"I was a premed student, Luke, and I have never seen a one-eyed surgeon. I will never have the life I wanted!"

Luke paused, sniffed, and apologized again. "When I found out what Ben was doing, I wanted to run," he told Amanda. "To leave and never return, but I couldn't do that."

"Why not?"

"Because he's my brother." Tears on his lashes, Luke took both of her small hands in his. She sat there, skeptical, staring at him, watching him plead with his eyes. Amanda knew it was way more than that. She bit her bottom lip, stifling a rude comment.

"Gosh, that's just awful," she said instead. Why would he risk his freedom for a brother he hadn't seen since elementary school? They were practically strangers. Beneath the designer clothes and shiny hair was an admitted street hustler, a con artist.

What could be the one thing he wanted more than staying out of prison?

And then it dawned on her: money.

And above all else, money changes people. It had changed her parents when her maternal grandmother left Amanda everything. It had given Amanda far more than financial freedom, though. It gave her something more important—independence and control over her future. And that had angered her parents.

"I can't do this," she said, her voice soft when she matched his gaze. With great care she removed her hands from his grasp.

"Can't do what?" he asked, his voice quiet.

"Be disingenuous. You really expect me to believe," she said, speaking louder, "that after nearly a dozen years you cared so much about Ben when you just told me you had, what? Five or six years before you went to find your family after your dad was jailed? Please, just be honest with me for a change, Luke," she implored, absentmindedly twirling the braids on her right shoulder.

Luke offered Amanda yet another blank stare. "Hey, Siri," he commanded. "Play 'In a Sentimental Mood.'"

"You helped Ben for a reason—and I'm not dumb enough to believe it was just because he's your brother. What's the con? I want to go home, and you want to get on with your life."

Outside, a strong gust of wind roared through the trees and the door to the isolated cabin flew wide open, surprising them both. The music played and Amanda noted how bright and full the moon was. Luke stood then and leaned against the sink, facing her. When she glanced up at him, his entire countenance had changed. His smirk was more noticeable now.

"You're a very smart girl, Amanda."

She sat on the edge of her seat. Her pulse quickened. She ignored the sweat sliding between her breasts. "It's an inheritance, isn't it?"

"Not exactly."

She racked her brain a moment. "Are you trying to get ahold of the land?"

"No," he told her. "Not the land. It's the house."

"What do you mean?"

"There's money in the house."

"You mean it's worth a lot?"

"I mean there's money in the house."

She cocked her head to one side and gave him a quizzical look. "Hidden in the house?"

He nodded.

"How much?"

"About one hundred and ten million dollars."

She raised both eyebrows. "That's a lot of money."

Luke hesitated before speaking again. Coltrane's sax stopped wailing.

"Look, I've been wanting to talk to you about this for some time. I just wasn't sure if I could rely on you. And now, to be honest, I'm out of options." Luke spoke so fast his words sounded tangled when they came out.

"What did you just say?"

"I said no one knows about the money except me and Ben and now you. My grandfather lived through the Depression, and he didn't trust banks. So over the course of his life he stashed the bulk of his fortune in the house.

Ben said that on her deathbed our grandmother made him promise not to tell our father about the money, but that he had to share it with me."

"All that cash is in that little guesthouse where Ben kept women prisoner?"

Luke shook his head. "No. In the main house." He took a deep breath. "Look, I helped Ben because he promised he'd split the money with me in exchange for me helping him evade the cops. I wanted him to stop killing people. Then he got caught."

Amanda frowned. "Why are you telling me this?"

Luke stared at his shoes for what seemed like an eternity. He then wiped the sweat from his brow, loosened his tie, and unbuttoned the top button on his shirt. He cleared his throat and met her gaze.

"Because I need you to get it out."

Amanda blinked a few times and the room grew silent—even the night music seemed to stop.

She exhaled, her voice weary. "And how am I supposed to do that? You've got me chained up like a damn slave."

Luke nodded. "For now. Listen, I know you don't trust me."

"You're right," she spat. "I don't."

Luke sat and moved his chair closer to hers, placing his well-heeled foot in between her bare ones. "But let's say you could trust me. Maybe we could work together to get that cash, Amanda. I would split it with you."

Amanda's chair screeched when she scooted away from him. "What makes you think I care about your grandparents' money, Luke? I. Lost. An. Eye!" she shouted. She stood up, the heavy chains on her ankle clattering. "I'm disfigured. I could have died! I just want to go home."

Luke tapped out another Marlboro but didn't light it. "Look at it this way: you've lost a whole hell of a lot," he told her. "No amount of money can compensate you for what you've been through. But at the end of all this, after you're free and you go home, wouldn't you rather have enough money to do whatever you want? For the rest of your life?"

Amanda contemplated his words.

"And I'd honestly love to let you go," he continued, flicking a lighter. "Once I get my money."

She stared at him in silence.

He leaned back. "Amanda, do you remember what happened after you attacked Ben in the guesthouse and Fiona ran and just left you there?"

That stung. "Yeah. Ben beat the living daylights out of me."

"Right. Until I stopped him."

"You?"

"Don't you remember? Think."

Amanda blinked a few times. She recalled two faces hovering over her, discussing her fate. One had wanted to kill her. The other intervened. Her mouth fell open when she gasped.

Luke nodded. "Well, you know now it wasn't Corinthia. Look, I've already saved your life. Twice, in fact, if you want to include me coming to New Jersey before Ben headed west."

Amanda was silent a moment. "Be honest with me. Did you help Ben kidnap Fiona?"

To her surprise, he nodded his head yes. "Yeah, we both dressed up as Batman on Halloween. I dropped him off at Dukes and waited for him to come outside the bar once he finished his surveillance."

"Even after you knew he killed all those women? After you buried Tallulah?"

The tip of the cigarette glowed orange between his clenched teeth when he lit it. He eyed her, as if sizing her up. "Consider this, clever Amanda. I may have held you against your will, but I have never physically hurt you. And I don't intend to. At the same time, I can't have you turn me over to the police." He leaned in very close to her ear. "I just want my money," he whispered. "And I'm willing to share it."

"In exchange for what?"

He flicked away some ashes. "That's simple. Your silence."

"So, fifty-five million dollars for my silence? Why don't you go and get that money yourself?"

"I can't. That place is crawling with lookie-loos. Plus, Luke Zanetti may not be in any government database because I've never been arrested, but my prints are all over that house. If I get caught, it's over for me. I won't go to jail for conspiracy to murder young women. It's something I didn't do."

Tell that to a judge. "You helped Ben dispose of a body. You knew he snatched Fiona after she left Dukes, and you didn't tell anyone."

Luke stuck out his lower lip, raised his eyebrows, and turned his head to the side. "True. I helped him kidnap Fiona, but I would never have let Ben kill her. Taking her last Halloween was a stopgap."

Amanda scowled. "For what?"

"To keep him from killing any more girls as Corinthia. Ben only wanted to touch them. I told you. I wouldn't have let him kill Fiona, Amanda. All I'm asking is for you to trust me."

The chain rattled. "Oh, that's all?"

He knelt before her. "I could have killed you a long time ago. I didn't because I need you."

Amanda searched his imploring blue eyes with her brown one, which moved rapidly back and forth, scanning his face. Still, she played along: "What do you need me to do?"

"Go inside and search for the money."

She shook her head, confused. "Search for it where?"

"I don't know exactly," Luke told her. When she opened her mouth to protest, he held up his index finger. "But I have an idea. You'll need to do it fast. The guesthouse is being torn down at the end of the year. The main house will be sold in a few months, and the proceeds added to a restitution fund for the families of Ben's victims."

Amanda looked away from him and crossed her arms. "That money should go to the families. I just want to go home, Luke."

"And I'll let you go, as soon as you go in that house and get me my share of it. What you do with yours is up to you."

"And if I don't?"

Without a word, Luke took his jacket off the back of the chair. From an inner pocket he pulled out three Polaroid photos and handed them to her one by one. The first was a photo of her father, entering their house. The second was a close-up of her mother at the hospital where she worked. She was dressed in a white lab coat, her long braids fanned around her shoulders, talking to what could only have been a patient. The third was a selfie of Luke with her mom. Amanda shivered when she peered at her mother's muted smile. She felt like ice water had been thrown in her face.

Luke's voice was soft when it interrupted her thoughts. "I'd hate to see anything happen."

Amanda's stomach dropped. She glanced at the floor and shook her head from side to side. She could go in, find the money, and both she and her parents would be safe. Her ordeal would be over, and with fifty-five million dollars she could live the rest of her life on her own terms. She'd be wealthy beyond belief. But why should she trust him? Why would he trust her?

"Aren't I good to you?" Luke pleaded.

"No!" Amanda said, raising the chains. "How the hell is this good?"

"Didn't I let you call your parents?"

Amanda looked away. With her index finger she wiped at her one good eye. For that she had been grateful. When Amanda had telephoned her parents on speaker to tell them she was alive, her mother dissolved into hysterics. But when Amanda screamed, "Mom, I'm being held by . . ." Luke ended the call. In the many months that he had held her captive, Amanda had come to realize that although Luke was crazy for keeping her, he was nothing like Ben. At times, he seemed earnest and sincere, but he had also just threatened her family. And on top of that, by his own admission, he was a con man. Hadn't she just glimpsed his duplicitous nature? He would say or do anything to get her to go into that house.

He needed her help, and with her parents' lives at stake, could she otherwise refuse?

Amanda's lips curled into a half smile, and she swallowed. "I'll get your money."

His shoulders relaxed. "Really?"

"What choice do I have?"

Luke's smile broadened as he headed for the door. "That's great! I'll be back in the morning with all the details. You won't regret this, Amanda."

She chuckled when he locked her inside.

"I won't," she whispered to herself. "But you might."

∽

~THE END~
Chantilly, Virginia
Jan. 11, 2020

ACKNOWLEDGMENTS

Many people encouraged me during the writing and production of this novel.

But especially my dear friend, thriller writer Tatsha Robertson, who coauthored *Media Circus* (BenBella, 2015) and the parenting book *The Formula* (BenBella, 2019). My agent, the insightful Jeff Ourvan; my terrific NYC writing tribe, which included Tatsha, as well as Jeremy Goldstein, Ashley Williams, Payal Kaur, Annie Rourke, Ann Harson, and Maxine Roel. Helpful, too, were friends David Davis, Norris Benns, James Williams, and my brother, Curtis Pinkney. I owe a debt of gratitude to my fabulous friend, prosecutor Stephanie Toussaint, whose advice made the courtroom scenes sparkle. I'm also grateful to countless others who answered my questions in the middle of the night, on holidays, vacations, and on Sundays—when I did most of my writing—in Starbucks cafes in Centreville and Chantilly, Virginia, and at the serene Wiawaka Center for Women in Lake George, New York.

I'd also like to thank the production, media, marketing, and editorial teams at Red Hen Press, including Rebeccah Sanhueza, Marc Gumbin, Monica Fernandez, Chloë Zofia, Shelby Wallace, Eleanor Peters, and Jaedyn Thomes; Publisher Mark Cull and, of course, my editor Kate Gale, who not only saw my vision but elevated it. I will never forget what she said about my "kick-ass novel" when we first met. That "the first job of a book is to be an exciting read . . . and [*Now You Owe Me*] brings up some great issues about family and how family affects who we become, and the issues about American culture." Her excitement about my book—and her belief in my talent—touched my heart and warmed my spirit. Lastly, I also cannot forget the love of my life. Thank you, my love. Your encouragement has meant the world to me.

And to you, dear reader, I—hand over heart—sincerely appreciate you! Thanks for putting down your phone for a bit (or for swiping open your e-reader) to live in Ben, Corinthia, and Amanda's world. I hope your trip through my imagination is as satisfying for you to read as it was for me to conceive.

Biographical Note

Aliah Wright worked her way through college simultaneously as an editorial assistant for the *Philadelphia Daily News* and as a stringer for the *Philadelphia Inquirer*. A successful journalist, she spent her career working for a variety of news outlets. Those include the *Associated Press*, where she was a political correspondent, and the Gannett | USA Today Network as the former entertainment editor for Gannett News Service. A graduate of Temple University, she lives with her family just outside her hometown of Philadelphia. This is her first novel.